MASQUERADE

SIERRA ST. JAMES

BOOKCRAFT

SALT LAKE CITY, UTAH

Visit us at www.deseretbook.com

Library of Congress Cataloging-in-Publication Data

St. James, Sierra, 1966–
  Masquerade / Sierra St. James.
     p.   cm.
  ISBN 1-57345-970-4
  1. Television actors and actresses—Fiction. 2. Divorced women—Fiction.
3. Deception—Fiction. 4. Nannies—Fiction. 5. Hawaii—Fiction.
I. Title.

PS3569 .T124 M3 2001
813' .54—dc21

2001001301

Printed in the United States of America   72082-6823
10 9 8 7 6 5 4 3 2

To Glen Larsen and Richard Hatch,
who to my thirteen-year-old heart created the perfect
romantic hero in their character of Apollo. (What's the
point of being a romance writer if you can't put
your teen idol in the dedication?)

And to my husband, Guy, who is better than
romantic. Instead of flowers, he brings me pizza,
because he knows me.

Also to all my loved ones who could use a
trip to paradise. Here's wishing you luck
the second time around.

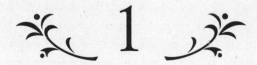

1

". . . and they lived happily ever after." Slade shut the book and looked down at his daughter. "Now it's time for you to go to bed."

Bella shifted in her bed, her small brows furrowed, and her lips pursed into a frown. "One more story," she said.

"We read one-more-story three stories ago." He leaned over and gave her a kiss on the forehead. "Now close your eyes."

She didn't reply, but as he pulled the blanket up around her, the frown still puckered her face. On an impulse he reached over and ran a hand over her light brown curls. The curls were just like her mother's, so was the frown. The only thing Bella seemed to have inherited from him was a pair of chocolate brown eyes. But this brought him comfort. As long as there was some part of him in his daughter, there was hope she would not turn out like his ex-wife.

Bella took hold of his hand and looked up at him pleadingly. "Just a tiny little story?"

He nearly relented, but the phone rang and saved him from the decision. He stood up, blew Bella a kiss, then turned out the light. The phone was on its fourth ring when he reached his own bedroom and picked it up.

"Hello?"

"Slade, take the next plane to Vegas and hit the tables because this is your lucky night."

Slade cocked his head to hold the phone in place. "Is that you, Tristan?" He didn't have to ask, though. He not only knew Tristan's voice but Slade could practically see his friend right now—his head tossed back, his feet kicked up on the nearest piece of furniture, a day's worth of stubble on that perfectly square jaw photographers were so crazy about, and of course, his blond hair carefully tousled.

"Don't think of me as Tristan," he said. "Think of me as the granter of favors, and I'm about to grant you a huge one."

Slade sat down on his bed, shifting the phone from one shoulder to the other as he settled against the headboard. "If this has anything to do with women, I'm not interested. The last one you set me up with had the personality of moss."

Tristan laughed. "Well, maybe, but she had other compensating qualities."

"Yes, she would have come in handy if I were ever lost in a forest and needed to know which way was north."

"This isn't about women. It's about the only creatures on the earth more desirable than women—producers."

Slade leaned forward. "I'm listening."

"You owe me big for this," Tristan said. "Someday I'm going to need something, and I'm going to remind you of this moment."

Slade didn't wait to hear any more of the bargain. "Did you get someone interested in my screenplay?"

"I said I was granting favors, not miracles. You're going to have to sell the script yourself. I'm just giving you the opportunity. A.J. is taking the entire cast of *Undercover Agents* to Oahu for a week-and-a-half-long shoot there. He's billing it as work, but you know A.J.—he just wants a chance to take a vacation before we start filming. Anyway, I booked a room for you at the Mahalo Regency Resort with the rest of us. I thought you could try to pitch the project to him between the time he's eating and swimming." Tristan paused for a moment and then added, "Now tell me I didn't do a better job for you than that overpaid agent of yours."

"You're certainly as resourceful."

"We leave in ten days. You just need to call the resort and confirm your spot."

Slade didn't answer for a moment. It was true, he'd been trying to find a producer for this manuscript for months. His agent had set up a few pitch meetings, but those hadn't been fruitful, so Slade had begged every friend and contact he had in the entire state of California for help. But he'd envisioned pushing the project in business offices or over dinner, not over hors d'oeuvres around a resort pool. There was also a little girl to consider.

"I don't know, Tristan. Bella always acts up when I'm away."

"And she always acts up when you're with her, too. What's the difference? Just pay your nanny extra, and you're set to go."

Slade hesitated. "Actually I'm between nannies right now."

"Bella chased *another* nanny away?"

"Bella didn't chase her away. The woman just wasn't capable of handling a spirited child. Besides, I think she only took the job in hopes it would give her an in for an acting career. She kept doing Angela Lansbury impersonations for me."

Tristan let out an impatient sigh. "So find someone else. Now that you've found religion you must know lots of those kinds of women. If I remember right, your baptism meeting was swarming with them. I couldn't turn around without bumping into some smiling, middle-aged, Mary-Poppinish woman."

Slade shook his head and leaned back against his pillows. "I'm surprised you remember anything from that day."

"I wasn't drunk," Tristan said. "I only had two Alabama Slammers beforehand, and how was I to know you weren't supposed to chant 'Hail Mary' after every prayer? No one told me otherwise."

There was no point arguing with Tristan, so Slade just shook his head again. "I'll try to find a nanny for Bella." And then as he thought about the idea he began to feel more positive about the whole thing. "You're probably right. Now that I've joined my church, it will be much easier for me to find the perfect woman."

Slade heard laughter on the line.

"What?" Slade asked.

"Oh, I'm just laughing at the new you. There used to be a

time when finding the perfect woman meant something entirely different to you."

Slade knew Tristan didn't understand, that he couldn't understand, and therefore he didn't try to explain anything to him. He simply said, "Thanks for the lead, Tristan. I'll see you in ten days," and then hung up the phone.

A few moments later Slade was rummaging through his desk drawer for the church phone list. He would call the stake Relief Society president and ask her if she knew—no wait, even better—he'd call the ward employment specialist. The man also worked as a temporary agent. Slade remembered this fact because after he'd started going to church, the man had stopped Slade in the hallway and asked him about acting jobs and if they ever used temp help to fill those positions. Peterson was his name. Somebody Peterson. That was the nice thing about being a Mormon. You never had to remember anyone's first name. Everyone was either Brother or Sister.

Slade pulled the ward list from underneath a pile of loose pencils, tithing envelopes, and a script he had been memorizing. He scanned down the list until he found the right number, then picked up the phone with confidence. Not only was Brother Peterson used to screening people, he was also a Mormon. That meant he'd know lots of sweet, wholesome, overly qualified little old ladies who belonged to the Church.

That's what Bella needed—someone who was used to children. Slade had seen those Mormon women in Primary. They could simultaneously control a whole row of squirming children, teach jazzy little songs about the scriptures, and tell stories using an assortment of hand puppets.

Slade smiled as he punched in Brother Peterson's phone number. Everything would turn out fine this time. Brother Peterson would find the perfect woman to fit the bill.

❖ ❖ ❖

Clarissa sat on a decoratively uncomfortable couch and sized up her competition. The other four people in the employment agency's waiting room appeared calm, perhaps even bored. A man with glassy eyes and a tight-fitting suit filled out his application in one corner. Two girls who looked as though they had skipped out of high school to be here chatted instead of filling out their applications in another. Both wore jeans, T-shirts, and too much makeup. Next to them a frumpled-looking older woman filled out her paperwork with a flourish, as though she thoroughly enjoyed dotting her i's.

Clarissa didn't enjoy filling out her application at all. Reducing her life history to one-sentence answers made her sound so . . . ordinary.

Accomplishments?

She tapped her pen against the clipboard her application was attached to. What had she accomplished lately? She'd survived a divorce. She'd single-handedly moved all her belongings into an apartment. She'd recently bought an ironing board, a blender, and two outfits for her three-year-old daughter at a garage sale and got change back from her ten dollar bill. That had seemed like a great accomplishment at the time.

What else?

She tapped the pen some more. How could it be that she was busy from seven in the morning until midnight every night and yet never accomplished anything?

Clarissa looked at the next space on the application. It read: *Hobbies*.

Oh, great. Not only was she supposed to accomplish things, she was also supposed to have hobbies. Somewhere in between her job at the fitness club, her job as a waitress, and all the quality time with Elaina she tried to wedge into the remaining hours of the day, she was supposed to be skiing, composing poetry, or playing chess.

Reciting Dr. Seuss probably didn't count as a hobby. Neither did turning old dish towels into Barbie fashions.

She looked at the space for a moment longer, then wrote *aerobics*. As part of her job at the fitness club she taught an aerobics class twice a week. It paid little enough, she supposed, to almost count as a hobby.

Clarissa glanced over her application again. It was unimpressive by anyone's standards. Perhaps she should embellish a few abilities and accomplishments for good measure. After all, she was justified because she really *needed* another job. Working two dead-end jobs had been all right in the short term. It had produced enough money to retain a lawyer and put down a deposit on an apartment, but she couldn't go on this way for very long. She had to think of her future. She had to think of Elaina's. She needed work that would allow her more time with her daughter, and enough money so she could eventually go back to school and finish her family science degree.

Clarissa held the pen poised over the application, but in the end couldn't bring herself to make up anything. It simply wasn't right.

She stood, walked to the receptionist, and handed her the clipboard. Then she slipped back onto the couch and picked up a magazine. She didn't read it, though. Instead she looked at the other people in the room and wondered what had brought them here. Then she wondered if they were thinking the same thing about her.

I'm not supposed to be here. This was never supposed to be a stopping place in my life. I planned on a career as a stay-at-home mom. I planned on baking bread, carting people to dance lessons, and teaching the joy of reading to a half dozen beautiful and talented children. That's what was supposed to have happened.

Clarissa closed her eyes, and pushed away the feeling of panic that assaulted her whenever she thought about the future. *It will be okay,* she told herself, and ignored the other voice in her head; the one that said, *You're a single mother with minimal job skills, an incomplete college degree, and a three-year-old daughter to support.*

A portly, middle-aged man appeared in the doorway of the waiting room, signaling that he was ready to see the next applicant. He looked down at the form in his hand and then called, "Clarissa Hancock?"

Clarissa flinched at the name. She'd meant to put down *Harrison* as her last name on the form. Instead, out of force of habit, she'd written *Hancock,* her married name. It was just one more way she hadn't fully adjusted to single life.

She got to her feet, smiled at the man who'd called her, and followed him into a small office.

He motioned her to have a seat, then sat down behind a desk, all the time keeping his gaze on her. As she settled into her chair, a smile broke across his face. "I *do* know you. It took me a moment to recognize you, but you're Alex Hancock's wife, right?"

She smiled back at him, trying to place him, and wondered how much of her current marital status to divulge.

Before she could say anything he added, "I'm an old friend of Alex's parents. Bill Peterson. I danced with you at your wedding reception, remember?"

She had to force the smile now, trying to pretend she wasn't uncomfortable talking about it. She shrugged and said, "I'm afraid that day is all a blur in my mind. I mean, I just remember smiling for a lot of pictures, shaking hands, and somewhere in all of that, we ate cake."

"Oh, well, in that case, I gave you the nicest wedding gift." He laughed a deep, rich laugh.

She didn't want to tell him. She somehow *couldn't* tell him the marriage was over, so she smiled and nodded at him instead.

"And how is that family of yours doing these days?" he asked.

"We have a daughter. Her name is Elaina and she's three."

He nodded. "Precious age."

"Yes." *I want to leave,* she thought. *I want to walk out of here and go where I'll never run into anyone who ever knew Alex.* She shouldn't have to explain, should she, all the personal details of her life? She shouldn't have to tell people that Alex was not as charming, or as kind, as the image he so carefully cultivated.

What would Bill Peterson's response be if she said, "Yes, three years old is a precious age—it's too bad my ex-husband could never see that. He always found things to yell at her about, until it became a daily ritual for her to break into tears every time he spoke to her."

One didn't say those kinds of things. One was supposed to keep it all inside and pretend everything was lovely. So she continued to smile and nod at him.

He looked over her application again, then set it aside. As he reached to flip through a card index on his desk he said, "I tell you what, I've always believed friends should help friends, and I'm going to see what I can do for you."

Clarissa gulped and hoped he didn't see the flush that suddenly touched her face. Before, her divorce had simply been a question of privacy. Now suddenly it was a secret, a secret that might help her get a job. It seemed dishonest to keep pretending she was Alex's wife, and yet how could she tell the truth now?

As Mr. Peterson searched through the cards, he recounted stories of all the cute things Alex had done on ward outings. Mr. Peterson had been Alex's Sunday School teacher and den leader. One simply didn't break into that kind of speech with: "Oh, I know exactly what you mean. Alex said the cutest thing to me the last time I saw him. He told me, 'I'll always be able to afford better lawyers than you can afford. I let you have full custody of Elaina, but don't think you'll ever get one cent more in child support from me.'"

Mr. Peterson looked up. "You don't have any accounting skills?"

"Not beyond balancing my checkbook. And I'm not all that good at that."

"Pity, that one paid well." He flipped to another card, then looked up again.

"Computer programming?"

She shook her head.

He returned his attention to the cards and looked through them for a minute more.

"Any experience in dental offices?"

"Only the kind where you sit in a chair with your mouth open for half an hour."

He smiled, then glanced down at her application again. "But you do have child-care skills."

"In spades."

He pushed the index cards away. "I should have thought about this before." Folding his arms, he leaned back in his chair and said, "Can you be an around-the-clock nanny for a week?"

One of Clarissa's visiting teachers watched Elaina while Clarissa worked, and she would probably consent to taking care of her for an entire week, but Clarissa balked at the idea of being away from her daughter for so long. "Well, I was really thinking of something more along the lines of eight to five."

Mr. Peterson smiled across the desk at her. He cocked one eyebrow. "It pays fifteen hundred dollars, with the possibility of callbacks."

"I'll take it."

He picked up a pen from his desk and jotted an address on a card. "This job offer came in yesterday. I already set up three people to be interviewed for it, but I'll add you to the list and tell him you come with the highest recommendation of all."

"Oh, that's very kind of you."

"The man's name is Slade Jacobson. He wants a nanny for his four-year-old daughter while he goes to Hawaii. It's going to be a sort of working vacation for him." Mr. Peterson leaned over his desk toward her. "Some life, huh?"

"Slade Jacobson?" Clarissa asked. "The Slade Jacobson who did all those movies?"

"The very one. I just loved him as Hawk Hawthorn in *Maximum Security*, which reminds me—don't give out his address to anyone. Actors are touchy that way."

Before she could promise to be discreet, he went on. "I know how these interviews go, so let me give you a few hints. Be on time. Dress professionally, and don't be afraid to emphasize your qualifications. Make sure he knows you're perfect for the job. You've got the schooling, you've got the experience, you're trustworthy, and you're married."

"I'm married?" she asked. "I mean, that's a qualification?"

He laughed again, the same deep laugh. "Officially no. Unofficially yes. I think he just didn't want any pretty young things taking the job for the wrong reasons."

"Oh, yes, I see." Well, there was no need to tell him the truth then. She wanted the job for only the right reasons.

"The interview will be Tuesday at three o'clock—" he stopped, leaned back in his chair, and waved his pen in the air thoughtfully. "Why don't you call and tell him you have a three-year-old daughter? She's about the same age as his Bella, and maybe he'd let you take her along as a playmate."

Clarissa nodded and looked at the card. His house was in Malibu. She didn't go there often, but she could find her way around.

She thanked Mr. Peterson and then stood up to go.

Mr. Peterson also stood and reached over the desk to shake her hand. "Say hello to Alex for me. And listen, if this interview doesn't work out, you come back, and we'll find something else for you."

She smiled and thanked him again. This interview had to work out because she could absolutely not come here again.

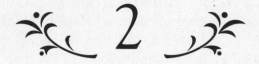

2

Clarissa looked in the rearview mirror for the umpteenth time. She wasn't checking traffic but making sure her hair was still in place and her makeup was still unsmeared. Such things were not likely to happen driving in a car with the windows rolled up, but she checked her appearance anyway. A sudden phobia of not being perfect had hit her.

Her outfit probably wasn't nice enough. And her shoes were scuffed. She hadn't thought much about them until she was getting ready for the interview, and then she remembered why she hadn't worn her wool blazer for so long. The only shoes that matched it were scuffed. But what could she do? This skirt and blazer were the only things that looked professional enough to wear to an interview. Everything else made her look like she was on her way to teach Primary.

Clarissa glanced in the mirror again, this time checking on Elaina in her car seat. "Are you all right back there?"

Elaina nodded, her twin blonde pigtails bobbing as she did. The pink bows Clarissa had tied in her hair were still in place, and her dress didn't even look wrinkled. It was pink, too. Elaina had decided it was her favorite color and lately refused to wear anything that wasn't some shade or hue of pink.

A pair of pale blue eyes looked up at her mother's reflection in the mirror. "Are we almost dere?"

"Yes, we're almost there. And while we're there, you're going to be what?"

"Good," Elaina said.

"And that means being what?"

"Quiet," Elaina said.

"And play nicely with the other little girl," Clarissa added. "And then what will we get after we're finished with the interview?"

"Ice cream," Elaina said, smiling.

"One more thing. Remember, we're not going to say anything about Daddy while we're there, okay?" Clarissa hoped Elaina wouldn't question why that was. It was just one more thing to worry about, and Clarissa was already worried about everything else.

It wasn't that she had any idealistic notions of celebrities. Clarissa had never been the type who pored over the tabloids or even watched the Oscars. Her knowledge of Hollywood was minimal by anyone's standards, but you simply couldn't be a Mormon and not know who Slade Jacobson was.

Slade had first thrust himself into the culture during an interview on a late night talk show. Clarissa hadn't seen the original show, but one of her neighbors taped the episode and showed it to her later. Slade, tall and tan, and looking totally at ease in front of the crowd, had talked about the difficulties of balancing a career and being a single parent. It was hard to think of this man as a father, since he looked like he was perpetually about to defeat a villain in rugged hand-to-hand combat and then carry off a swooning yet seductive maiden. Ordinary fathers didn't have shoulders like linebackers or dark brown eyes that seemed to look right through you.

"And if kids aren't hard enough to deal with," Slade said, "you've got to watch out for your parents, too. You turn your back, and they're off joining some cult."

The interviewer laughed and said, "What happened—did they shave their heads for their last Christmas photo?"

"No, two Mormon missionaries showed up on their doorstep, and now every phone call I get from them, they're talking about angels, temples, and prophets I've never heard of before."

"Where did you go wrong in raising them?"

Slade seemed unconcerned about it all. "I'm going back for a visit soon. I'll see if I can't get them straightened out."

"But you won't stay away for too long," the interviewer said. "Aren't you starting work on the sequel to *Maximum Security* soon?"

"It won't take long," Slade said.

This conversation set off a wildfire of opinions from anybody and everybody who had an opinion on Mormonism, cults, Christianity, talk shows, or the role celebrities have in society. It did nothing to diminish these flames when a month later Slade not only apologized for his remarks but announced he'd set a baptismal date. The same talk show host who had interviewed Slade before his conversion included Slade Jacobson jokes in the opening monologue for two solid weeks.

"I think Slade is confused by this whole church thing. You see, when the missionaries asked him if he thought he should be Mormon, he answered, 'Well, yeah, I've always wanted to be more man.'"

✦ ✦ ✦

Clarissa turned away from the busyness of the main streets and toward Malibu Canyon. The farther she drove up the hill, the harder her heart pounded. *I'm really going to do this*, she thought. *I'm going to walk up to Slade Jacobson's house and knock on the door. Then he's going to open the door, and I'll look at him, and my brain will stop working, and my tongue will start, and the first thing I'll blurt out is, "I'm not really married."*

Clarissa gripped the steering wheel and resolved to remain poised and in control of her tongue. Her marital status didn't matter. Slade had only requested a married woman so he didn't have to worry about getting applicants who were just conniving little flirts in sheep's clothing—or in this case, wool blazers. But Clarissa had no designs on Slade. In fact, after spending the last five years with Alex, she was likely to remain designless, as far as men went, on a permanent basis. If she ever felt lonely again for someone whose main purpose in life was to point out her every shortcoming, she'd buy a subscription to a beauty magazine.

She pulled up Ocean View Drive, and then into a long driveway. She stopped in front of an imposing metal gate. The agency hadn't mentioned this gate, or what she was supposed to do now that she was here. She saw an intercom button on the gate and pressed it tentatively.

"Yes?" a faraway sounding female voice said.

"I'm here for an interview," she said, "and I can't get past the gate."

"Just a moment," the voice said. A few seconds of silence ticked by, and then the gate slowly swung open.

Clarissa continued down the driveway until she reached a two-story colonial house, a gray brick splendor with dark green shutters and a crisp white porch that extended the length of the house. Although the house was impressive, the landscaping was what caught her attention. Rose bushes bordered the porch; their red and pink blossoms splashing color against the wood. To the side of the house, a grove of oak trees towered over an expanse of plush green lawn. It looked like a place fairies would visit, and not at all like a home for Hawk Hawthorn.

Clarissa took Elaina's hand, and they walked silently up the walk. She glanced at her watch. They were fifteen minutes early, but Clarissa hadn't been sure how long it would take to make the drive and didn't want to be late. Now she walked to the door as slowly as possible.

On the doorstep she squeezed Elaina's hand again. "Remember to be good."

Elaina nodded. "Ice cream," she said.

Clarissa rang the doorbell, and moments later it opened to reveal a well-dressed, trim, middle-aged woman. Her gray hair was cut in a bob and neatly curled under, and even from where Clarissa stood, she could tell her lip color exactly matched the shade of her fingernail polish.

And now the flowers suddenly made sense. Clarissa was at the wrong house. Somehow there had been a horrible mistake, and Slade Jacobson was waiting for her somewhere in a house decorated with cactus, boulders, and the skulls of small animals that had wandered onto his property.

"I . . . uh . . . was looking for Slade Jacobson," Clarissa said.

"Are you his three o'clock appointment?"

"Yes."

The woman smiled and opened the door farther. "Come in. He isn't finished with the last interview, but I'll show you to a waiting room."

Clarissa took in the entryway in a glance. A crystal chandelier cascaded from the high ceiling. The walls were cream, hung with large paintings of parochial hunting scenes above a border of hip-high wood molding. A vase of lilies overpowered a glass-topped table at the foot of a curved stairway, and the mahogany floor shone as though just recently buffed. There were still no signs of cactus or animal skulls.

As they walked through the entryway, the woman then extended a hand to Clarissa. "I'm Meredith Allen, Slade's assistant."

Clarissa shook her hand. "Clarissa Hancock." And then, because she thought she should say something else, she added, "This is a lovely home."

The woman smiled. "Thank you. I decorated it myself." She leaned a little closer to Clarissa. "Slade hasn't quite forgiven me for all the florals, but he'll get over it eventually."

Meredith then bent down and surveyed Elaina. "You must be here for the job of playmate, is that right?"

"I get ice cream if I'm good," Elaina said.

This was perhaps not the best way to start out an interview on child-rearing practices, and Clarissa cleared her throat uncomfortably. "It isn't bribery," she said. "It's rewarding appropriate behavior."

Meredith straightened and the smile was still intact. "Oh, you don't have to convince me. I frequently reward myself with ice cream. What's the point of being good otherwise?" She walked a few paces down the hallway and motioned through a doorway. "You can wait in here until Slade is ready for you."

Clarissa gave a soft "Thank you" to Meredith and led Elaina into the room. It was the size of a small living room with an oversized couch in one corner and a matching chair in the other. Several silk trees stood against the walls, and a rustic-looking coffee table displayed an assortment of magazines. A floor-to-ceiling bookcase completely covered one wall, and two large ceramic dogs lay sprawled on the floor.

There was another door—a slightly open door—directly across the room. Clarissa deposited Elaina on the couch, told her to sit still, and then went to investigate the door. She planned on closing it, but as she got closer she heard voices coming from the room beyond it. One voice she recognized immediately. It was Slade.

"And discipline?" he asked. "How do you handle that?"

Instead of closing the door, Clarissa walked beyond it and sat down in the chair beside it. It wasn't really eavesdropping, she told herself. Meredith had told her to wait here, and the door was already open. It wasn't her fault if she overheard the interview questions, and after all, it would help her prepare her own answers.

"I'm firm where discipline is concerned," the woman said. "I let parents set the rules but expect children to follow them."

Elaina bounced up and down slightly on the couch.

"Sweetheart, sit still," Clarissa whispered.

Elaina stopped bouncing and slid off the couch. She started toward her mother, then stopped in front of the ceramic dogs. "Look, Mommy, doggies!"

"Yes, sweetheart. Don't touch."

From the other room Slade asked, "And when do you think is the right time to ask for the parent to intervene?"

Clarissa tried to judge from the sound of his voice whether or not he approved of the woman's last answer. His voice sounded clipped, but perhaps that was just his interviewing voice.

"I don't expect a parent to have to intervene when I'm tending," the woman said. "That's my job."

"I see." His voice definitely sounded disapproving that time, but Clarissa had no idea what he disapproved of.

She glanced over at Elaina and saw her gingerly touching one of the dog's heads.

"Elaina, I told you not to touch that."

"But I's petting it nicely," Elaina said.

"Mommy said no."

Elaina frowned. "I want to go home."

"In a little while. Here, come look at these stickers in my purse. You can play with them when it's time for me to talk to Mr. Jacobson."

Elaina walked toward her mother but stopped and looked at the trees by the couch instead.

Clarissa tuned back to the conversation in the next room and heard Slade ask, "What are your favorite activities to do with children?"

This was an important question, and one she hadn't considered before. She would answer . . . reading. No one could take issue with that. And to make the answer more authentic, she'd mention how she and Elaina loved to spend time at the library.

Cooking was another good answer. It sounded homey, and educational. She could talk about the way Elaina liked to stand beside her as she made dinner and help dump ingredients into the bowl. But then, perhaps Slade wouldn't approve of that. He probably had someone do all his cooking for him, and besides, maybe he'd worry about his daughter being burned or cut or something. Cooking was definitely out. Board games, perhaps.

Elaina moved behind the trees and giggled mischievously. "You can't find me," she cooed, and then giggled again.

"Where is my sweetheart?" Clarissa asked. She knew this question would prolong the game and keep Elaina busy for a few more minutes. Then she blocked out the giggling and listened to the conversation in the next room again. They were talking about children's self-esteem, although Clarissa wasn't sure how they'd gotten on that subject. Slade seemed to think it was of the utmost importance though, and Clarissa tucked that information into her list of possible discussion topics to bring up during her interview. When she went over her background in family science she could slip in something about how appropriate achievements boost a child's self-esteem.

And—oh, she had it . . . the perfect answer to the "What are your favorite activities to do with children?" question. When Slade asked her, she'd simply smile and say, "Whatever the child's favorite activity is. I find children are happiest when they're pursuing areas of their own natural interest and talent." How could Slade find fault with that answer?

I might have a chance at this job, Clarissa thought. *I just might be able to pull it off.*

She heard Slade say, "Well, thank you for coming, Mrs. McGrath. I'll call you tonight and let you know my decision."

Clarissa's gaze instantly swung back to the silk plants. "Elaina, come here. It's our turn now."

The plants remained still and silent.

Clarissa stood and walked to the trees. Pushing aside the foliage she said, "Elaina?"

There was no answer, and no little girl.

Clarissa's eyes now swept over the room, looking for her daughter's hiding place. She could hear the click of heels across the floor in the next room and knew Mrs. McGrath was leaving.

"Elaina," Clarissa hissed, "come here, right now!" She looked behind the chair, and then, because it was the only hiding place left in the room, Clarissa knelt down beside the couch. The couch stood high off the floor with a ruffled skirt, which concealed everything underneath. It probably could have accommodated several small children. Clarissa lifted the ruffle and looked to see if it hid hers. The area was dark, and it was impossible to see anything, so Clarissa reached out her hand to see if she could touch something that felt like a three-year-old.

"We evicted all the dust bunnies from underneath the furniture, but if you're interested, we have a fine lint collection behind the washing machine."

Clarissa jumped at the sound of Slade's voice behind her, and in doing so banged the side of her face into the bottom of the couch. Then, more slowly, she turned to look up at him. He was taller than she'd expected and even more striking. In real life his hair seemed darker, his features stronger, and his eyes had an intensity she never saw on TV.

"I was looking for my daughter. She seems to have wandered off."

"Under the couch?"

"Well, no. I just figured she must be in here someplace, and I've looked everywhere else."

He appraised her silently for a moment. "You lost your daughter?" and although he didn't actually come right out and say, "And yet you want a job taking care of mine?" the question hung in the air.

"She was just here and I . . ." but how could she explain? She couldn't very well tell him she'd been so busy eavesdropping she hadn't been paying attention to Elaina. "I'm sure she can't have gone far."

Clarissa glanced over at the door to the hallway and noticed it stood slightly ajar. She went to it, and glanced down the hallway.

Empty.

"Elaina?" she called.

No one replied.

She stood for a moment, feeling her heart pound, and looked hopelessly from the room to the hallway.

Slade came up beside her and peered down the hallway himself. "How far did you say she usually wanders?"

She wasn't sure whether his voice was laced with amusement

or just amazement. At this point it didn't matter. "Look," she told him, "you probably don't consider me capable of watching children. You don't have to hire me to watch yours. But could you please help me find my daughter?"

He nodded slowly. "All right." He stepped out into the hallway, looked up and down it, then tilted his head back a little. "Meredith?"

She appeared in one of the doorways down the hall. "Yes?"

"Mrs. Hancock has misplaced her daughter. Could you help her look around down here, and I'll try upstairs?"

Meredith's gaze turned to Clarissa, and for a moment she saw sympathy there. "Certainly."

Slade walked leisurely down to the end of the hallway and disappeared through one of the corridors. Meredith walked to the other end of the hallway and began peering in rooms. Clarissa followed her, scanning everything for movement, and every once in a while called out, "Elaina, come here right now!"

She tried to quell the sense of panic that nipped at her. After all, Elaina wasn't really lost. It wasn't as if someone had spirited her off. At least, Clarissa hoped not. She suddenly wondered how many servants Slade Jacobson had working in his house and if all of them had had background checks. She shook off the thought. Elaina wasn't kidnapped, she'd simply wandered off, and they would find her any moment. Still, as she searched, Clarissa said a silent prayer that Elaina wasn't somewhere hurt, or scared, or breaking priceless antiques.

They systematically went from one room to another, which proved to be quite a task. Clarissa didn't see any signs of a little girl, but she did see enough cherry wood furniture to convince her that somewhere there was a large empty space in a cherry orchard with Slade Jacobson's name on it.

Finally they reached a spacious living room. Clarissa was checking inside a fireplace that could have comfortably accommodated a band, when Slade reappeared at the top of a winding staircase.

"Bella's not in the playroom anymore," he called to Meredith. "Have you seen her anywhere downstairs?"

Meredith shook her head.

Slade's jaw clenched, then he banged his hand against the banister and yelled, "Isabel Jacobson!"

Only silence followed his call.

He stomped down the stairs, mumbling something Clarissa was glad she couldn't hear, then walked into the kitchen.

Meredith sighed and resumed her head shaking. She leaned toward Clarissa and in a confidential tone said, "This is why I don't look after Bella anymore. I'm too old to be chasing wild fillies."

Wild fillies? So Slade Jacobson—Mr. "We Have No Dust Bunnies under the Couch"—had a daughter who could be classified as a wild filly? It made Clarissa feel a little better about blowing her interview. At least she knew Mrs. McGrath would have to work for her money.

Slade came from the kitchen with a little black mop of a dog happily trailing behind him. The dog stared expectantly up at Slade, wagging his tail so fiercely it looked like it would topple him over in a moment.

"Blitzer," Slade spoke slowly to the dog. "Where's Bella? Go find Bella."

The dog's droopy ears lifted momentarily, and he looked about the room intently. He then put his nose down and ran, in what seemed a random manner, around the room. Clarissa watched all of this with her mouth slightly open.

Slade glanced at her, cleared his throat, and shrugged. "It's Bella's dog," he said. "They play hide-and-go-seek together, and he can always find her."

"Yes, but that's usually because Blitzer cheats," Meredith said. Then to Clarissa she added, "He counts to ten but never closes his eyes."

The dog apparently caught a whiff of the little girl because he charged into the kitchen. Slade followed after him, and Meredith and Clarissa followed after Slade. The dog sniffed around the kitchen for a few moments, then ran through an archway into the dining room. Once there, he went straight to the dining room table and stuck his head and front paws under the tablecloth. It was a tablecloth that, like the matching curtains nearby, puddled lace onto the floor and so only the backside of Blitzer stuck out, his tail once again wagging wildly.

Blitzer gave one sharp, happy bark, which was followed by giggling. Two pairs of giggles.

Slade crossed his arms and glared down at the table. "Bella!"

The giggles stopped.

"Bella Jacobson, what are you doing?"

Two little heads peered out from underneath the tablecloth. The one with light brown curls said, "We're having a hot chocolate party, Daddy." Her smile grew wider. "Because we don't drink tea anymore."

Slade started to grin, but forced his lips back into a stern line. "Bella, you were supposed to stay in the playroom until Meredith called you to come down."

Bella's smile instantly turned to a pout that made her look even more charming.

"But you said I was going to get to play with a little girl, and then she *came* and you *forgot* to get me." She pulled Blitzer into a hug, and he licked her face until she laughed and let him go. He then disappeared under the tablecloth completely.

"No one forgot to get you," Slade said. "It just wasn't your turn to play yet."

Clarissa motioned to her daughter and said, "Come here, Elaina."

Elaina crawled from underneath the table with a frown. "But I didn't get to play enough."

"You have to ask me before you play. You know that. I was worried when I couldn't find you."

Elaina sighed dramatically and with her ponytails bobbing,

stomped over to her mother. "But that girl said she wanted to play."

Slade cocked his head and gave Bella another stern look. "Isabel, did you go into the waiting room and tell Elaina to come with you?"

Bella nodded and her curls bounced around her shoulders.

"Why didn't you ask her mother if it was all right for her to play?"

"Because we're playing spy and it's 'posed to be a secret. That's why we're in our secret hideout."

Slade nodded. His voice had a crispness to it when he spoke. "We will talk about your career as a spy later. Right now I want you to go back into the playroom so I can talk to Elaina's mother."

"You still want to interview me?" Clarissa asked.

"Are you still interested in the position—" he turned toward the table where Bella still looked up at them, "even now that you know my daughter is an underworld spy who lures unsuspecting bystanders underneath the dining room table?"

"Well, that depends," Clarissa said. "Does the dog come along as part of the job description?"

Slade smiled a broad, even smile, the same one she'd seen plastered on the cover of *TV Guide* not long ago. "I'll talk to Bella about hiding."

Without a trace of emotion Meredith said, "And perhaps you could put a bell around her neck."

Slade shot Meredith a look, but when he turned back to Clarissa, he seemed all at once to be the person she'd first seen in the waiting room—professional and impatient. "Well, let's get this interview underway. Where did I leave my notebook?"

He looked toward the door, but before he could move in that direction Meredith spoke up, "I'll get it for you." She smiled coolly, turned, and her heels clicked sharply across the floor as she left.

Slade looked over at Bella. "Why don't you and Elaina make a secret hideout in the playroom now?"

"But the table is the best hideout." Her pout was back. "Pleeees . . ."

Slade shook his head, and Clarissa could see the answer forming on his lips, but then just as quickly he stopped, half smiled, and said, "I suppose we can do the interview in here." He glanced over at Clarissa. "If you don't mind."

Clarissa shrugged and let go of Elaina's hand. Her daughter happily skipped over to the table and disappeared back underneath.

Slade walked to the table and pulled two chairs a little way from it. He motioned for her to sit down on one of them. As she did, he scrutinized her carefully.

"Now then, Mrs. Hancock, I looked over the resumé the agency sent on you, and it seems very nice, but tell me one thing, do you have an acting background?"

Clarissa shifted in her chair uneasily. "I was Liesl in my high school's production of *The Sound of Music* . . ."

"Anything more recent?"

"I did a skit at my ward's talent show."

"But you have no aspiration to be a professional actress?"

Not unless one considered pretending to be married, acting. "No," she said.

"Good. The last nanny I hired was more interested in my agent than in my daughter."

"Oh. Well, you don't have to worry about that in my case."

He folded his arms and leaned back in his chair. "Now then, on to your references."

She nodded, glad she had called all three of the friends she'd written down for references and instructed them what to say.

In a professional voice he said, "Your references spoke well of you, but I have yet to speak to your most important reference, Elaina."

"Elaina?"

"She's had the most on-the-job experience with you. And besides," he smiled at her mischievously, "kids tell the unvarnished truth."

Yes, exactly, which was why Clarissa suddenly felt like her heart would knock through her chest.

Without waiting for her to formulate a decent protest, Slade left his chair and sat down on the floor by the table. Flipping up the tablecloth, he looked under the table at the girls. They lay sprawled out on their stomachs, and in between them was both a furry black dog and a pink plastic tea set.

"May I join your party?" Slade asked.

"Of course, Daddy." Bella put her hand out as though giving him something. "Here's a cookie for you. It's pretend because Blitzer just ate all the real ones."

Blitzer wagged his tail.

"Thank you," Slade said. "I've always had a fondness for pretend cookies. What kind was it?"

"Peanut butter chip," Bella said.

Slade put his hand to his mouth and chewed thoughtfully. "Delicious." Then he leaned toward Elaina. "So, Elaina, how old are you?"

"Almost four."

"And you have a mother, right?"

Elaina nodded.

"What's her name?"

"Mommy."

"A lovely name. One of my favorites. And what type of thing does Mommy do at home?"

Elaina tilted her head to one side. "The dishes."

Slade took another bite from his invisible cookie. "Ahh, I specialize in that myself. Is she a good mommy?"

Elaina held her arms wide in a gesture that had become a daily ritual between her and her mother. "She's the *b-e-s-t* mommy in the whole world."

Slade looked over at Clarissa with raised eyebrows and

nodded. "Stunning references." He then turned back to Elaina. "What's the nicest thing your mommy has ever done for you?"

"She's gonna give me ice cream if I'm good."

"Oh, that *is* nice. Tell her you want Haagan Daas. It's the best."

"Just what she needs to hear," Clarissa called over.

"Does your mommy play with you?"

"Yup."

"What sorts of things do you play?"

"Shoot and batter."

"Chutes and Ladders," Clarissa corrected. "It's Chutes and Ladders."

"Yeah," Elaina said. "We also play Go Flesh."

"Fish," Clarissa said.

Slade smiled and nodded. "Do you ever get in trouble?"

Elaina hesitated, sheepishly tilting her head to her shoulder. "Yes."

"What happens when you get in trouble?"

"Mommy sends me to the chair and then says, 'Do you want to grow up to be like Aunt Renea?'"

"Who's Aunt Renea?"

With the exact same inflection Clarissa must have sometime used, Elaina loudly proclaimed, "She's a pain in the neck."

Slade bit back a smile and nodded.

Before he could formulate another question, Bella put a plastic pink spoon into the sugar bowl, lifted it out again and said, "Daddy, would you like one or two spoonfuls of sugar in your hot chocolate?"

"None. You don't put sugar in hot chocolate."

"I do." Bella put the spoon into her cup, then picked up the teapot and poured something into her father's cup.

Slade took it from her. "Hey, this is real water. Bella, you know you're not supposed to take water out of the kitchen."

Bella blinked her large brown eyes up at him. "But this is the outside-of-the-kitchen water."

"There is no outside-of-the-kitchen water." He took a sip and then spit the contents back into his cup. "This is awful. Where did you get it?"

"Out of the watering can." She smiled proudly. "Because you said that's the only water that goes outside the kitchen."

Slade picked up his cup and dumped the contents back into the teapot. "Great. Now I've ingested Miracle Grow." He picked up the teapot and looked in the girls' cups. "Have you been drinking this?"

"Just a little," Bella said.

Clarissa immediately went to the table and dropped to her knees so she could get a better look at Elaina. "Did you drink any, sweetheart?"

Elaina nodded solemnly.

Clarissa turned to Slade. "Would Miracle Grow hurt them?"

Meredith's tailored pumps suddenly appeared by the table. Clarissa hadn't noticed her come back into the room, but she must have been there for some time because she said, "Shall I call the poison control center?"

"Yes." Slade handed her the teapot. "Do that right away."

"I can call," Clarissa said. "I have the phone number memorized."

"So do I," Meredith replied tiredly. She left the room carrying the teapot slightly away from her as though she didn't want to spill any of its contents on her clothes.

Still sitting, Slade looked over at Clarissa with one eyebrow raised. "How come you have the poison control center number memorized?"

"I like to be prepared. I have all the emergency numbers memorized. In time of crisis you don't want to be fumbling through a phone book."

"Oh." From the tone of his voice Clarissa could tell this was not the reason he expected.

"Why does Meredith have the poison control number memorized?" Clarissa asked.

"Well," Slade cleared his throat, "not too long ago Bella got into some of those chewable multivitamins with iron. She ate half the bottle, and we had to take her to the emergency room."

"Oh." Clarissa nodded her head.

"And then a little before that Bella got into my liquor cabinet. She was playing wedding and got into the peppermint schnapps. After that I got rid of all the alcohol in the house."

"Oh," Clarissa said again.

"And then there was the time she picked a bunch of oleander seed pods, put them in her dishes, and said they were beans. She didn't actually eat any, thank goodness, but those things are so poisonous it gave us all a scare. That was another night spent in the emergency room."

"Oh, dear," Clarissa said.

"She's a very imaginative child," Slade said.

Meredith came clicking back across the floor. "Poison control said it wasn't a problem. Miracle Grow in water is too diluted to hurt anybody. Oh, and Vivian sends her regards."

Slade shifted his weight a bit and glanced back at Clarissa. "They only remember me because of my name."

"Vivian asked if we'd be sending her a Christmas card again this year."

Slade said, "I didn't know we sent one to her last year."

Meredith shrugged. "It only seemed proper after the way she helped us through the toothpaste affair."

"The toothpaste affair?" Clarissa asked.

"The bubblegum flavored kind in the squeeze bottle," Meredith said. "Bella pretended it was frosting."

"All right, all right." Slade held up one hand as though conceding the point. "Maybe we are on a first name basis with the ladies at the poison control center." He reached over and tilted Bella's face so she was looking at him. "But all of that is going to change from now on, right?"

She smiled happily up at him. "Right."

"Because what is rule number four?"

"We don't eat anything Daddy didn't serve us," she chimed.

"What's rule number one?" Clarissa asked.

With the same enthusiasm, Bella said, "We don't put Daddy's keys into the ignition."

Clarissa nodded slowly. "I see. And exactly how many rules are there?"

"Sixteen," Bella said.

"Seventeen," Slade corrected. "I just made another one. No going to secret hideouts when Daddy doesn't know where you are."

"Okay, Daddy." She reached over and gave him a kiss that melted the sternness from his face. He shook his head and ran his hand over her hair.

Clarissa watched them silently. They looked like a scene from a Norman Rockwell calendar. Father and daughter sitting by the pink tea set smiling at each other as though they were sharing some irresistible secret. It was hard to remember that this was the same man who'd been serving up those sharp, You-lost-your-daughter? comments only minutes earlier. He seemed so gentle now.

Men. You could never figure them out. It was a good thing Clarissa had sworn off them. Who needed the aggravation of trying to second-guess them?

Bella glanced up at Clarissa and said, "Is that lady going to take care of me?"

"We haven't decided yet," Slade said. "What with two crises in one afternoon, we may have scared her off . . . "

Elaina giggled as though he'd just told a joke. "My mom's not afraid of anything."

"Another good qualification for this job," Meredith said.

Again, Slade shot her a look. "Why don't you take the girls into the playroom for a few moments, so I can finish this interview."

She nodded and said, "Come along, girls."

Bella dragged herself out from underneath the table, and

Elaina trotted along behind her. Blitzer sniffed around the carpet where the girls had been playing. He must have found something of interest because suddenly a soft crunching noise came from that area.

Clarissa expected Slade to return to his chair and to his professional manner. Instead he stayed on the floor, leaned back with both arms stretched out behind him, and sighed in an almost defeated way.

"Kids," he said slowly. "You know, I never realized how hard parenting was going to be."

"I know," Clarissa said. "Just when you think you understand them, they come up with something else to baffle you with."

Slade cocked his head at Clarissa. "You understand your child? You must be doing a better job than I am. I always feel baffled."

"Your daughter adores you. You must be doing something right."

"I hope so," he said. He looked not at Clarissa, but blankly behind her at the wall, then he shook his head. "Sometimes I just don't know how to get through to Bella. She doesn't seem to remember anything I tell her—or at least not the seventeen important things."

"She's four years old. It's amazing she can even count to seventeen." Clarissa smiled sheepishly. "And you saw how well my daughter remembered to stay by her mother. I've told her a hundred times not to even talk to strangers, and here she went off with one to pursue a life of espionage."

Slade's gaze slid over to Clarissa, and he returned her grin. "Look at us. I've known you for a total of fifteen minutes, and we're sitting underneath the dining room table sharing parenting woes." He shook his head. "As soon as I involved the children, I should have known the interview would end up this way. Kids just have a way of doing that. We walk around wearing all sorts of masks, and they find a way to strip them off. If I'd had a few more moments with your daughter I would have known all your family secrets."

Clarissa laughed and hoped he didn't notice it was nervous laughter.

"Who's Aunt Renea, anyway?"

"Alex's sister. She's just sort of . . ."

"Ah, there you go. You're putting on a mask. I can see you doing it."

"All right," Clarissa said, "I'll tell you. She's the type of person who thinks she can do whatever she wants, whenever she wants, and is always surprised the world doesn't spin around to accommodate her."

"Spoiled and selfish."

"Yes."

Slade nodded. "I've known a few of those myself. You're right not to let Elaina grow up like her."

"Well, I'm trying, anyway."

He looked at her silently for a minute and then said, "So, do you want the job?"

"Yes."

"Good." He held his hand out and shook hers. "I'll see you Thursday morning."

He stood up then and pulled her up along with him. "I still have some travel plans to attend to, but Meredith can go over Bella's schedule with you."

She nodded and thanked him, and then as she turned to leave, thanked him again. He walked her to the front room where Meredith gave her an employment contract, a copy of Bella's daily schedule, a list of house rules, and directions to Bella's preschool. She was shown the guest room, Bella's bedroom, and where they kept the fire extinguishers.

Meredith also gave her a list of phone numbers, including Bella's dentist, doctor, and the nearest emergency room.

Clarissa smiled weakly as she looked them over. "But I probably won't ever have to use these, right?"

Meredith smiled back at her. "That's the spirit."

Clarissa must have looked frightened because Meredith quickly added, "Oh, you don't have to worry too much. I'm here in the office most of the day. If you run into anything you can't handle, I'll help you out. I mean, my week just doesn't seem complete unless I get to chat with the ladies at the poison control center."

Clarissa's expression apparently didn't change because after a moment Meredith patted her arm and said, "I'm joking, dear. You'll do fine."

The two women then walked to the playroom to retrieve Elaina. Clarissa was half afraid the girls wouldn't be there, but both were playing happily beside what looked to be an entire Barbie village. Elaina was pushing a shiny red Corvette up to the dream house and looked so enthralled that Clarissa didn't let her know right away she'd come to end her playtime. She just folded her arms and glanced around the room.

It was easily the size of Clarissa's entire apartment and had a built-in playhouse on one side. An assortment of child-sized furniture sat in the middle, and so many toy shelves covered the far side of the room, it could have passed for KB's.

Rather than gasp at it, Clarissa kept smiling. "Well, I guess this sort of takes the anticipation out of Christmas morning."

"Slade doesn't mean to spoil her," Meredith said. "He just tries to keep her busy. And to her credit, Bella is a sweet girl most of the time. It's not her fault, really, that she goes through nannies like some people go through socks."

"Oh," Clarissa said, "then whose fault is it?"

"Some of it's just bad luck . . . bad timing . . . the nature of help . . . the nature of children—and, of course, some of it really is Bella's fault. The way she used to run away from Nancy." Meredith shook her head. "I didn't blame her at all for leaving."

"She ran away?"

"With only a day's notice, too. Her next employer called and asked for a reference, but I didn't know what to tell them. I mean,

I didn't blame Nancy for quitting, but really, one needs more than a day's notice to replace a nanny. Especially a nanny for Bella."

Clarissa had been asking about Bella running away, not the nanny, and was not at all comforted by this new piece of information.

Meredith appraised Clarissa for a moment. "I'm sure you'll do fine with Bella, though. You look like a sturdy individual."

"I'd, um, like to think so." Clarissa's gaze stopped at Bella, who held her Barbie as though it was diving into a plastic pool. Bella's curls lay against the side of her face, and she spoke softly to her doll. She looked cherubic and cuddly, and not at all like the type who could intimidate a slew of nannies.

"Don't let my grumblings worry you," Meredith added. "Bella will probably be so busy playing with Elaina she won't give you any trouble at all. And you know, when Slade starts work on his miniseries, he'll need a full-time nanny for Bella. You might want to keep that in mind."

"Full-time?"

"Actors work terrible hours, and when he's on location it's even worse. He can't take Bella with him then—at least not after the last scenery disaster." Meredith shook her head, but still smiled as though she found it amusing.

"Well, I hope he'll think I'm capable of the job."

She said, "I'm sure you'll do marvelously," but there was a look in Meredith's eyes that said something else. Clarissa wasn't sure what.

Clarissa called to Elaina then, and they walked hand-in-hand from the house. Elaina practically jumped up and down at the prospect of ice cream, and Clarissa herself walked with an extra bounce in her step. If Slade paid as well for a permanent position as he did for this temporary one, it would be the perfect job. Better than perfect, because she could keep Elaina with her. All she had to do was be prepared, sturdy, attentive as a watchdog, and make sure she had all the emergency numbers memorized.

3

Slade was standing by his bed, tossing shirts into his suitcase, when Bella walked into the room. She looked at his things with a frown, then climbed up onto his bed and watched him as he added a pair of shorts to the pile.

After a moment she said, "I don't want you to go."

He folded a pair of jeans without looking at her. "I won't be gone long. Only a week. And I'll call every night."

"What about Halloween?"

"The ward is having a party for the kids. Clarissa can take you."

This answer didn't seem to satisfy her. She continued watching Slade with a frown. "What if you don't come back?"

"I always come back."

"Mommy didn't."

His hands froze in midair over the suitcase. He looked at his daughter, at her soft brown eyes, and then he dropped his clothes on the bed and sat next to her. He pulled her onto his lap and said, "That's different, Bella. I've explained this before. Mommy left because things changed between her and me, and she didn't think it was a good idea to live here anymore, but I love you and that will never change."

The soft brown eyes still looked up at him, filling with tears.

"Not that Mommy doesn't love you anymore," he said. "She still does. It's just that . . ." he groped for the words to make a four-year-old understand the things he still couldn't quite comprehend himself.

He rubbed her back gently for a moment and then said, "I'll tell you what. Why don't you come with me to Hawaii?"

Her eyes brightened, and she threw her arms around his neck. He couldn't have said any more if he had wanted to because she began to sing, "I get to go to Hawaii!" over and over again.

❖ ❖ ❖

Clarissa loaded the last of the dishes into the dishwasher and was about to reach for the Cascade box when the phone rang. She picked up the receiver, holding it between her shoulder and her ear, so she could pour the soap into the dispenser. "Hello?"

"Mrs. Hancock?" a deep and familiar voice asked.

She hesitated at the name, hesitated because she couldn't place the voice, then answered, "Yes?"

"This is Slade Jacobson. Listen, there's been a change in plans that I wanted to talk to you about."

Clarissa's heart fell. He didn't need her after all. He'd changed his mind and hired someone else. All of her planning was for nothing. She was back where she had started, with no job.

"I wanted to know if you could possibly come to Hawaii for the week and watch after Bella when I'm busy there." He quickly added, "I'll pay for Elaina's and your flight and room, of course."

"Hawaii?" she asked, because it was the only word her lips could currently utter.

"Bella was having a hard time with me leaving, and I thought it would be better for everyone if I took her along." He paused for a moment, then said, "I realize though, that your husband might not approve of you going off to Hawaii for a week with me, and if you have to decline I'll—"

"He won't mind." Perhaps she said the words too quickly because Slade didn't answer for a moment. She should have added some explanation such as, "because he trusts me," but couldn't bring herself to deepen the lie. So she let the words stand and waited for his reply.

"Well," he said lightly, "that goes to show you what *In Step* magazine knows. It said most husbands wouldn't allow their wives to go to a Ricky Martin concert unattended, but you . . . your husband doesn't mind you going off for a week with me."

"Well, only because it's business, I mean . . ."

She could tell from the tone of his voice he was smiling. "No, don't try to explain. My ego will recover eventually. I'm just trying to make sure I'm not creating any problems before I buy your plane tickets."

"Yes," she said.

"Yes, to the problems or the plane tickets?"

"The tickets. Not the problems. There are absolutely no problems where my husband is concerned."

"Really? A husband with no problems? Count yourself lucky, Mrs. Hancock."

"Yes, I'm very lucky." Again she said the words too quickly. They seemed forced even to her ear, but he didn't question her about it.

"Very well then, be here at 10:30 Thursday morning with your bags packed."

"Ten-thirty Thursday morning. Bags packed. Right. Thank you. I'll see you then." She vaguely remembered saying good-bye before she hung up the phone, but it was hard to think of phone etiquette when she'd just learned she was going to Hawaii.

How wonderful. How symbolic. She'd gotten a divorce and was now on her way to paradise. What could be better?

It wasn't until later that the full implications of what was happening hit her.

First of all, she'd learned Slade's four-year-old daughter had the ability to rearrange her father's schedule just by getting upset. That didn't bode well for her future as a disciplinarian in this child's life. If Slade was willing to pay for flights and a room just to keep Bella from being cross, how long would he keep a nanny who similarly upset her?

Second of all, it was one thing to tell a man you were married and then not have to see him again for a week. But now, he, she, and Elaina would be together off and on for the entire job.

Elaina was not even four yet. She didn't fully grasp the concept of keeping secrets. Without much prodding she would probably let the cat, her kittens, and an entire assortment of farm animals out of the bag. How would Slade react if he found out she'd lied to him?

These thoughts continued to press in on her during the evening, and by the time she went to bed, Hawaii didn't seem nearly the paradise she had first imagined it to be.

✦ ✦ ✦

It wasn't until Slade lay in the darkness of his bedroom, trying to sleep, that he realized he'd made a mistake in hiring the new nanny. He'd felt a certain uneasiness about it ever since his phone call, but he hadn't been able to put his finger on what it was that was wrong with her. Now he knew.

She was too pretty.

Of course he had noticed this before. He noticed it the first time she looked up at him from beside the couch. But he tried not to hold it against her then. After all, just because she was pretty didn't mean she wasn't also competent. Looks didn't matter in a nanny position. Clarissa Hancock was an experienced mother who was working on a degree in family science, and judging from her interview, was the type of person who could roll with the punches. All necessary qualifications in a caretaker for Bella.

So he hadn't held it against Clarissa that she had eyes like an angel and legs that made a man feel, well, less than angelic. He was, after all, open-minded where beautiful women were concerned.

But it occurred to him that the press wouldn't be nearly as lenient in their views. If some of the media people covering the *Undercover Agents* shooting happened to see him check into the resort with Clarissa at his side, the quality of childcare she provided would be the last thing they'd consider. Rumors would fly. Would Clarissa's problem-free husband still be so understanding then? And what about Slade's newly acquired reputation as a

Mormon? He winced even thinking about the monologue jokes that would follow such a report.

Slade tossed from one side of his bed to the other in an attempt to get more comfortable. He should have gone with that McGrath woman. She looked like someone who could play Mrs. Claus at the mall. No one would make anything of seeing the two of them together.

Of course, it was too late to change his mind now. He'd already offered the job to Clarissa, so he'd just have to make the best of it. They would be discreet. They would check in to the resort late, after any and all stray media people had left the cast alone. He'd make sure he never stood too close to Clarissa. And a child would be between them at all times. Better yet, he'd invite Meredith to come along on the trip with them. She hadn't taken a vacation in a while. She deserved a trip to Hawaii. And besides, that way he could make sure a child *and* Meredith stood between him and Clarissa at all times.

Slade stretched out his legs and felt a little better. Everything in Hollywood took jimmying and gerrymandering, and this was just one more thing to work around in order to sell his script.

❖ ❖ ❖

The next day Clarissa ran around collecting everything she needed for the trip. It felt odd digging out her summer clothes in October. Even though California generally didn't get too cold, most people at least made a pretense that fall had come. Instead of sandals they wore regular shoes. Instead of shorts, they wore jeans.

Clarissa took her old blue swimsuit from the box and held it up to herself. She looked over at the mirror and tried to imagine lying on the beach wearing it. Then she grimaced. Swimsuits were never a pleasant consideration, and the thought of wearing one while Slade Jacobson was around was doubly unwelcome.

He had probably never even seen a woman in a swimsuit who hadn't had a skilled team of professionals create her for the occasion.

Perhaps if she got a new suit . . . and a tan . . . and. . . . She touched a strand of her shoulder-length blonde hair. Well, it was almost blonde. It had been blonde when she was younger, but now seemed determined to turn light brown. Perhaps she could highlight it. And while she was giving herself a complete makeover, some work on a Thighmaster wouldn't hurt either. All those aerobics classes—all those hours on the stair climber, and she still didn't like her thighs.

Clarissa threw the swimsuit into her suitcase and looked for her old terrycloth robe. It was ridiculous to even contemplate spending a lot of money to go on this trip. She was supposed to be earning money. And what was the point in trying to impress her boss, anyway? He thought she was married. A housewife. The dowdier she appeared the better. Besides, she couldn't pull off being glamorous if she tried.

The phone rang, and she answered it while searching through her closet for her sandals.

"Clarissa?" The voice on the other line asked.

"This is she."

"I'm so glad I was able to track down the right number. I've wanted to call you for ages."

Clarissa didn't have to ask who it was. She recognized the musical tone of the voice. "Renea, what have you been up to?"

"Therapy. And I feel absolutely wonderful."

Clarissa didn't ask for what. It didn't matter, and it was all the same anyway. Renea had gone through every single pop psychology fad, spa treatment, and herbal remedy in existence. Renea wasn't a person who tried to solve her problems—she celebrated them.

Clarissa shifted the phone to the other ear so she could better reach the back of her closet. "I'm glad you're doing well."

"During my last session with Dr. Blumen, I told him about you and Alex, and it suddenly occurred to me that what the two of you really need is to come in and see him."

Clarissa momentarily stopped rummaging through shoes. She

examined a pair of worn tennis shoes, then threw them into the suitcase and said, "I think the time for that is past."

"It's never too late to recover."

"Alex and I are divorced, Renea. There's nothing left to recover."

"You see, you're in the first stage of grief: denial."

With a great effort to keep her voice pleasant, Clarissa said, "It's nice you're concerned about us, but I think it's best if we both just try to get on with our lives."

"Denial, denial, denial."

"It isn't denial. It's a statement of fact. We're divorced."

"If you'd come to therapy you'd learn you can change, Clarissa."

" *I* can change?"

"It isn't too late to fix things with Alex."

Clarissa took a deep breath, her resolve to keep a pleasant voice quickly evaporating. "Listen, as much as I'd love to sit and chat with you, I'm packing for a trip to Hawaii with Slade Jacobson, so I'm a bit pressed for time."

For a moment nothing but silence came across the phone, and then Renea said, "This is so sad, Clarissa. Now you've moved on to the next stage of grief: delusion."

"I've got to go, Renea. I'll send you a postcard." Clarissa didn't wait to hear more. She simply hung up the phone and went back to packing.

✦ ✦ ✦

The flight to Hawaii was uneventful. Well, as uneventful as five and a half hours on a plane with two young children could be. Bella and Elaina went through eighteen storybooks, four sticker books, a paper doll community, an entire bag of potato chips, and the patience of at least three adults and two cabin attendants before the plane touched down in Honolulu.

After retrieving their luggage, they took a limo to an upscale Chinese restaurant for dinner. It was there that Bella taught Elaina the joy of knock-knock jokes. Neither of the girls understood the concept of a punch line, but they still laughed uproariously at the end of each joke, and sometimes in the middle too.

Everyone was tired when they finally got into the limo that would take them to Oahu's north shore and the Mahalo Regency. Slade seemed especially tired. None of the charm, none of the gentleness she'd felt from him when they had sat on his dining room floor discussing parenting, surrounded him now. He was distant and aloof. He hardly said anything to Clarissa, and when he did speak, he seemed tense and irritable.

Actors, Clarissa supposed, thought they had a right to be moody. She decided to ignore him the best she could and looked out the car window. They left the crowds of Honolulu behind them and now drove along a two-lane road that hugged the jutting hills of Oahu. In the darkness she caught glimpses of the foliage they passed, and she strained to see it better. Earlier, as they had driven from the airport, she noticed a lot of the plants in Honolulu were identical to those in California: palm trees, bougainvillea, lantana, and thornberi trees. But somehow this island foliage seemed more exotic. These trees and bushes were bigger and more lush, as if they knew they belonged in Hawaii. Those same plants in California were just sadly making do because they'd been planted there.

Clarissa suddenly wished she had one of those job skills that could be used anywhere. A doctor, or professor—if she'd stayed in school and gotten a Ph.D., she could be here on her way to teach at BYU–Hawaii instead of being somebody's nanny. Then she looked over at Elaina, and those thoughts vanished. Her little girl was holding a Dalmatian Beanie Baby, her favorite stuffed animal, and was saying softly, "You've got to be a good dog in Y-ee or no ice cream."

How could Clarissa regret staying home to raise Elaina instead of continuing her education? She treasured every moment they'd spent together. If she had it to do all over again, she'd make the same choice.

The limo pulled off the main road and onto another. Clarissa saw the lights of a large building glowing off in the distance and knew they would soon be pulling up to the resort. She ran her hand across Elaina's shiny blonde hair and said, "We're almost there."

Slade said something sharply under his breath, then Bella said loudly, "Daddy, we don't swear anymore, remember?"

"I know. I'm sorry, Bella."

Clarissa looked over at Slade to see what had angered him. He was staring out the window at the now imminent resort.

"The press," he said. "They have vans all over the parking lot." He shook his head with a clenched jaw. "*Undercover Agents* must have some publicity thing going on, and we're walking right into it."

Clarissa glanced over at Meredith to see if she were similarly distressed, but she was calmly rearranging items in her carry-on bag. "You'll find a way to handle it," she said.

"I thought actors liked publicity," Clarissa said.

"Sure. You like it when you're working on a project, but not when you're checking into a hotel with . . ." He waved a hand toward Clarissa.

When he didn't explain further she said, "Small children?"

"A beautiful woman," he said, and didn't sound at all pleased.

She continued to stare at him. "You don't mean me, do you?"

"Well, I don't think he's referring to me," Meredith said with exaggerated offense.

Slade colored and looked over at Meredith. "Stop fishing for compliments, Meredith. You're an attractive woman, but not one the press will think I'm having an affair with. But Clarissa . . ."

The car came to a stop in front of the resort, and the limo driver looked back at them. "Where do you want me to let you off?"

Slade glanced over his shoulder. "Drive around to the back of the parking lot until we figure something out."

The car started again and moved smoothly away from the front entrance of the hotel.

Clarissa looked from the building back to Slade. "Certainly no one would report that we're having an affair. You'll just explain to them that I'm the nanny."

"Mrs. Hancock," Slade said slowly, "you're either extremely naïve, or you've never paid attention to the tabloids as you've gone through the checkout line at the grocery store. These are the people who report on who's currently dating Elvis. Facts aren't a big concern for them."

Meredith finished shuffling around the last of the contents in her carry-on bag. Slade said, "So we'll ignore each other. It's as simple as that."

Clarissa smiled at him. "I've never seen you before in my life."

Bella chimed in with, "What's an affair, Daddy?"

"Something Clarissa and your daddy are not having," Meredith said back cheerily.

"Okay," Slade said, "this is what we'll do. You four go into the resort ahead of me and check in. The reporters will leave you alone because you're not important—"

"Thanks," Meredith said.

"You know what I mean," he told her. "Then after about fifteen minutes I'll come in. After I'm checked in, I'll give Clarissa's room a call, and she can bring Bella to my room. Everybody got that?"

"I've never seen you before in my life," Clarissa said again.

Elaina nodded solemnly. "Me either."

"Are reporters bad guys?" Bella asked.

"No," Meredith said.

"Yes," Slade said, "and you're to stay away from them."

Clarissa undid the girls' seatbelts, while Meredith opened the door. As they got out of the car she asked, "What about our luggage?"

Slade glanced at Meredith's bag on the limo floor. "I'll have

43

a porter bring them all in." And then Slade shut the door behind them with a heavy thud, disappearing behind the tinted windows.

Clarissa took each little girl by the hand, and they began trudging across the parking lot.

Meredith looked down at her feet. "I wish they'd dropped us off closer to the building. These are not the most comfortable shoes, and I'm not as young as I used to be—as Slade so kindly pointed out in the car."

"I'm sure he didn't mean—"

"Oh, you don't need to defend him. Slade and I go way back." A smile crept across her face. "I love him like a son. It's just that he never thinks about what he's going to say before he says it. That's not a good quality in Hollywood, and I'm constantly telling him to work on it. The problem is, he listens to me like a son—which is to say, not at all."

Elaina shuffled her feet as she walked, kicking tiny bits of gravel across the parking lot. Clarissa tried to hurry her for a moment, then gave up, bent down, and picked her up. Bella looked up at Elaina and frowned.

"I want someone to carry me, too."

"We're almost there," Meredith said. "If I can make it, then so can you."

"I want Daddy." Bella looked across the parking lot, and her voice took on a high-pitched whine. "I want him to carry me."

"Your daddy will come in a few minutes," Clarissa said. "We just have to get to that building, and then he'll come."

Bella glanced over at the building, but her frown didn't disappear. "I want Daddy now."

"Here," Meredith said, "let me carry you, Bella."

Now the frown turned to tears, and Bella pulled her hand away from Clarissa. "No! I want Daddy."

Clarissa had known these moments would come when she accepted the job, but she hadn't expected them to take place just seconds after she was first left in charge of Bella. She bent down to Bella's level and looked her in the eyes. Softly, reasonably, she said, "Bella, don't you remember what your daddy said in the car? We have to go check into our rooms, and then we'll get your daddy. But if you stay here crying, he won't be able to find us, will he?"

Logic did not do the trick. Bella stood fixed to the spot and let out deep dramatic sobs. Clarissa stared at her for a moment, sighed, and then put Elaina down. Without another word she picked up Bella and continued toward the building again. "Come on, Elaina," she told her daughter. "Mommy needs you to walk now."

Elaina furrowed her brows, and she didn't seem at all eager to move forward.

Meredith looked from one little girl to the next. "Do you want me to carry someone?"

"I can manage it. After all, I'm the nanny. I'm supposed to be able to deal with these situations." She walked slowly forward and was grateful Elaina followed instead of staying put. "Besides," she told Meredith, "Bella must weigh forty pounds. You shouldn't have to lug her around."

"Ah, yes," Meredith said. "I forgot that everyone thinks I'm old. Between you and Slade reminding me, I can tell this will be a fabulous vacation."

"I didn't mean to imply that," Clarissa said, and then to change the subject added, "Elaina, can you walk a little bit faster?"

Meredith took Elaina's hand, smiled down at her, and said in an overly loud voice, "Thank you, Elaina, for walking and being such a good girl. We appreciate it."

Bella sobbed a little less noisily at this, as though she really were trying her best to be good, but couldn't quite manage it, what with a broken heart, and all.

When they at last made it to the courtyard in front of the building, they walked past a crowd of people gathered outside the resort. Most of them were teenage girls, standing in clumps, talking loudly, and fidgeting with excitement. A few reporters were scattered here and there. Instead of jeans, they wore business attire, had crisply hairsprayed hair, and had cameramen trailing behind them. Every few seconds the reporters looked anxiously around, as though they didn't want to miss anything important, but they didn't pay any attention to Clarissa and her entourage of tired little girls.

At last they reached the resort doors. Meredith pushed open one large glass door, and the four of them entered the lobby. It was spacious and done in mahogany with splashes of emerald green. Potted palm trees lined the walls, and a large stone fountain gurgled and splashed in the center of the room. It was surrounded by overstuffed chairs and a long couch, but no one sat there.

On the other side of the room a broad staircase wound up to a balcony that overlooked the lobby, but Clarissa only glanced at all these things. As soon as she saw the front desk, she carried the still sniffling Bella toward it. Bella quieted down considerably as they crossed the room, perhaps because she had now completely won the I-don't-want-to-walk battle, and whispered into Clarissa's ear, "Where's Daddy?"

"He'll be here soon."

A well-dressed man and woman already stood in front of them at the counter, arguing with the desk clerk about something. Clarissa shifted Bella in her arms as they waited for their turn.

"But I requested that room back in January," the man told the clerk sharply.

The clerk was only a young woman but didn't flinch at his tone. "I know, sir, and we try to honor requests, but we can't always manage it. Number 112 is still a nice room."

He let out a sigh and waved a hand to one side. "All right, 435 was our first choice, but if we can't have it, then just give us something else on the west wing."

The clerk's voice stayed even. "I'm sorry, sir, our entire west wing is booked."

"Booked? All of it? Before last January? I don't believe you."

Bella wiggled and twisted to look around at the lobby, so Clarissa set her down, but kept hold of her hand. As soon as Elaina saw that her mother's arms were free she raised her own in a request to be carried. Clarissa's arms ached from holding Bella the entire walk, but she couldn't refuse Elaina. After all, she had been so patient in walking all the way. Clarissa picked up her daughter and held her in one arm while holding onto Bella with her free hand.

"The crew of *Undercover Agents* is shooting a show here, and they have the entire west wing blocked off," the clerk explained. She nodded toward the front doors. "That's what's going on outside. Any minute now the cast is coming out to sign autographs and talk to fans about their show."

The man glanced through the glass doors, then back at the clerk with the same expression of disapproval. "I've seen that program, and there aren't more than a dozen people in it. Why do they need the whole west wing?"

"For production people, camera people, lighting crews, that type of thing."

"Well, what rooms do you have left then?"

The clerk rattled off several numbers, and the man shook his head, as though familiar with all these rooms, rejecting each of them on an individual basis.

Clarissa glanced at her watch. It was 8:10 now. What time had it been when they'd left the car? 8:00? Perhaps even 7:55. It had taken them some time to cross the parking lot because of Bella's stubbornness and Elaina's tiredness. So any time now Slade would make the same journey, and he'd do it in considerably quicker time. Perhaps he'd even have the limo drop him off at the front of the building. Would they still be waiting in the lobby when he arrived?

She tried not to think what this would do to Slade's mood if, despite all his plans, the press still found out they were here together.

The man in front of them shook his head, then pointed a finger at the clerk. "You know, we've been coming here for years, and there used to be a time you didn't have to be a movie star to get a good room in the place."

The clerk shrugged her shoulders and held out one hand in a gesture of apology. "I'm sorry you're not happy, but I can only do so much about the scheduling."

"The least you could do is offer us some sort of an upgrade."

Clarissa looked down at her watch. It was 8:12, and they hadn't even reached the check-in counter yet. Shouldn't the resort have more than one clerk working the desk? She strained to see if someone else was around but didn't see anyone. Maybe all the other employees had joined the crowd outside.

Clarissa squeezed Bella's hand and bent closer to her, trying to balance Elaina with her other arm. "Bella, would you like to play a funny game?" she whispered. "How about we play an ignore-your-father game? If he comes in here, let's pretend we don't know him, okay?"

Bella didn't say anything, but her brows wrinkled together unhappily. It was a bad sign.

Clarissa then leaned closer to Elaina and said, "We've never seen a movie star before in our lives, remember?"

Elaina smiled and nodded. At least she was willing to cooperate.

The man in front of them crossed his arms forcefully. "Well, I'm not sure if we want a room here then. I'll need to discuss our options with my wife." The couple moved farther down the counter to talk.

Clarissa quickly stepped up to the counter. "Clarissa Hancock and Meredith Allen."

The clerk checked through names on a ledger and then opened a drawer and took out two key cards. She put them on her side of the counter, then picked up a piece of paper with an outline of the resort on it. Holding the map over for them to see, she said, "You'll be staying in rooms 420 and 421." She quickly drew a circle around the little boxes with these numbers. "They're off to your—"

"Wait a minute, wait a minute!" The man stormed back to the front of the counter, standing directly beside them. "You just told me the west wing was all booked up."

"It is," the clerk said, this time a little less patiently. "These women are part of that group."

The man looked from the little girls, to Meredith, and then at Clarissa. "You mean to tell me you're movie people?"

Elaina smiled up at the man. "We've neber seen movie stars before in our lives."

"I thought as much." He turned to the clerk and waved a finger at her. "I want to see the manager, right now."

Clarissa took a step forward until she was leaning over the counter. "Can we just get our keys, please?"

And then from outside, clapping and hollering erupted.

"It sounds like the Agents just showed up," Meredith said.

Clarissa swallowed. "Or someone else." She let go of Bella's hand to take her key card from the clerk, and as she did, Bella shot off toward the front doors.

"Come back here," Clarissa called.

"Right now," Meredith added.

Bella peered out the glass doors for only a second. "It's Daddy!" she said, and then just as quickly, pushed open the door.

For Clarissa it was one of those awful moments, like when you knock a glass off a table and watch the thing falling in slow motion to the floor. You want to stop it, but you can't. Clarissa stood holding Elaina and willed Bella to turn and come back, but instead the little girl went crashing outside.

Clarissa turned and without a word handed Elaina to Meredith, then took off after Bella.

Bella had a head start, but she also had shorter legs, and Clarissa was determined to catch her.

The little girl darted into the crowd, and Clarissa followed. For a moment Clarissa couldn't see her at all, and felt the trappings of panic. What if she lost her altogether? Clarissa called out, "Bella!" and got no answer.

Then Clarissa caught sight of her weaving through a group of teenagers. She called out her name again, but Bella only glanced back at her and went quicker. Clarissa sprinted after her, trying to keep her in sight, while simultaneously avoiding plowing into bystanders. Bella slowed, staring up at the faces around her, looking for her father, and Clarissa narrowed the ground between them. The end of the chase came when Bella started to go one way, then changed her mind and went the other. Clarissa reached out and caught her. She took hold of Bella's arm and said, "You're coming with me right now, young lady."

Bella lunged toward the nearest pant leg and held on. "Daddy!" she screamed.

Still pulling on Bella's arm, Clarissa looked up at the owner of the pant leg to apologize for Bella's behavior and found herself looking directly into Slade's eyes.

He stared back at her, coldly, and hoisted Bella up into his arms. Then he took hold of Clarissa's elbow and propelled her forward. "We've had enough of a scene for one night," he said quietly into her ear. "Let's gather what dignity we can and go to the lobby."

Clarissa moved forward, in a shocked sort of way, and noticed for the first time that all eyes were on her. She gulped, and walked stiffly, hoping that if there were ever a time in her life when she could manage to walk without tripping, this would be it.

As they walked, one of the well-dressed, well-hairsprayed women stepped into their path. She called out, "Slade, is this your daughter?"

Slade paused in front of the reporter and smiled casually, confidently, as though he'd meant to take this opportunity to show off Bella all along. That, Clarissa supposed, was why they called it acting.

"Yes, this is my daughter, and," Slade motioned to Clarissa with a nod, "this is my daughter's nanny, Mrs. Hancock." He emphasized both the words *nanny* and *Mrs.*

The reporter gave Bella a big smile. "You are just a *doll.*"

"Are you a reporter?" Bella asked.

The smile got even bigger. "Yes, honey, I am."

In a matter-of-fact tone Bella said, "Reporters are bad people."

Slade laughed, in a choking sort of way. "I don't know where kids come up with these things."

"You told me so, Daddy," Bella said.

Slade laughed again, and this time it definitely sounded more like choking. "Of course, I wasn't talking about *you,*" he told the woman.

She smiled back at him stiffly. "Of course."

"My daddy and Clarissa aren't having an affair," Bella added.

Slade didn't wait for any questions after that. He started walking toward the lobby again, quite quickly this time, and Clarissa matched his pace.

Bella hugged her father's neck happily, as though it had been years and not just minutes since she'd last seen him and then kissed him on the cheek. It must have made an irresistible picture. Which is why, Clarissa told herself, there were suddenly flashes going off all around them.

4

Clarissa stood outside Slade's hotel door and knocked softly. She tried to appear as poised as possible for a person about to face the wrath of a man who had—at least in the movies—single-handedly stormed the White House, killed dozens of terrorists, and brought down a drug dynasty.

She fidgeted with her hands, forced herself to stop that, then found herself biting her bottom lip.

She had known ever since the instant she looked up from Bella's arm into Slade's eyes that this time would come. He had said nothing to her the entire time they were checking in at the hotel desk, or even on the way to their rooms. Now the girls had their pajamas on, their teeth brushed, and lay on Meredith's bed watching *Nick at Nite* so Slade could—as he'd explained to Meredith—have a moment alone to speak with Clarissa.

She stood outside his door and waited for his reply. She didn't have to wait long. After a moment he opened the door, moved aside, and very curtly said, "Come in."

She did. She stood in the middle of the room, looking first at the couch and then the chair. "Do you want me to sit down, or would you rather I stand while you yell at me?"

"One thing . . ." he told her. "I asked you for one simple thing." With his hands thrust in his pockets and his eyes darkened by anger, he paced back and forth across the floor of the suite. "I simply requested that you check in before me so I could spare myself any negative press. Was that so much to ask?"

"I only let go of Bella's hand for one second to get my key,

52

and she took off outside. I had to go after her. What else could I do?"

Slade stopped pacing and turned to face Clarissa. "Bella called reporters bad people and then specifically told one we weren't having an affair. How do you suppose *that* story will go over in the news room?"

"I didn't put those words into her mouth. You did."

"Yes, but I hired *you* to take care of her. You were supposed to be keeping her away from the reporters." He held one hand up in the air and began pacing again. "Do you have any idea what you've done? Do you have any idea what could happen now?"

She shrugged, but he wasn't watching her anyway.

"Reporters want a story, and you gave them a story." He emphasized his next words as though each one were a headline. "Slade Jacobson turns back on religious vows. Slade Jacobson trades heaven for a week in paradise with an angel. Slade Jacobson is a monumental hypocrite." Now he threw both hands upward. "I can hardly wait to see what Jay Leno has to say about *this*."

"I was doing my best to control Bella—"

"I certainly hope that wasn't your best," he cut in. "One would hope your best efforts would see you past the first hour of your job."

For one horrible moment Clarissa wasn't in Hawaii at all. She was back in her old house with Alex, and he was standing there berating her.

She couldn't keep the house clean. She couldn't control her daughter. Somehow Elaina had always been too loud, too messy, or up too late, and it was Clarissa's fault. Now with Slade Jacobson standing here saying the same things, she felt crushed by the thought that perhaps Alex had been right all along. Perhaps everything was her fault.

She bit her lip to keep the tears from coming, but felt them stinging in her eyes anyway. "I'm sorry," she said. "I tried not to let go of her."

He must have heard the quaver in her voice, because he suddenly stopped walking and looked at her more closely. Once he did, he sighed and tilted back his head. "Oh, no. Don't cry. What is it with women? They can't ever take a performance review."

"Is that what this is?" she coughed out. "A performance review?"

A quick sharp knock sounded on the door, and they both turned to look at it.

"Who's there?" Slade called.

"It's me, Tristan. Hurry and open the door."

Slade hesitated, but stepped toward the door. "This isn't the best time, Tristan. Can I give you a call later?"

"I don't care if you're in your pajamas," Tristan said. "Just open the door, and hurry."

Without another word Slade swung open the door. Tristan instantly came through, then pushed the door shut behind him. He was a young man, perhaps in his late twenties, with sandy blond hair that was a bit too long, but looked good on him anyway. He had clear blue eyes, a square jaw, and perfect features. Without looking at Slade, he put one shoulder against the door and listened to the sounds in the hallway. "Three teenage girls are after me. I don't know how they got past security, but I don't dare go to my room or I won't have a minute's peace."

"So you led them to my room," Slade said dryly. "How considerate."

Tristan shrugged, a smirk stealing across his features. "I figured you could use some female company even if—" and then he turned and saw Clarissa for the first time. A smile lit up his face. "Or perhaps not."

Slade spoke in a flat, expressionless voice. "This is Clarissa Hancock. Bella's nanny for the vacation."

Still smiling, Tristan walked to Clarissa and shook her hand, slowly, caressingly. He then winked over at Slade. "You don't have to explain to me."

It was just a smile, but it instantly became much more than

that. With this single act of admiration, Tristan gave Clarissa her confidence back. Everything was not her fault. Alex had been wrong, and so was Slade. They were just a pair of impossible men.

Slade folded his arms across his chest and looked over at his friend. "Oh, for heaven's sake, Tristan. She really is the nanny."

Clarissa smiled back at Tristan. "He's a little touchy about the subject right now."

Another knock sounded on the door. This one followed by giggles. Slade rolled his eyes and walked farther away from the door. "Great. Your fan club has arrived."

Tristan, in a voice much deeper than his own called, "Who is it?"

"Is this Tristan McKellips's room?" came a voice from the hallway.

"No," Tristan boomed. "It's Slade Jacobson's."

"Oh!" A chorus of shrieks and giggles penetrated the door and then, "Can he autograph our shirts?" More giggles. "Please?"

Tristan leaned toward Slade and in a low voice said, "Shall I call security, or do you want to go out there? They looked older than eighteen . . ."

Slade turned to Clarissa and whispered, "Can you convince them to leave, please?"

"How?"

"I don't know. Tell them I'm busy, tell them anything, just get rid of them."

"Tell them anything," Clarissa slowly repeated, and then smiled. "All right."

She strode to the door, unlocked it, and opened it wide enough to stick her head out. Three young girls stood in front of her, dressed up, made up, and questionably older than eighteen.

"Is Slade Jacobson really in there?" the one in the middle asked in an awed tone.

"Yes," Clarissa said. "But trust me. You don't want his autograph."

"Why not?" asked the first one.

"Well, I'm his daughter's nanny, and I can tell you, he's the most overbearing, egotistical man you'd ever hope not to meet. He asks the impossible and then acts like a tyrant when he doesn't get it."

All three faces fell. "Really?" they asked together.

Clarissa nodded. "Really. He's horrible." She then looked down the hallway. "If you want to meet someone nice, though, keep looking for Tristan McKellips. He's very friendly."

The smiles returned. "Thanks," the last one said, and then they started down the hallway, heads bobbing close together, already talking about this new information.

Clarissa shut the door, fastened the safety bolt, and then turned back to face the room.

Slade stood with his arms folded and glared at her. "I'm horrible?"

"They left, didn't they?"

"I'm overbearing?"

"See, you're doing it right now," she said. "You ask the impossible and now you're unhappy."

"I think the phrase you used was, 'He's a tyrant.'"

She leaned against the door because there was no place else to go. "You said you wanted me to get rid of them."

"But not like *that*."

"Ohhh," she drew out the word as though she at last understood. "Well, I'll think of something else to tell the next group."

"No you won't. I don't want you to say anything to anyone for the rest of the time we're here. Do you understand?"

"That's a little overbearing, don't you think?"

Tristan laughed. Slade didn't.

She cocked her head and looked at her boss. "So are you firing me?"

"No. And don't you dare quit and leave me without a nanny, either. You agreed to work for the whole time we're here."

"All right," she said. "Then I think it's time I go to bed so I won't be dead on my feet tomorrow."

Slade nodded, but his eyes still smoldered with anger. "Good night, then."

"Good night. I'll have Meredith bring Bella to you."

She opened the door and slipped outside. Just as the door closed she heard Slade's voice, still crisp with emotion, say, "This is exactly the reason I'm single."

Clarissa shook her head and walked over to Meredith's room. "Ditto," she said out loud.

✢ ✢ ✢

Early the next morning Slade dropped Bella off at Clarissa's room. She greeted Bella with the exaggerated happy voice adults use when they talk to children. She greeted Slade with less enthusiasm.

He almost—almost—said, "I'm sorry about last night," but instead he mumbled, "I don't know how long I'll be."

She shrugged. "That's all right."

He handed her a cell phone. "I always give this to Bella's nannies to keep with them. That way we can keep track of each other."

She took the phone. "Fine."

He then handed her one of his key cards. "If you need to get into my room for toys or clothes for Bella you can use this."

"Thanks," she said.

"And be sure to take your key card with you if you leave this floor. After last night's teenage invasion, the hotel has set security guards at the end of the hallway."

"Okay," Clarissa said.

They stared at one another for a moment longer, and then Slade said, "Well, I'll see you later then." He turned, started down the hallway, and heard the door close behind him.

In brisk, heavy steps he walked to the elevator. He hated apologies. It was just like rehashing the event all over again. And women made it even harder than it had to be. With guys, apologies were easy. You just said, "Hey, you're not nearly as obnoxious as you were yesterday," and the other guy said, "And you're not nearly as ugly!" Then you slapped each other on the shoulders and the thing was over.

Women always wanted to discuss their feelings, analyze every word you said, and point out all your many flaws along the way. They expected things like candy and flowers; and the prettier the woman, the more she expected. Clarissa probably pulled in quite a haul after every argument.

He would have to pick up something for her later, though he wasn't sure what. With her big blue eyes she probably got stuff like jewelry. He wondered, but only for a moment, what Clarissa's perfect husband would do if she came home wearing jewelry Slade had given her. It would probably cause a big argument, and more apologies, and then she would get another installment of jewelry. Love didn't keep jewelers in business, apologies did.

Maybe he'd just give her a bonus after the trip.

Slade ate breakfast in the hotel restaurant in hopes of seeing A.J. there, but no one he knew came in. In between the time he spent pushing his eggs around on his plate, and the time he spent checking the door, he stared out at the ocean.

He'd grown up in California, so he'd put in a good deal of time at the beach. Still, he never tired of watching the waves— the way they rose up, as though reaching for something, then rolled over in a great churning mass and spilled onto the shore. This time as Slade watched them, he wondered what they were reaching for.

And he hoped he had better luck in reaching his goals.

After breakfast he made his way to a meeting room off of the lobby, which had been turned into a prop storage area. He wasn't actually expecting A.J. to be there, but perhaps someone from the crew might know where he was.

An odd assortment of crates and boxes created a maze in the room, and a few people milled around between them, unloading things here and there. He sauntered in, stepping over cables and wires from the lighting equipment, and looked for a familiar face. It took him only moments to find one.

Nataly Granger knelt beside a box, digging through its contents with her long, tanned arms. He hadn't seen her in over a year, not since they'd worked together on the film *Mermaid Island*. Her platinum blonde hair was shorter than it had been, but her eyes were still the same bright blue, and her body still looked a perpetual twenty years old.

She wore a pair of tight blue jeans and a halter top, but he could almost see her decked out in her mermaid outfit and being carried onto the set because she couldn't walk in her fins.

He had teased her mercilessly throughout the production, telling her one crippled mermaid joke after another. She got back at him by making their love scene difficult. Every time they practiced, she changed it on him. Instead of murmuring softly into his ear that she loved him, she'd put her head on his shoulder and whisper anything else. "I was attacked by a rabid tuna," she told him once breathlessly, "and now I feel like biting you."

She made such a joke of the whole thing he could barely keep a straight face during the actual shooting of the scene.

Slade shook his head and took in the sight of her for another moment. "Nataly, if they're making you unload your own props, I suggest you find a new agent."

She looked over at him, and recognition warmed her face. "Slade!" She got to her feet and gave him a hug, holding her body tightly against him. As he held her he got a faint whiff of her Giorgio perfume. Even that was the same.

She released him, then glanced back at the boxes. "I was looking for my laptop. I think it got packed up with the props back in California." Smiling, she tucked her hands into her back pockets. "This is such a surprise to see you again. What are you doing here?"

"Mostly just visiting Tristan."

Nataly tilted her head, and her eyes narrowed slightly. "Men never visit Tristan. And besides, the two of you can see each other in L.A. Why are you *really* here?"

He laughed and ran a hand across the back of his neck. "Well, actually I'm trying to pitch a script."

"Ahhh. Business. I should have known. Everything is always business with you." She leaned closer to him. "If I recall, you were always too busy to devote any time to our budding relationship."

"Yes, but as you remember, you were a fish. And besides, you died tragically in the end." He snapped his fingers in the air as if trying to remember. "What was it that finally did you in? Was it the rabid tuna or the oil spill? I've forgotten."

"It was those little plastic rings they use in six packs," she said. "They're deadly to marine life."

"Ah, yes, well, it's good that the old saying is true then. 'There's more than one fish in the sea.'"

She reached out and put a hand on his arm, her pale pink lips parted slightly, seductively. "It's also true you always remember the fish that got away."

And then Slade recalled the other thing about Nataly. Back when they were working on *Mermaid Island*, she made passes at him on a daily basis. He considered it harmless flirting at first, but then one day she showed up in his dressing room wearing nothing but seashells. He'd had to emphasize, strenuously, that he was married. Happily married. Back then he still believed it was a happy marriage.

Nataly leaned toward Slade and ran a finger across his arm. "I was really sorry when I read in the papers that you and Evelyn split up. All that fidelity for nothing."

"Yes, well, sometimes that's how it goes." Slade looked around him to see if the other prop people were watching them. They had all disappeared except for one guy across the room. With his back to them, he pulled what looked to be a bunch of assault rifles from a box, looked them over, and then put them back into the box.

"Fidelity is overrated in my opinion," Nataly purred.

"And underrated in mine."

She took her hand from his arm and slowly pushed a strand

of blonde hair behind her ear. Her long fingernails were striped gold and silver, matching the rings she wore on each finger. "The cast is having a luau tonight—a dinner and a dance here at the resort to celebrate being in Hawaii. You'll come, won't you?"

He took a step away from her and pretended to look at a box full of police hats. "What are you doing here with the cast, anyway? Are you guest starring?"

Casually, she leaned up against one of the crates and watched him. The pose was calculated. Alluring. "No. Actually, I'm here with my boyfriend."

"And does he share your views about fidelity?"

She laughed, a soft tinkling sound like water falling. "Drinks are at 5:30. Roasted pig is at 6:00. A.J. is hosting. Is he the one you want to pitch your script to?"

Slade nodded. "He's the man."

"I can help you with it then."

Somehow he knew, before he even asked, what the answer to his next question would be. Still, he had to ask it. "And how would you do that?"

"I'll get you a seat at our table. A.J.'s and mine."

"He's your boyfriend." It was more of a statement than a question.

"I don't mind helping you out, Slade. I want to do it." She flashed him a smile that lit up the blue in her eyes. "Oh, and of course the dress is Hawaiian. So shall I put you on the guest list? The security is going to be very tight."

"Having trouble with fans?"

"No, with the press."

"You didn't seem to have problems with them last night." He tapped his thumb against the crate and tried not to cringe at the memory. "It looked like you invited every reporter on this side of the Pacific to come out and meet you."

"It's not the local press that's giving us grief. It's the tabloids. Ever hear of Sylvia Stoddard?"

The name rang a bell, and not a smooth melodic bell, but the shrill clanging of an alarm clock. "Sylvia Stoddard?" he repeated.

"*The Scoop* magazine." Nataly overpronounced each word, as though the syllables themselves were sharp.

"Ah, yes, *The Scoop*." One of those horrible tell-alls that only tells enough to fuel the imagination of its readers. "I've always wondered what exactly it was scooping out."

"Well, not only is Sylvia producing fiction for it, she's also started one of those TV gossip bits they do on the news shows. It's called the *Hollywood Dish*, and lately the *Undercover Agents* cast has been the main course. It's driving us all crazy."

Now he remembered Sylvia. He could picture her clearly, sitting behind her desk, her shoulder-length dark hair pulled back into a bun, a full set of shiny white teeth set in the middle of wide cheeks. The cheeks were wide because she was on the plump side, but also because she smiled so continually that her cheek muscles had probably grown to be the strongest in her body.

That was the thing about Sylvia. She smiled in a calm regal manner as she sat on TV devouring people's lives.

Nataly reached over and placed a hand on Slade's arm, tilting her face up at him. "So are you brave enough to hang out with us, or should I leave you off the guest list?"

For a moment Slade considered refusing the invitation, because of Nataly, not Sylvia.

But that was silly, wasn't it? After all, there was nothing wrong in having dinner with the cast of *Undercover Agents*. It was exactly the type of opportunity he needed. And Nataly wasn't likely to try any of her old tricks with A.J. sitting right next to her. He was her boyfriend, for heaven's sake. Chances were she was madly in love with him, and all of this stuff now was just flirting for old time's sake.

"Dinner sounds great," he said, and then to be on the safe side added, "I'll bring my secretary along. She just, you know, loves mingling with celebrities."

"The woman who used to bring Bella to the set?"

"Yes, Meredith. That's the one."

One of Nataly's perfectly shaped eyebrows arched up. "She's still with you, even after the tropical fish fiasco?"

Slade shifted his weight uncomfortably and turned away from the police hat box. "It wasn't Meredith's fault that Bella shattered the aquarium. Bella is just accident prone." He glanced up at the ceiling, then let out a slow breath. "It was my fault, really. I should have known better than to let her be within throwing distance of it."

Nataly smiled in a reminiscing sort of way. "I'll never forget the way the water flooded all over the studio floor—how all the fish flopped around on the ground while we raced around trying to save them . . ."

"The lighting guys and I tried to save them," Slade said. "You just sat there in your fins laughing at us."

". . . and you threw some of them into the water cooler. . . . That might actually have worked if they had been fresh-water fish . . ."

Slade shook his head ruefully. "You wouldn't think dying fish would be so picky."

". . . so then you stood over the cooler with a salt shaker trying to save them. It was very noble."

"Yes, I'm sure that's what you thought while you were doubled up laughing."

She grinned at him, but it wasn't the grin he noticed. It was the way her gaze locked onto him, as though trying to hold him captive in it. "I've always thought you were very noble." She leaned closer to him again. "You'll save me a dance tonight, won't you?"

"Sure. We'll request the theme song to *Mermaid Island*."

"Good." The grin melted from her face, but the gaze was still going full blast. "I guess I ought to get back to my room. I have tons of unpacking to do." She took a few steps toward the door, then turned back to face him. "Oh, and Slade, since we're in

Hawaii, who knows—maybe I'll be able to find some seashells you like."

Nataly finished her exit out the door, but Slade stood in the room for several moments longer. He rubbed one hand over his brow and stared at the door. He hadn't planned on walking any tightropes, but suddenly found himself teetering on one. If he offended Nataly, she'd destroy his chance with A.J. If he didn't offend Nataly—well, there was no way around offending her if she planned to resurrect her seashell wardrobe. He'd have to just do his best to avoid her until he'd worked things out with A.J.

Of all people, he had to run into Nataly here.

Slade shook his head again and resolved never to become a gambler, because nobody, he was sure, had worse luck.

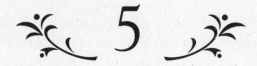

5

After Clarissa shut the door behind Slade, she smiled down at Bella in the most confident manner she could muster. Clarissa had spent half of last night mentally reviewing every child-rearing technique she'd ever learned about—coming up with contingencies for every possible Bella situation, until she felt she was ready for anything.

After all, Clarissa was a trained professional. During her family science classes she'd studied Piaget, Brazelton, Skinner, Freud, and most importantly James Jones. She knew all about developmental needs, motivation, consequences, the subconscious, boundaries, and a myriad of complexes. She had years of experience in child care and the experts on her side.

Now she bent down until she was eye level with her charge and asked cheerfully, "Are you ready to play with us?"

Bella glanced around the room, taking in Elaina, who sat at the coffee table sleepily chomping on pieces of French toast. Bella looked back at Clarissa and said, "I want to go swimming."

"Maybe we'll do that later then."

"Why can't we go now?"

"Because we just ate, and we don't want to get cramps." Okay, Clarissa told herself, I'm thirty seconds into this day, and I just reverted to an old wives' tale. Next I'll be telling her the stork brings babies and if she steps on a crack her mother will be doomed to a life of chiropractic care. But Clarissa didn't want to tell Bella the real reason they weren't going outside right now, which was that Clarissa felt she had to get some ground rules down, inside, before they faced another crowd. Bella needed to understand that Clarissa was in charge, that she had authority to enforce the rules, and that consequences would follow if Bella didn't obey. Last night, as far as Clarissa could tell, Slade hadn't even reprimanded Bella for running away. It was a performance Clarissa didn't want to have repeated—that she couldn't afford to have repeated.

In the same cheerful voice Clarissa asked, "Would you like to color while Elaina eats breakfast?"

Bella ignored Clarissa's question and went and stood beside Elaina. Looking down at the pieces of French toast she said, "Are you done yet, 'Laina?"

Elaina shook her head, then slowly lifted another forkful of syrup-drenched French toast to her mouth.

"Are you done now?" Bella asked.

Clarissa tried to curb the questioning. "Bella, we're going to play inside for an hour or so. Then if the two of you are good we can go to the pool."

"But I want to go to the ocean and look for sharks."

"We'll try the kiddy pool first."

Bella's brows knitted together, and she frowned over at Clarissa. "You're 'posed to be playing with me."

"I'd be happy to play some inside games."

Bella crossed her arms tightly across her chest. "I want to go to the ocean."

"I understand that," Clarissa said, "but nevertheless the answer is no."

The tears sprung immediately to Bella's eyes. Her face almost seemed to scrunch into itself, and she let out a low wail of, "You're not playing with me!"

Clarissa tried to reason with her for a moment longer, but Bella's wails only got louder and more shrill. In between her, "I want to see the waves right now!" and "I'm telling my dad that you're not nice!" she also added a few, "My daddy can make people disappear!"

How nice for him. Along with being a movie star, and an impromptu spokesman for the Church, he was also a magician. Life must be easy for those with so many talents.

Holding tightly onto the last vestige of her cheerfulness, Clarissa scooped up the little girl, sat her down on the desk chair, and called over the din, "You can get off of the chair, Bella, when you're quiet."

Clarissa then walked over to the coffee table and wiped Elaina's face and hands off with a napkin. Elaina sat, wide eyed and unblinking, staring at Bella. She was quite done with her breakfast now, and clearly wondered what horrible thing was going to happen next.

"Bella just needs to learn she can't always have her way," Clarissa told her daughter softly. "Let's play with a sticker book while we wait for her to calm down."

Elaina allowed Clarissa to propel her to the couch, but still kept her gaze fixed on Bella. Clarissa picked up a book filled with vinyl zoo animal stickers and set it on her lap. For half an hour she put animals in and out of cages in an attempt to ignore Bella's screams, which rose by octaves as time progressed. Any moment now they would shatter glass.

Clarissa glanced down at her watch. If this were to go on for much longer the hotel staff would probably call to see who was being tortured. Perhaps the security guards were even now on their way to the room—or worse yet, Slade himself might be striding down the hallway.

And what would Slade do if he found out that his daughter had sat screaming on a chair all morning? Perhaps for her job's sake, she ought to take Bella off the chair, go directly to the beach, and decide that if Slade wanted to teach Bella discipline, he could do it himself. Clarissa wasn't her parent. Clarissa just got paid to keep Bella happy while Slade worked.

Clarissa glanced over at Bella, and then at the hotel room door. If they left now, they could reach the beach in ten minutes. Ten minutes to quiet, happiness, and job security.

But even as she thought about it, Clarissa knew she couldn't give in. She couldn't let Bella get her way by screaming. Bella had already had a succession of revolving caregivers, and someone, somewhere along the line, had to be firm with this child. If for no one else's sake, for Bella herself.

Clarissa shut her eyes for a moment as though trying to see all of the text she'd ever studied on the subject. Somewhere in those pages were the tools she needed. The experts, the men with the doctorate degrees . . . she reached out to them.

Skinner, yes, he said behavioral extinction takes time. Sometimes a lot of time. Jones said a parent couldn't control a child's behavior, just the consequences that followed. So she was on the right track. And Freud—he said repressed anxiety needed psychotherapy. Well, rather than go into dream analysis, she would just ignore Freud. It had been her standard practice during her years of studying family science.

Clarissa took a pack of cards from the table and said in an overly loud voice to Elaina, "Why don't we play a game of Go Fish while we wait for Bella to calm down?"

Bella's voice dropped to a low whine, and in between broken sobs she asked, "Can we go to the beach if I calm down?"

Clarissa shuffled the deck of cards and without looking at Bella dealt them out into three stacks. "If you calm down, you can get off the chair and play cards with us. Then later on we can go to the swimming pool."

Bella crossed her arms over the chair back and buried her head in her arms. From underneath her mass of curls she moaned, "I'm telling my daddy I want you to go away."

Clarissa handed one stack of cards to Elaina, then picked up her own hand and arranged the cards. "I understand that you're angry with me."

Bella continued to lie half flung over the back of the chair, muttering things into her arms. Clarissa supposed it was quiet enough to count as 'calmed down' and softly called up to her, "Would you like to play Go Fish with Elaina and me now?"

Bella lifted her head, looked at the cards, and then sniffed. Clarissa was sure the little girl would snarl, "No," and turn away again, but instead Bella slipped from the chair, went to the third stack of cards, and plopped down in front of them.

"Do I get to go first?" she asked.

"That would be fine," Clarissa said, and then, while Bella was arranging her cards, Clarissa let out a slow breath. It was only one hurdle, she knew, but it felt like success to have cleared it.

❖ ❖ ❖

After three rounds of Go Fish, four storybooks, and two trips to the bathroom, Clarissa decided she was secure enough, ready enough, to try an outing at the pool with Bella.

But just to be certain, she decided to take along Piaget, Brazelton, Skinner, and Jones anyway. Freud would undoubtedly bring his id and tag along, too. That was the thing about Freud. Once he popped up, it was hard to get rid of him.

Clarissa gathered up towels, sunblock, snacks, toys, keys, the cell phone, and basically anything and everything else she could think of that might come in handy at the pool, then put it all in a big plastic beach bag. She needed to be prepared for anything, so she would be.

Next she had the girls put on their swimming suits. Bella looked like a fairy princess in hers. It was covered in ribbons and ruffles—no doubt created by some chic boutique on Rodeo Drive. Elaina, although less conspicuous, also looked darling in a pink checked suit with small white ruffles. Clarissa looked considerably less darling in her old blue suit. As she slipped the straps over her shoulders, she noticed some snags in the material she hadn't seen before, and the elastic was giving way around one of the legs. It also looked decidedly faded next to the crisp brightness of the girls' swimming suits.

She had meant to buy a new one last summer, perhaps even the summer before that, but every time she spent money it led to a fight with Alex, and so finally she just stopped buying herself anything. And of course since the divorce she hadn't had the

means to buy such frivolities as swimming suits. Not when Elaina
needed so many things.

Clarissa took one last depressing look at herself in the mirror,
then tossed her white terry cloth robe into the beach bag. It was
short and thin and could pass for a swimming suit cover-up. If
there were a lot of people at the pool, if she got to feeling too
insecure, she would just throw it on.

As they walked to the kiddy pool, Clarissa told the girls several times that whether or not they went to the beach depended
on how well they minded her at the pool. Bella, in her haste to
get to the pool, only half listened. She skipped all the way there,
stopping every few feet to turn around and call, "Come on. I can
see it!"

A large clover-shaped pool, with a fountain spraying up in
the middle, lay spread out in back of the resort. The kiddy pool
lay right beside it, only it wasn't merely a shallow pool, it also had
fountains tossing water in different directions, and a slide shaped
like a sunken ship.

As they weaved through the sunbathers Clarissa said,
"Remember, I'm responsible for looking after you, and the first
time you so much as go near the big pool, we're done swimming,
and we'll go back to our rooms for naps."

"I don't take naps anymore," Bella said.

"You will if you go near the big pool," Clarissa told her.

Neither child seemed especially worried about her threats,
and they both ran, squealing, into the fountains, without looking
back at her.

Clarissa tossed their towels on a patio table, pulled a beach
chair closer to the pool, and sat down to watch the girls. Bella
had no fear of anything. She jumped from one fountain to the
next, then slid down the slide with hands raised as though trying
to take hold of the sky. Elaina eyed everything cautiously. She
tried something new only after she saw Bella do it first.

Clarissa wished her daughter were a little more confident.
Perhaps some of Bella would rub off on Elaina during this trip.

After Clarissa watched the girls for about twenty minutes, a middle-aged woman walked over and sat down in the chair next to her. The woman's dark hair was pulled back in a bun and wrapped in a brightly colored tropical scarf that matched her skirted swimsuit. Dark sunglasses hid her eyes, but she trained a red lipsticked smile on Clarissa as she said, "It's a beautiful day to sit out at the pool, isn't it?"

"Yes, it's gorgeous out." Clarissa vaguely wondered why the woman had come to the kiddy pool. She looked too old to be the mother of any of the children tromping about in the water, but then, sometimes women had children late in life, and other times they were early grandmothers.

"Of course, kids don't care what kind of day it is so long as they can play something," the woman said. "Mine always liked the rain as much as the sunshine. Rain made mud, and that, as you know, is great fun."

Clarissa nodded. "And fun to clean up after, too."

The woman looked out over the pool. "Which children are yours?"

"The one coming down the slide and the one . . ." Clarissa searched for a moment to find Bella. "And the one sitting on that fountain."

"Two girls. How sweet. Are they twins?"

"No, I'm just tending the fountain-sitter."

The lipstick smile grew. "Well, that's a generous thing to do while on your vacation. I hope her parents appreciate it."

"I'm being paid to do it," Clarissa said. "I'm here as a nanny."

"Oh, a nanny." The woman turned her gaze back on Bella, and she nodded. "I had a friend who nannied years ago. It didn't work out very well for her though, poor thing. The little boy she watched was a terror, and the parents were impossible to deal with." The woman shook her head. "I'm afraid most nannies are vastly underappreciated. It's a hard job."

It has been so far, Clarissa thought, but she didn't say it.

When Clarissa didn't comment, the woman went on. "But

71

then, of course, you're watching a little girl, and they're not half the terrors boys are."

"I don't know," Clarissa said. "I imagine Bella could take on anyone for that title."

The woman laughed lightly and stretched her legs out a bit farther against the pool deck. "Oh? Does she give you trouble?"

Clarissa didn't answer right away. She suddenly felt pangs of disloyalty for saying what she had.

Skinner: Labels damage a child's self-esteem.

Jones: Bella needs positive reinforcement.

Freud: Your subconscious is trying to assert itself independently of your ego.

When you came right down to it, Freud didn't make a lot of sense.

Clarissa shrugged. "I imagine all children, both boys and girls, come with their own amount of trouble. It's part of raising them. I'm just happy I can work and still have my little girl with me."

The woman turned her gaze to Elaina. "Yes," she said slowly. "That is wonderful. Some employers wouldn't allow it. Yours must be very fond of you."

Not really. "He's a very nice man," Clarissa said.

The woman leaned in a bit closer to Clarissa. "How lucky for you that you get along. How much time do you spend together?"

Before she could answer, a booming voice came from behind her. "Sylvia! Yes, I thought that was you. How are you doing?"

Clarissa turned around and saw Tristan striding toward them. He wore a pair of khaki swimming trunks and had a towel draped around his neck. His hair was wet, and water droplets glistened all over his tanned body, as though he had just stepped out of the pool and hadn't had a chance to dry off yet.

Sylvia slipped the sunglasses from her face and smiled up at him. "I'm fine, Tristan. And I don't need to ask you. I can tell you're doing wonderfully."

Tristan sat down on the other side of Sylvia and gave Clarissa a forced smile. "I see you've met Sylvia Stoddard. She's one of the reporters for *The Scoop* magazine."

Clarissa didn't say anything at all. She just shut her eyes momentarily and gulped. A reporter. She'd been talking to a reporter—something her employment contract specifically stated she could not do. But it wasn't her fault. She hadn't known. And she hadn't said anything bad . . . well, except that Bella could compete with anyone for the title of "Terror."

Slade was not going to understand this. Clarissa laid her head back against the chair and gulped again.

Sylvia's attention turned to Tristan; however, and she didn't seem to notice Clarissa's discomfort. She tapped her sunglasses against Tristan's leg with an air of familiarity. "When are you going to let me interview you for *The Scoop*? I've always wanted to do you, you know."

Tristan's smile was still forced. "Oh, I think your magazine has already done me quite a few times. The last time I read it I learned I was secretly engaged to half a dozen show girls, and in drug rehab all at the same time."

Sylvia didn't even wince. She leaned toward Tristan and said, "Consider it your opportunity to set the record straight."

Tristan's gaze traveled back to Clarissa. His voice was still light, and yet felt very heavy to her. "Is that what you were doing talking to Slade's nanny? Trying to get the record straight?"

Sylvia glanced back at Clarissa as if just remembering she sat beside her. "We were just passing the time. Friendly chitchat. That's all. Weren't we, dear?"

"Bella is a lovely child," Clarissa said quickly, "and Slade is only nice to me in a professional sort of way."

"Yes, of course, dear," Sylvia said.

Tristan shook his head slightly and rolled his eyes, but before Sylvia turned back to him he put on his smile again. In a low voice, as though he and Sylvia were conspirators, he said, "I wouldn't want you to use anything Slade's nanny said in your magazine. Slade likes to keep his family life private, and I'd hate to see her in trouble, since I'm the one who got her the job as nanny."

Sylvia tilted her head a bit, seeming every bit as surprised as Clarissa was by this information. "You're in the nanny business now?"

"No, but Slade needed a nanny, and . . ." He hesitated only a moment before he came up with her name. "Clarissa is a friend of mine, so I got them hooked up with one another." Tristan leaned forward and put one tanned hand on Sylvia's not-so-tan knee. "How about this. You forget you talked to Clarissa, and I'll buy you lunch. While we eat you can interview me to your heart's content."

Sylvia's smile grew so wide it seemed to cut her face in half. "I'll take you up on that offer, and I just so happen to be famished right now."

"Great," he said. "Let's go see what the hotel is serving."

They both got up, and Sylvia didn't even give Clarissa another glance as they walked away from the pool. That was all right though. The look Tristan shot her was enough.

For quite some time Clarissa just sat in the chair, limply watching the girls splash around, while she chastised herself.

She should have known better than to talk to that woman. Well, okay, she wasn't sure *how* she should have known better, but she should have. She was in a different world now, a world where words, where the mere innuendo of words, was a dangerous thing. She couldn't forget that again. If needs be she'd take up sign language and pretend to be mute—that was, if she actually had a job after this afternoon.

When the cell phone rang in the beach bag, Clarissa jumped. Slade was calling. What should she tell him?

"Hello?" she said meekly.

"Hi. Where are you guys?"

"We're at the kiddy pool."

"Okay. I'll be there in ten minutes. Good-bye." He hung up without waiting for her good-bye. It was just as well he didn't say anything else. If he had, he would have probably asked, "How did things go?" and then she would have had to tell him something. At least this way she didn't have to tell him over the phone. She could tell him in person his daughter had spent half the morning screaming and threatening to get her fired. And then Clarissa could mention that she'd just told a reporter that Bella was a terror and at this very moment, Tristan was out having lunch with the woman to try to rectify the situation.

Clarissa let out a small groan, shut her eyes, and leaned her head into her hands. She didn't want to face Slade. She really didn't.

When she opened her eyes the first thing she saw were the snags in her bathing suit. And she especially didn't want to face Slade wearing this beat-up old bathing suit. If she was going to be fired, she should do it with as much dignity as possible.

Hadn't that same thought flashed through her mind last night?

Clarissa shook her head as she pulled her robe from the beach bag. It just wasn't a good sign that this sentence had become the theme of her career as a nanny.

She slipped into her robe but didn't actually feel any more confident. Then she forced herself to look at the girls, and not at her watch, counting down the minutes until Slade came.

It was seventeen minutes later, not ten, that Slade showed up, and he didn't come by himself. Two men and a woman walked with him toward the pool. The men were perhaps in their forties but in good shape. One had a receding hairline, but wore what hair he had left tied behind his neck in a ponytail. The other man had jet-black hair, a mustache, and wore metallic sunglasses. The woman Clarissa vaguely recognized as one of the actresses from *Undercover Agents*, although she couldn't think of her name offhand. Long red hair swung around her shoulders, and large green eyes looked out from the midst of flawless skin. She was easily 5'-10" tall, and most of that was willowy legs. Her swimming suit looked as though it were made of black velvet and showed off a Barbie-perfect figure.

Next Clarissa's gaze moved to Slade, and she couldn't keep it from lingering there as he approached. He wore navy blue trunks, dark sunglasses, and had a pool towel slung over one of his shoulders. Clarissa had never particularly appreciated how broad Slade's shoulders were before, and now as he walked toward her, she tried not to stare at them. It probably wasn't professional behavior for someone who was about to be fired.

When Slade reached Clarissa he dropped his towel on the chair next to her, then stepped out of his sandals. Those with him followed suit and began settling into the row of chairs by Clarissa.

Slade nodded at the group with him. "This is Bella's nanny, Mrs. Hancock." He then held his hand out to point at each of the people with him. "This is Brandy, the hardworking, streetwise junior agent; and two narcotic thugs, Joe and Breck, who get killed in a bloody shoot-out at the end of the next show."

Joe, the one with the ponytail, reached over, shook Clarissa's hand, and winked. "Only the good die young."

Brandy laughed, sat down, and adjusted her pool chair so it leaned back. "Slade, that's the last time I tell you the plot line to one of our episodes."

"You don't have to tell anyone the plots," Breck said, plopping down on the chair next to her. "They're all the same. Just for variety, I'm going to try and convince A.J. to let us kill off one of the agents in our crossfire."

"Don't let it be me," Brandy said. "Nataly would be buttoning up my uniform before they could even shoot the tender and poignant scene where everyone comes to my funeral and cries their eyes out."

Slade was the only one still standing. He looked out over the kiddy pool and fountain area. "Where's Bella?"

Clarissa pointed to the far corner of the pool where Elaina and Bella were bent over on their hands and knees, periodically jumping across the pool. "They're being sharks," she said.

"Ah, yes, my daughter the shark." He sat down in the chair between Clarissa and Brandy and leaned back in a relaxed fashion. "How has Bella been today?"

And here it was. The time to confess all, only Clarissa couldn't exactly bring herself to do it with three other people sitting with them. And Slade wouldn't want these other people to know what had gone on this morning anyway. Hadn't Tristan just emphasized what a private person Slade was when it came to his family life?

Still Clarissa had to say something. She smiled weakly and said, "Bella wanted to go to the beach, but I thought it was best if we tried the kiddy pool first. She got quite upset about that."

Slade looked back over at Bella. "Upset how?"

"You know, yelling and crying," and *issuing threats like a three-foot dictator.*

Slade continued to look at Bella and at last shrugged. "She seems to be fine now."

Clarissa let out a slow breath. That was easier than she expected. Of course, Slade's attitude might change after he talked to Bella. It all depended on whether Bella actually carried through on her plans to tell Slade what an awful nanny she was. And there was still the matter of the reporter. Clarissa hadn't formulated a casual way to tell Slade about that.

Before she could think of anything he said, "I thought I'd watch the girls for a while and give you the afternoon off. That way you won't be mad at me when I ask you to watch Bella later this evening."

"Oh, you have something planned?"

"The *Agents'* cast has a dinner and dance tonight. A.J. will be there, and the press won't."

"The press?" Clarissa repeated.

Joe leaned toward her. "Vultures," he said. "And may I someday be famous enough to have them circling me."

She should have said something about Sylvia then. She should have said, "Yeah, the press is really horrible. Why, just a little while ago . . ." But she couldn't do it. Slade had already yelled at her in front of Tristan. She didn't want to add three more actors to that list of witnesses. Pretty soon she wouldn't be able to turn on the TV without spotting all the people who'd seen her chewed out.

Clarissa twisted one finger around the tie of her robe. "So you're going to a dance tonight? That sounds fun." Her voice sounded unnaturally high, and she hoped Slade didn't notice.

Breck slapped suntan lotion across his arms and shoulders and shook his head. "It should be another one of A.J.'s big affairs. I swear, he doesn't think he's running a production, he thinks he's running a cruise ship, and he's Captain Stubing."

Joe nodded. "He must have taken Fred Astaire courses and wants to get his money's worth."

Brandy stretched out her long legs, then slipped a pair of sunglasses over her eyes. "Some people enjoy dancing."

Breck elbowed Joe and smirked. "Yeah, and those people are called women."

Clarissa's gaze momentarily fluttered over to Brandy. She couldn't help but wonder if she was the one who had invited Slade. They would make such a striking couple together. All of Brandy's long red hair next to Slade's thick, dark, I'd-love-to-run-my-fingers-through-it brown hair.

She suddenly felt enormously dowdy in her terry cloth robe.

It wasn't fair. No one should have to sit next to a starlet at a swimming pool while wearing an old terry cloth robe. These men were probably all comparing Brandy's long tanned legs to Clarissa's pale ones . . . and Brandy's shiny, curled-just-right hair to Clarissa's dull, limp, pulled-back-in-a-ponytail blonde hair. She hated to think what else they might be comparing.

Clarissa had the sudden urge to name off her good qualities. *Okay, so I've never appeared in* People *magazine, but I'm a caring mother, and I got straight A's in college. I know how to can peaches, make life-like flowers out of crepe paper, and can sing all of Handel's*

Messiah *on key. I have lots of friends back home. Not famous friends,
but still people of the highest caliber.*

It wouldn't have mattered to them, she supposed. Somehow
in the great scale of life, being able to can peaches and be a good
mother never seemed to outweigh looking stunning in a black
velvet swimsuit.

Slade leaned over to Clarissa. "I'm serious about you taking
the afternoon off. Have you given the girls lunch yet?"

"Lunch? Um, no. I was just about to order something for
them."

"I can do it," Slade said. "Go have some fun, and I'll bring the
girls to your room at 4:30."

Clarissa glanced over at Bella and Elaina. They were leaping
toward the chairs now, making tremendous splashes as they came.
Any moment Bella would look up and see her father, and then
what would happen? Perhaps Clarissa should take Slade up on
the offer and bolt before Bella had the chance to make even more
waves.

"But are you sure you're up to watching two children?"

He rolled his eyes. "I am a parent, Clarissa. Over the past four
years I have managed to pick up a few child-rearing abilities."

Bella let out a squeal, followed by a loud, "Daddy!" and then
tromped up to the chairs and flung herself onto her father's lap.

"Hey, princess." He took his towel off the chair and wrapped
it around her until she looked like a big mound of fluff with eyes.
"Are you having fun?"

"I'm a shark," she said.

"I see. And did you have a good morning with Clarissa and
Elaina?"

Clarissa wrapped her own towel around Elaina and held her
breath, waiting for the tell-all: The ocean. The chair. The I'm-
going-to-tell-my-daddy-to-send-you-away story. To what degree
would Slade take his daughter's side, over that of the nanny?

Bella's gaze brushed across Clarissa for a moment, then she
said, "We played Go Fish. I won three times."

"Ah, you're a *card* shark then. It all makes sense now."

Breck looked over his sunglasses at Slade. "What type of things are you teaching your child, Slade? You got her running a card racket?"

Joe leaned over and tousled some of Bella's wet curls. "Hey, kid, if you're really tough we could use you during our shoot-out. We got some namby-pamby agents we got to teach a lesson to."

Bella slipped off her father's lap, probably to get out of Joe's reach, and let the towel fall from her shoulders. She took hold of her father's hand and said, "Come play with me, Daddy."

Slade said, "In a minute, Bella," and turned his attention back to Joe.

Clarissa felt Elaina shiver and pulled the towel around her a little tighter. Then she leaned down, and so as not to disturb Slade and Joe's conversation, she whispered, "Do you want to stay out here and have lunch with Bella and Slade, or do you want to come back to the hotel with Mommy, and have lunch there?"

Elaina looked back out at the slide and fountains. "I want to stay here."

Oh.

Clarissa wasn't sure whether to be happy or disappointed. On one hand, she couldn't remember the last time she had more than five minutes to herself. On the other hand, her daughter— her daughter, who usually couldn't be pried from Clarissa's side, had just voluntarily chosen to spend time away from her. That sort of hurt.

Then from the recesses of her mind, the child experts spoke again. They all seemed to be nodding approvingly and murmuring things about a child's quest for independence and a child's ability to make her own choices.

Clarissa rubbed her hand up and down Elaina's back. "Okay, honey, I'll let Slade know you want to play out here for a bit longer, but if you change your mind Slade can always . . ." She broke off as she noticed Bella. The little girl had given up tugging on her father's hand and now, with hands on hips, let out a heavy sigh. She looked over at Clarissa, and something flickered in her eyes. Then without a word she circled around the back of the chairs.

Before Clarissa could even call out to her, Bella skipped over to the big pool and went directly over the edge. Her parting into the water made little more than a whispered splash.

At first Clarissa could neither move nor breathe, then her body suddenly worked again, and she yelled, "Slade!"

She leapt from her chair without waiting to see his response. Her sandals made it hard to run, but she didn't have time to take them off. In seconds she reached the pool. She saw the form of Bella beneath the water's surface and immediately jumped into the pool next to her.

The water felt cool and heavy, too heavy. Her robe, now saturated, weighed her down, and every motion seemed to take aggravatingly long. She reached out for Bella, kept reaching, but the little girl seemed to always be just beyond her grasp. Then a moment later she grabbed hold of Bella's hand and pulled her into her arms. Clarissa then turned and pushed through the surface, holding Bella's head up into the air. The water was not terribly deep, perhaps about five feet, and Clarissa was able to stand as she checked the little girl's face to make sure she was breathing.

"Are you all right?" she asked Bella.

Bella nodded, her eyes wide with surprise.

Clarissa pushed her way to the stairs, hugging Bella to her, and tried to keep herself from shaking. "You scared me to death, Bella. Didn't I tell you not to go near the big pool—didn't I?"

"But you weren't watching me anymore. Daddy was."

"That matters?" Clarissa looked up and saw Elaina, Slade, Joe, Breck, and Brandy, all standing and staring at her from the side of the pool.

Slade looked at her without the worry, without the terror, Clarissa had expected to see. On his face was only puzzlement. "What in the world are you doing?"

"Bella jumped in the pool. I went in to save her."

"Oh," Slade said, and a smile played on his lips. "That's very sweet of you. Very heroic." He held out his hands and took Bella from her arms. "Of course, it would have been more meaningful if Bella didn't already know how to swim."

Clarissa stood on the top stair, her robe heavy with water, which now streamed down around her ankles. Slowly she said, "Bella knows how to swim?"

"Well, yes. I've got a pool at the house, so naturally she's had lessons since she was a baby. She probably swims as well as I do."

Clarissa stepped out onto the pool deck, and for the first time noticed that one of her sandals was now dangling halfway off her foot. She kicked her foot into it angrily. "You never told me she knew how to swim."

"I never told you she didn't."

Clarissa glared at him but didn't dare look at the other faces. It was one thing to feel like a fool, it was another thing to see the proof that everyone agreed with you. Instead Clarissa pushed the clinging strands of hair away from her face, then peeled off her bathrobe and rung it out. She held the still-dripping bundle in her hands and wondered what to do with it.

"Who says good help is hard to find?" Brandy said cheerily.

Clarissa glared at her, too.

Slade took the robe from her hands. "If we drape this across one of the pool chairs it should dry out soon."

She'd already had enough humiliation for the day; the thought of staying here for even one more moment did not appeal to her. She shook her head and said, "I'll just hang it up in the bathroom." She reached for the robe, gave it another twist, and watched as more water pooled onto the concrete. "Maybe I should take Elaina with me. She doesn't know how to swim, and I wouldn't want you to worry—"

Slade held his hand up in a Boy Scout sign. "I'll keep both girls safely in the kiddy pool, we'll have lunch, and then go up to the hotel room and play a few rounds of Shoot and Batter or something." His eyes ran over Clarissa's figure, and stopped at the water accumulating at her feet. "Really. You deserve the afternoon off."

Clarissa shot a last look at Elaina, then said, "Fine," and turned around and headed toward the hotel. Her wet skin felt cold against the air, and her sandals made a squishing sound with every step she took.

Step. Squish. Step. Squish. She probably wouldn't stop dripping until she reached the elevator. One leg of her suit began to twist unnaturally, but she didn't dare try to stop and fix it. She'd already created enough of a spectacle to amuse the movie stars.

Step. Squish. Step. Squish.

She hated the way Slade looked so at ease in every situation while she always floundered around, looking incompetent. And she hated the smug humor she'd seen on Brandy's face before she turned around. But most of all she hated the way Bella could send Clarissa into a pool one moment and then blink innocently up at her nanny from her father's arms—the image of an angel—the next.

"Somehow," Clarissa muttered, "I just know she did this all on purpose."

And from the recesses of her mind Clarissa could hear the voice of Freud laughing. "You'd better listen to me next time."

6

Clarissa changed into dry clothes, did some damage control to her hair and makeup, then went out on her hotel room's balcony to read a novel. It should have been easy to relax against the backdrop of the bright blue ocean spilling onto the white sand. But it wasn't. She reread the same paragraph over and over again while wondering how Slade was managing with the girls. Finally she put the book down. *Pitiful,* she scolded herself. *It's been so long since you had any time to yourself you don't know what to do anymore.*

She looked out at the beach, sunny and inviting, and wished her balcony faced the pool instead. That way she'd be able to see whether or not Slade had already taken the girls inside.

She was beyond pitiful; she had reached pathetic.

I should go for a walk along the beach, she thought, and pictured herself for a moment strolling along the shore with the other sunbathers. Then she pictured herself in her old blue swimming suit and sighed. She didn't want to go for a walk; she wanted to buy a new swimming suit.

Before she had time to talk herself out of it, she went back into her hotel room, grabbed her purse and her key card, and was out the door.

✦ ✦ ✦

Clarissa had expected the hotel gift shop to be small, but it was also a pro shop and ended up being bigger than some of the stores she'd been to in the mall. It carried everything from toothbrushes to sports equipment. In the back of the store, in between the golf shirts and beach towels, stood a rack of women's swimming suits.

As Clarissa flipped through them she chastised herself for not buying a suit before she came. In California she could have shopped around and found a bargain. Here she'd just have to accept the price.

She turned over the tag on a bright, floral-printed, one-piece suit and winced. Too much. It was a week's worth of groceries. She couldn't justify spending this much . . . and yet even as she thought about returning the suit to the rack, she also thought of Brandy stretched out on the pool chair in her velvet black suit, looking sleek and elegant. For just a little while Clarissa wanted to feel that way. The old blue suit seemed symbolic of all Clarissa's problems, and she didn't want to put it on again. Ever.

She took not only the floral suit, but also grabbed a hot pink suit and a black suit from the rack. Then she took them all to the dressing room.

The whole time she was disrobing she mourned her lack of willpower and the amount of chocolate she'd consumed over her lifetime. Chocolate. It seemed to cancel out all the time she'd put in at aerobics class. She ought to have done better. If she were perfect it wouldn't matter what she wore. She would always feel confident.

Clarissa turned sideways to the mirror and threw back her shoulders a bit. It was a good thing, really, that she and Elaina would be here for Halloween instead of back home. Who needed half a dozen bags of fun-sized Snickers lying around the house to tempt you? As of this moment, she promised herself she would never overindulge in chocolate again—at least not when there was a chance she would have to face people while wearing only half a yard of tight spandex.

These thoughts were reaffirmed upon seeing herself in the floral suit. It made her feel like she had just put on bumpy wallpaper. The black suit wasn't much better. She took one glance in the mirror and muttered, "It would be perfect to wear to an Esther Williams funeral."

The pink suit had promise, but felt a bit tight. Clarissa remembered seeing the next size up on the rack and now peered over the top of the fitting room door in search of a wandering sales clerk. Of course, she saw no one.

She thought about getting dressed to walk back to the swimming suit rack but then chided herself for being silly. After all, if she planned on wearing the swimming suit outside in front of the whole world, she ought to be brave enough to walk ten feet across the store. Besides, the store was nearly empty, and maybe no one would notice her.

She took a deep breath, then darted out to the swimming suit rack. It took her a moment to locate the pink suit in a larger size; and once she did, she also found the same style in yellow and turquoise blue. She held all of them in her hands and tried to decide which color she liked best. She had just decided to take all three back to the dressing room, when she looked up and saw Tristan approaching her.

He came, stood beside her, and put one hand on the swimming suit rack. As though it were a perfectly normal way to start a conversation, he said, "You may have heard the saying, 'There is no such thing as bad publicity.'" Now he leaned toward her, keeping his gaze cool, serious, and directly trained at her eyes. "But let me warn you that Slade doesn't think that saying applies to him."

Clarissa stared back at Tristan, clutching the swimsuits to her chest in an attempt to create some sort of spandex shield. "I didn't know Sylvia was a reporter. I wouldn't have said a word to her if I did. I hardly said a word to her as it was."

One of Tristan's eyebrows raised in disbelief. "Then you must have a really direct conversational manner, because she told me you loved Slade but thought Bella was a terror."

Clarissa nearly dropped the swimming suits altogether. She caught hold of the hangers before they completely slipped from her fingers and held them to her in one massive tangle of material and tags. "I didn't say that!" She swallowed hard and gripped the hangers tighter. "Well, I mean, I didn't say it like *that*." She shut her eyes momentarily so she wouldn't have to return Tristan's stare and whispered, "She's not going to print that, is she?"

"No, but only because I gave her a better story instead." He ran a hand through his shaggy blond hair and shook his head. "For forty-five minutes I talked to that woman about my career plans, personal life, and promised if I ever have any illegitimate children, she'd be the first to know."

"I'm so sorry."

Tristan folded both arms across his chest, and his eyes narrowed. "You and Slade both owe me a really big favor for this."

She almost volunteered to have a few illegitimate children for him, but then decided against it. He might not realize she was joking. Women probably actually did make those types of propositions to him on a regular basis. Instead she gulped and said, "Just name it."

He looked at her for a moment, and then his gaze slid down her figure, as though realizing for the first time she wore only a tight pink swimming suit. A ghost of a smile appeared on his lips, and his whole expression softened. "Just name it, huh?"

She felt herself flushing and wondered if she had turned the same shade as her suit. "Well, I mean, you know, what I meant to say was that I hope someday I can return the favor."

His smile grew. "I hope so, too."

This line of talk was getting her nowhere. Well, actually it was getting her somewhere, but she was pretty sure she shouldn't be there. Just being in the same room with Tristan McKellips was enough to make any woman sweat; being six inches away from him while he smiled down at her was positively dangerous. She nervously pushed a strand of hair behind her ear and tried to change the subject. "I haven't told Slade about Sylvia yet. I didn't have the time at first, but I'm still not sure what to say to him." She was babbling now, and looking steadfastly at the clothes rack beside Tristan, but it didn't make any difference. Anything was better than facing Tristan's sultry stare. "I mean, despite what she told you, I didn't actually say any of that, and what I did say she tricked me into saying—"

"Clarissa." He said the word slowly, soothingly. "It's all right. You don't have to tell Slade anything. It's taken care of."

"I should tell him *something*," Clarissa said.

He shrugged as though it didn't matter, then casually reached over and took the turquoise swimming suit from her hand. It was one foot less of spandex in her shield, and she blushed anew as he held it up to her. "The pink looks good, but I don't know. I like the way the blue brings out the color in your eyes."

"Do you? Well, blue it is then." She took it from his hand and started backing away toward the dressing room, still clutching all the suits in front of her as she went. "I'm going to get dressed now. Thanks for your opinion."

He smiled and called after her, "Are you sure you don't want to try on a few more? I can give you my opinion on all of them."

"No, that's okay. I mean, I'll go with the blue."

Once inside the dressing room she locked the door, leaned against the wall, and cursed the fashion industry for ever doing away with suits with bloomers. She also cursed herself for being so easily embarrassed. A modern woman shouldn't blush in a swimsuit.

He must think of her as incredibly backward.

Of course, she shouldn't care what Tristan thought of her.

But somehow she did.

Well, she couldn't help herself, after all. Three days ago she'd been an unimpressive, unimportant, struggling single mother. The only men she ever saw were home teachers and such, and the only feelings those men had toward her had to do with sympathy, pity, and duty.

Now she was here in Hawaii. She was still an unimpressive, unimportant, struggling single mother, but Tristan McKellips had just flirted with her. Of course she cared. If she could have videotaped the event to replay for herself every time she got depressed, she would have.

Well, maybe not. If she videotaped the event, then she'd have to watch herself blushing, and fumbling, and looking awkward. Some things were better just to forget.

Clarissa sighed, changed back into her shorts and top, and stepped out of the dressing room. She hadn't expected to see Tristan still in the shop. In fact, she was relatively certain she'd never see him again, but there he stood beside the closest wall, glancing at the golf shirts, and clearly waiting for her.

He was waiting for her. Oh, for a video camera.

As she came out of the dressing room, he turned and then strolled casually back to her. His head tilted slightly, and his blue eyes sparkled. "Can I ask you a question?"

Yes, I will have your illegitimate children, and yes, I'll even be the one to send the birth announcements to Sylvia. "Sure," she said calmly.

"Are you really Bella's nanny? I mean, is there really nothing going on between you and Slade?"

"No. I mean yes. I mean no." She took a deep breath and tried again. "No, there's nothing going on between us, and yes, I really am Bella's nanny." Clarissa ran her fingers around the swimming suit hanger and tried to subdue her heart rate. What she thought was going to come next, couldn't really come next. Not between someone rich and famous like Tristan, and someone men just pitied, like her.

"Well, I'm glad to hear it," Tristan said softly. "That being the case, do you have plans for dinner tonight?"

She had just been asked for her first date since the divorce. Ever since her relationship with Alex ended, she'd wondered about this moment. She wondered if she would be ready. She wondered if the question would come from someone she'd be eager to accept or someone she'd have to avoid for the rest of her life. But she never—not even once—imagined it would happen in a Hawaiian resort by Tristan McKellips, teen idol and Hollywood hunk.

And to think Alex had told her she would never find someone to replace him. She smiled at this fact even though she knew she had to turn Tristan down. "I'm sorry, I'm watching Bella tonight while Slade goes to a luau."

Tristan shook his head and moaned. "That's the same party I was asking you to. Can't you get someone else to watch her while you come with me?"

"It's my job to watch her," and then because Clarissa suddenly remembered she had to say it, she added, "and besides, I'm married."

He tilted his head at her. "You said that pretty much as an afterthought."

"What?" she asked, because she didn't want to admit he was right.

"Well, usually, if a woman is married that thought stays pretty much foremost in her mind. I mean her excuse isn't, 'I'm sorry, I'm busy, and oh, by the way, I'm married, too.'"

"I'm sorry," Clarissa said, and she felt the blushing come back. "I didn't think that you thought, I mean, I just thought you were being friendly and . . . I'm sorry."

He smiled, and it was still a confident smile. "You're not really Slade's nanny, are you?"

"Yes I am. It's just that . . ." In spite of her embarrassment, she kept her eyes on him. His tousled, sunbleached hair, his half-parted lips, his blue eyes all seemed to pull her toward him. For a moment she considered telling him everything, then decided that was her stupidest idea since she swore off chocolate.

No one could know the truth. No one. If it got back to Slade, it would ruin whatever inkling of a chance she still had for a permanent position. So she was married, and that was that, even if it did mean turning down a date with the most handsome man who'd ever asked her out.

"It's just that what?" Tristan asked.

"Nothing," she said. "I really need to go. But thanks for your opinion on the swimsuit."

She walked toward the front counter to pay for the suit, and he didn't follow her.

"And thank *you*," he called after her, "for leaving me with that visual image."

✦ ✦ ✦

At 4:15 Slade knocked on the door. Clarissa didn't even care that he was early. She'd missed Elaina and scooped her up in her arms the moment she saw her.

"Did you have a fun time this afternoon?"

"Yep," Elaina said. "Slade let us jump on the bed."

Clarissa raised an eyebrow as she looked over at Slade. "You did?"

He thrust his hands into his pockets and didn't move from his place in the doorway. "Well, *you* try to play seven games of Chutes and Ladders and see how long you last."

"Poor thing. No wonder you brought them by early."

"I didn't mean to show up early. It's just that I keep calling Meredith's room and can't get ahold of her. Did she tell you where she was going?"

Elaina started to squirm, so Clarissa put her down. The little girl immediately ran over to the full-length mirror into which Bella was making faces and sat down beside her.

Clarissa turned back to Slade. "Sorry, I haven't talked to Meredith all day."

"She's supposed to go to this luau thing with me."

"Then I'm sure she'll turn up."

Slade paused for a moment, then sighed. "Well, I haven't actually told her about it yet."

Clarissa raised another eyebrow at him.

"I haven't seen her since I found out about it, but I don't want to go alone." Slade looked down at his watch and then glanced back down the hallway. "Perhaps I should check with the front desk and see if she rented a car."

91

As soon as he'd said this, Meredith rounded the corner. She wore a large brimmed hat, a swimming suit cover-up, and held not only a towel but a large beach bag.

"Where have you been?" Slade called to her. "I've been trying to get hold of you all day."

"I'm on vacation," she told him slowly. "I went to the beach." She put her things down by her door and ran her key card through the slot. "I had a lovely afternoon and met a very nice banker from Idaho." She opened the door and gave them another smile. "He didn't seem to think I was too old at all."

Before she went into the room Slade said, "I need you to come to dinner with me in an hour. Wear something Hawaiian. It's a luau."

She turned back toward him and smiled graciously. "I had a late lunch with Bill, so I'm not hungry, but thanks anyway."

"It's one of A.J.'s affairs, and he'll be there with Nataly Granger. She's already threatened to go seashell hunting for me. I need you with me."

Meredith sighed but then shook her head. "I'm tired and sunburned. The last thing I want to do is stay up all night trying to keep Nataly Granger away from you. Besides, you know how I hate mingling with celebrities. It's awful. You always have to try and think up compliments about their work no matter how pathetic it is."

"You won't have to talk business tonight," Slade said.

"That's what you said when we went to the network charity dinner. I was trapped in a corner with Kevin Kline for a complete hour. The things I had to say about *Wild, Wild, West*—" She looked at the ceiling and breathed out slowly. "It burns my soul just to think about it."

Meredith then glanced back over at them, and her gaze locked onto Clarissa. Perhaps a little desperately, she said, "Why don't you take Clarissa?"

"She's watching the girls."

"I'll watch them."

"They're too much for you to handle."

"Nonsense. I watched them for a bit last night and survived just fine. Besides, they'll be going to bed in a few hours, which means I'll be able to relax." Without waiting for further protests, she walked into Clarissa's room and said, "Come along, girls, we're going to have a slumber party in my room."

"A party?" Elaina asked. "Do we get balloons?"

"Of course," Meredith replied. "Go grab your jammies and toothbrush." Both girls got to their feet and chattered to each other happily.

"I want a pink balloon," Bella said.

"I want anoder pink one," Elaina added.

"We'll take whatever colors we can bribe the housekeeping staff to get for us," Meredith answered.

While Meredith started to gather Elaina's belongings, Clarissa turned to Slade, "But what about our affair? I mean, I thought you didn't want us to be seen together."

"Seeing the two of you together will help dispel any rumors," Meredith said cheerily and patted Clarissa's arm. "Just talk about your husband every few minutes."

"I don't have anything to wear," Clarissa said weakly, but it was too late. Meredith was already shooing the girls toward the door.

"Just keep repeating, 'The cinematography was breathtaking!' and you'll be fine," she said and was gone from the room.

Slade glanced at his watch. He didn't look entirely pleased by the turn of events, either, but he seemed resigned. "Can you be ready in an hour?"

"I suppose so," she said, because she knew she didn't have a choice.

"Wear your hair up," he told her as he left the room. "That looks more matronly."

✤ ✤ ✤

At quarter to six Slade knocked on her door. He wore tan pants and a Hawaiian shirt, but still seemed crisp, professional, and utterly handsome. She hadn't brought anything tropical to wear, so had put on a straight khaki skirt, a beige blouse, and the lei she'd been given by the flight attendant as she left the airplane on their arrival in Honolulu. The tiny white flowers were a little wilted around the edges, but it was the only Hawaiian thing she had.

Slade looked her up and down in an appraising manner. With evident disapproval he said, "You don't look at all matronly."

"Do you want me to bring Elaina along to prove the point?"

"No." He sighed and then moved away from the door so she could come out of the room. "I suppose I'm just asking the impossible again."

She would have taken this as a compliment if he hadn't looked so displeased as he said it.

As they walked to the elevator Clarissa could feel his gaze run over her again. "Remember to bring up your husband every few minutes. You know, in that annoying gloating sort of way married people always talk about their spouses."

She glanced over at him. "Women don't generally accuse you of being charming, do they?"

He smiled as he reached to push the elevator button. "I'm sorry. I just don't want anything else to go wrong."

The door opened, and Clarissa stepped in and waited for Slade to join her. They both reached for the button to the lobby at the same time, and their hands brushed together for a moment. Clarissa quickly withdrew hers. She suddenly felt awkward, as though without Elaina's hand to hold, Clarissa wasn't sure what to do with her hands. She finally folded them together. They stood in silence for a moment, then Clarissa said, "Who is this Nataly Granger, anyway?"

"An old colleague. She used to have some ideas about the two of us, and apparently time hasn't changed her mind. It's going to be especially tricky because she's here with A.J. He's the one I'm trying to pitch my script to."

"She's A.J.'s girlfriend?"

"Yes."

"But she's coming on to you?"

"Oh, yes."

The elevator door opened and as Clarissa stepped out, she lost her footing and wobbled for a moment. It wasn't the surprise that nearly tumbled her but the heels she wore. She'd purchased them on one of her post-divorce, bargain hunting shopping trips. At the time they'd seemed carefree, young, something a single woman would buy—as it turned out, they were something that only people who didn't actually have to wear them would buy. She did her best to keep pace next to Slade as he walked down the hallway and was thankful he walked slowly. "And what exactly am I supposed to do about Nataly tonight?" she asked.

"You just have to be around. That way I'm obligated to stick by you and make sure you have a good time. I have a built-in excuse not to disappear anywhere with Nataly."

"Oh."

He smiled over at her again. "Now you know where all those soap opera plot ideas come from."

The luau was being held in the hotel garden overlooking the beach. As they exited the lobby and crossed the hotel lanai, Clarissa stopped momentarily to take in the view around her. Beyond the resort gardens and through a row of tall palm trees, a bank of purple clouds on the horizon of the ocean was turning shades of pink, yellow, and red. The surf rolled in long white lines toward the beach, and from somewhere through the dense foliage, strains of soft Hawaiian music drifted over the garden. Paradise. Clarissa breathed in the fragrance of tropical flowers and wished she could capture this scene, this moment, and hold it forever.

Slade motioned for her to follow him, and she pulled her gaze away from the beach. Across the garden terrace stood a dozen circular tables, covered in crisp white linen and pineapple centerpieces. A long table stood in the middle of these, loaded with fresh flowers and an assortment of salads, rolls, and condiments.

A parquet dance floor spread out in front of the band, but no one was dancing. Those who had already arrived were congregated in groups, talking, or lined up at the bar for drinks. It all looked very informal, except for the presence of a number of husky men in hotel uniforms who stood around the perimeter of the banquet site. Clarissa could tell without asking that they were security men, charged to keep unwanted guests out.

The next thing Clarissa noticed as they walked around were the familiar faces. People she had seen often but had never met. It wasn't just the *Undercover Agents* who were scattered about. She also noticed a tennis pro, a former NBA star, a couple of Spice Girls, and an assortment of supermodels.

Clarissa stayed next to Slade as he slowly circulated through the crowd. He introduced her to everyone as Mrs. Hancock, but no one seemed at all concerned about who she was or why she was with Slade. In fact, hardly anyone spoke to her beyond the introductions. They all wanted to talk to Slade, ask him what he'd been doing and why he was in Hawaii.

Clarissa didn't mind being ignored. It saved her from having to admit she knew nothing about the movie business, the modeling industry, tennis, basketball, or exactly which spices were scary. So she simply smiled, nodded, sipped her orange juice, and concentrated on keeping her balance in shoes she was now convinced were designed for people with foot abnormalities that *required* them to walk on their tiptoes.

As she followed Slade around on his mingling tour she saw both Joe and Breck. Joe just looked over at her, grinned, and then laughed softly into his drink for the rest of the time she stood near him. Breck wasn't as subtle. When they reached the group he was standing in, he winked at her and said, "Clarissa, find anyone else to save today?"

Then because everyone looked at him for an explanation, he gave a blow-by-blow description of the whole event, sound effects included. He finished off the story with an aside to Clarissa. "And if you're ever concerned about Bella getting trapped in an elevator, don't worry. I have it on good authority she already knows how to push the buttons."

"Thanks," Clarissa said. "Thanks so much."

She expected more of the same treatment when they reached Brandy's group, but Brandy barely glanced at her. It was as if she'd not only forgotten the whole event at the pool but also forgotten Clarissa altogether. Clarissa didn't mind the snub. In fact, she was grateful.

At one point Tristan, with drink in hand, sauntered up to the group Slade and Clarissa had joined. He wore a black shirt with a gaudy silver pendant of an eagle around his neck. An average person would have looked absurd wearing it to a luau, but on Tristan it looked chic.

"Hello, Slade." He nodded at his friend, then turned to look at Clarissa. "Mrs. Hancock, what a surprise to see you here. I thought you were busy tonight."

Clarissa gulped and shifted the glass in her hands. "I was. I mean, Meredith volunteered to watch the girls."

"Oh, you got someone else to watch Bella." He nodded again. "It's a pity you didn't think of that when I suggested it to you."

Slade said, "When you suggested it, Tristan? What are you talking about?"

"Oh, nothing," Tristan said. "I'm just making idle chitchat. Mingling and all that." He looked over at Clarissa again. "But tell me, Mrs. Hancock, do you think you'll be too busy to spare me a dance later?"

"I'm sure I'll have the time."

"Good, then I'll talk to you later." He smiled at her rather forcefully and then turned and walked away.

Slade watched him go. "What was that all about?"

Clarissa just shook her head. "Nothing really."

"Nothing? It didn't sound like nothing." He didn't press the point because another couple approached them. The man was tall, lanky, and probably in his fifties. Streaks of gray lightened his brown hair, and wrinkles lined the corners of his eyes. His maroon shirt looked more western than Hawaiian and matched the pair of cowboy boots he wore. The woman at his side was much younger. She could have been his daughter, except a daughter wouldn't have hung onto his arm so possessively. Her platinum blonde hair, expertly styled, just brushed against her bare shoulders. Her flowered sundress was short, tight, and showed off her tan exceptionally.

The man extended his hand. "Slade, glad you could make it tonight."

"I wouldn't want to miss one of your events, A.J."

The woman turned huge blue eyes on Slade. "Your secretary just looks better and better every time I see her."

"Oh, I forgot to make introductions." Slade held out his hand as he spoke the names. "A.J., Nataly, this is Bella's nanny, Mrs. Clarissa Hancock. My secretary couldn't make it tonight, but Clarissa is a big fan of the movie industry, so I brought her along."

All eyes turned on Clarissa as though they expected her to make some comment about her love of movies, and she stammered out, "Movies are . . . well . . . the cinematography is breathtaking." It made no sense, and she quickly took a drink of her orange juice so she wouldn't have to say anything else.

Nataly cast her a half-sincere smile. "How nice of you to come then. I can tell just by looking at you that you must be very good with children."

"Thank you," Clarissa answered, even though she had the distinct feeling she'd just been insulted.

"Slade," A.J. said, "I haven't seen you since that night at the Oscars. What are you up to these days?"

Slade smiled broadly at him. "I've written a screenplay. A wonderful screenplay some astute producer is going to pick up soon."

Nataly turned her eyes back onto A.J. "You're as astute as they come, A.J. You'd better set up a pitch meeting."

A.J. laughed and pulled Nataly close. With one arm draped

around her shoulder he said, "Sure thing. We'll have lunch sometime."

"Why don't we have Slade sit at our table?" Nataly said. "Then he can tell you about it over dinner."

A.J. wrinkled his nose. "I don't talk business at parties. That's the fastest way to give everyone heartburn, but we'll save a spot for you at the table anyway. And I'll tell you what—you give me a call tomorrow, and we'll set something up."

"Great," Slade said. "I look forward to it."

A.J. and Nataly drifted away after that, and Slade didn't seem any worse for his encounter with the actress. Still, every once in a while when Slade was busy talking, Clarissa glanced over to where Nataly was circulating through the crowd. There was no doubt; she had a knack for displaying herself. She didn't just walk; she glided, she flowed, she drew glances to her like a magnet, and Clarissa was suddenly glad Slade wanted to stay away from her.

Dinner was a continuation of the mingling session, only sitting down. Clarissa still felt like an outsider who had nothing to say and no idea what anyone else was talking about. She ate silently, occasionally nodding at the conversation just so people would think she was paying attention.

Tristan sat a few tables over. Clarissa glanced over and noticed him talking animatedly with the group of people there, but as she watched him, he turned and saw her. She looked away quickly, embarrassed to be caught staring at him. She gazed intently at her plate, the pineapple centerpiece, anything but Tristan.

It was ridiculous to feel guilty for showing up with Slade when Tristan had asked her first. She hadn't planned on purpose to slight him. And besides, he couldn't be slighted by her anyway. He was a movie star. All he had to do was walk into a room that had more than three women in it, and he could find a date—or two. Tristan knew that. He'd only asked her out in the first place on a whim—because she was standing in the store wearing a swimsuit, and he'd enjoyed embarrassing her over it. He didn't care what she did or who she was with. In this crowd, she was a nobody. It didn't hurt when a nobody turned you down.

Almost against her will, she glanced over at Tristan's table again and saw him staring back at her. This time he turned away, but he smiled before he did it.

Clarissa blushed and tried to rethink the logic. It shouldn't have mattered to Tristan that she'd turned him down . . . unless he was so bothered by the fact that a nobody had turned him down, that he now saw her as a challenge.

That was probably it. Certainly he couldn't have any real intentions toward her. That was too unlikely for a man like Tristan.

Of course, now that she thought about it, she realized she didn't really know what sort of man Tristan was. She just knew what sort of man he portrayed in movies. Perhaps he wasn't like those wicked but charming scoundrels at all.

"Clarissa is married and has a three-year-old daughter," she suddenly heard Slade say.

He smiled over at her like she ought to have some commentary on that statement, but she had no idea what he wanted her to say. She simply smiled back and said, "That's right."

"Clarissa's husband is a great guy," Slade said. "She just talks about what a great guy he is all the time."

"That's right," Clarissa said again, because now everyone at the table was staring at her.

Slade snapped his fingers and put his finger to his lips as though trying to remember something. "What was that funny thing you told me about your husband on the way up here?"

Clarissa blinked at him and said the first thing she thought of. "He's a perfectionist."

"What's so funny about that?" Nataly asked.

Clarissa swallowed hard and willed her brain to think of something to say that actually made sense. "Well, it's not funny in a humorous way," she finally decided on. "It's just funny that with so many things in life to think about, a person would zero in on the crumbs in the silverware tray."

"Oh," Nataly said, and then with a shrug of her shoulders, laughed. "I can't tell you the last time I cleaned out my silverware tray."

A.J. winked at her. "That's because you always eat out."

"Still," Nataly said, "it's nice to know if I ever want to be a perfectionist, all I have to do is dump out the silverware tray once in a while."

Clarissa suddenly felt strangely detached from her marriage, as though here, thousands of miles away from Alex, she could just begin to see him clearly. "It's not just the silverware tray," she said. "It's also the hangers in the closet. They have to face the same direction. The shoes have to be lined up in a row, and the paper towel roll in the kitchen has to have the flap in the front and not the back."

A.J. shook his head sadly. "Your husband is definitely neurotic. . . . Except for the paper towel thing. I do that, too."

"And he watches every single football game during the entire season," Clarissa said.

"What's perfectionistic about that?" Nataly asked.

"Nothing," Clarissa said. "It's just something else I find annoying."

Slade smiled at her, but it was a stiff unhappy smile, like he wanted to kick her underneath the table. She cleared her throat and tried to think of a way to redirect her comments. She was supposed to say happy things about Alex, no matter how hard that was.

"Alex is just thorough about everything. He's an accountant for an engineering firm. I suppose that's about as opposite of an actor as you can get. Although . . ." she picked up her glass and slowly swirled the water in it, "I guess it's hard to tell what an actor is really like. I mean . . ." She looked across the room as though searching for an example. "Take Tristan McKellips. He always plays the part of a womanizing playboy, but for all I know he's completely different from that in real life."

"No," Slade said. "He's actually like that."

Clarissa shrugged and then tried to look thoughtful. "One woman is about the same as the next to him?"

Slade cocked his head and stared at her. "Why do you ask?"

She knew she ought to change the subject, to forget Tristan, and yet she felt compelled to reach some sort of understanding about him. She couldn't be so close to the answer and not ask the question. She shrugged as casually as she could. "I'm just thinking about different types of men. You know, perfectionists. Womanizers. I mean, in theory, it wouldn't hurt Tristan's feelings for long if a woman turned him down. He'd just move on to the next woman. It wouldn't even faze him, right?"

"It would faze him," A.J. said. "He'd probably go into shock from the surprise."

"I don't think anyone has ever turned down Tristan," Nataly said, and she grinned in a way that made Clarissa wonder if she spoke from experience.

Slade's eyes narrowed as he looked over at Clarissa. "How did we suddenly start talking about Tristan? What do womanizers have to do with perfectionists?"

Clarissa cleared her throat to give her a moment to think. "They, uh, both try to determine their self-worth by using . . . um . . . outside props."

The group all stared at her for a moment. "Well," Slade said at last, "that will give me something to think about the next time I clean out my silverware tray."

"If I had to choose to be either a perfectionist or a woman-izer," A.J. said, "I think I'd be the womanizer."

Nataly swatted him playfully and said to Clarissa, "See, you ought to be glad your husband just watches football. He could be watching something else." Then she gave a perfectly charming pout to A.J. "When are you going to take me dancing, you wom-anizer, you?"

A.J. took his napkin from his lap, tossed it on the tabletop, and stood. He held his hand out to Nataly, and her pout instantly turned to a smile. They left the table without saying good-bye.

They were the first ones out to dance, but as soon as they took the floor, several couples followed, then several more, until Clarissa felt she was one of the only people left still working on dinner.

Slade sat beside her. He ripped his dinner roll in half but didn't eat it. "When I told you I wanted you to talk about your husband, I was thinking along the lines of endearing little stories that would let everyone know you were happily married, not an exposé on his faults."

She slunk down in her chair a bit. "I'm sorry. I just said the first thing that came into my head."

"The first thing that came into your head was which direction your husband puts the hangers in the closet?"

Clarissa looked out at the dance floor, wondering if it would be impolite to ignore the question altogether, and then saw Tristan striding toward her.

He smiled down at her, a knowing smile, as if he knew she'd been discussing him during dinner—not because anyone had told him, but simply because he knew women. "Are you too busy for that dance you promised me?"

She glanced at Slade. He rolled his eyes. If she stayed here, Slade would just continue his lecture on her shortcomings as a dinner guest. She smiled up at Tristan, took his hand, and said, "I'd love to." They walked onto the dance floor, and she noticed once, as she turned in Tristan's arms, that Slade was watching her. His lips were drawn tight into a scowl, but she tried not to think about what that might mean.

For a few minutes Tristan said nothing to her. He just moved her around the dance floor, looking down at her in a manner that could have been classified as 'lazily' if there hadn't been an intensity behind his eyes.

Finally, tired of the silence and the intensity, she said, "I'm

sorry about turning you down this afternoon. I really was planning on staying in my room tending Bella and my daughter. It
was a last-minute thing that I came, honest."

"You're sorry?" His voice was sultry.

"I just said so."

He pulled her closer to him and bent to whisper into her ear.
"Then make it up to me."

"Make it up to you?"

His fingers momentarily tightened on her waist. "Clarissa,
remember how you told me to name a favor, and you'd do it?"

Yes, well, and apparently that had been a mistake, but how
in the world was she supposed to know this afternoon that he'd
be whispering things into her ear tonight? She hadn't expected
him to even remember her name, let alone whisper it.

"You're blushing," he said, and actually sounded surprised.
"That's so refreshing. I don't recall the last time a woman blushed
around me."

"I can help you with that. It was this afternoon by the swimsuit rack."

She felt the chuckle, rather than heard it. "I meant besides
you."

For a moment Clarissa thought the subject of favors had been
dropped and was about to sigh in relief, but Tristan leaned toward
her ear again and said, "Well, are you going to keep your word? I
want to name a favor."

"I, uh . . ."

"You don't need to start blushing again. I just want you to
have dinner with me tomorrow night."

For a moment, she actually considered saying yes, but she
swallowed back the word and instead said, "I did mention to you
that I am married, didn't I?"

"You mentioned it. I promise to take you somewhere
respectable."

"But that's the point. It wouldn't be respectable."

The intensity in his eyes grew until she felt as though she

wasn't looking at him at all, that she was just looking at a picture of him. It was like watching a movie, and this was the part where he swings the heroine into his arms and kisses her passionately. "Couldn't you be disrespectable for one night?"

She laughed. She hadn't meant to, but suddenly it all seemed so . . . so Tristan—as if he'd rehearsed for the part of being himself. "You're very good at this," she said. "No wonder they pay you so much to look that way on the screen."

"I can be better." He glanced around the dance floor. "It's a little crowded here. Let's take a walk to the beach." He drew back from her and gave her a playful look, as though he had already anticipated her protest. "A very respectable walk."

"I can't disappear anywhere. It would defeat my whole purpose for being here." And because she'd reminded herself of this fact, she glanced back at their table. Slade had left his seat, but a moment later she located him, standing with some of the production people he'd introduced her to earlier. It could have been her imagination, but his gaze seemed to connect with hers, and his lips were still drawn into a tight line.

"Your whole purpose?" Tristan asked. "And what would that be?"

Clarissa tried to think of a way to explain it to him without implicating Nataly, then realized she couldn't do it. "Never mind. It's nothing."

"No, really, tell me."

"I can't. Forget I said anything."

"Hmm." Tristan nodded. "You're gorgeous and now mysterious, too."

Clarissa smiled at him. She probably shouldn't have. She probably should have found some proper way to put an end to Tristan's flirting, but she couldn't think of anything that wouldn't be rude. And besides, it had been so long since anyone told her she was gorgeous, that the compliment was like water on parched ground. She hated to turn it off.

Besides, it wasn't wrong to smile up at him this way, because she wasn't really married. And none of it mattered to Tristan anyway. He undoubtedly flirted with everyone. He wouldn't even remember her next week, let alone that she smiled back at him while they danced. She'd just bask in his attention for a few more moments before she returned to being a dowdy, unnoticed house-wife.

"Your purpose . . ." Tristan said again. "Let me guess. You're an undercover reporter?"

"Nope."

"An actress? A spy?"

"Sorry."

"All right, you don't have to tell me, but at least admit I'm right. You have a secret, don't you?"

She stumbled momentarily in her dance step, and he laughed and shook his head. "That's as good as an answer."

"It's just these heels. You'd fall every once in a while if your feet were balancing on these things."

The intensity returned to his gaze. "Have dinner with me tomorrow night."

"I really can't."

Tristan smiled at her again and seemed anything but defeated. "Very well, then, I guess I'll have to be satisfied with holding your picture."

"My picture?"

"The one in the paper. As soon as I get back to my hotel room I'm going to cut it out."

"What paper?" she asked.

He cocked his head at her. "The morning's paper. Didn't you see the picture of you and Slade in it?"

"No," she said and then, "Oh, no." She felt a ball of anxiety tightening in her stomach. "What did it say?"

He shrugged. "Nothing really. Just that Slade was here with the cast."

She hadn't even realized she was holding her breath, but now exhaled slowly. "Well, that doesn't sound too bad."

Of course it wasn't bad. If the paper had printed anything unfavorable, she would have heard about it by now from Slade. Repeatedly. In a loud angry voice.

Tristan shook his head. "Yeah, every once in a while the papers have an off day and print something nice. But I'm sure their next article will call us all *Under-the-Covers Agents*, and they'll write an exposé on how we trashed the hotel during our wild parties."

"Well, I'm not talking to anyone from here on out. In fact, I'm going to insist on some sort of identification and proof of occupation before I even discuss the weather."

He laughed softly. "It won't matter. The press is like Santa Claus. They know when you've been sleeping. They know when you're awake. And they pretty much know about anything that happens in between those two times."

"Doesn't that bother you?"

"Sometimes. It's been worse lately. I think the whole cast is getting tired of being food for the gossip columns. We're all afraid to cough for fear of being written up as having contracted the plague."

Which only made Clarissa feel more guilty about her slipup at the pool. In a quiet voice she asked, "Why did you tell Sylvia I was an old friend of yours?"

He looked down at her and shrugged. "Because I know how those trashy reporters think. Sylvia won't believe you're simply a nanny. She thinks you have some ulterior motive, some connection. I just let her believe your connection is to me instead of to Slade. I don't have Slade's reputation to uphold." Now he winked at her. "In fact, I like being linked with beautiful young women. You see, this isn't just a dance—I'm helping your cover story."

She shifted a bit in Tristan's arms, uncertain how to reply to the compliment. She looked at his shoulder and not at him. "Well, thanks again for pulling Sylvia away from me."

"You still owe me a favor," he said.

The song ended, but Tristan didn't let go of her. "You're not ready to go sit down again, are you?"

She didn't have time to formulate a reason for doing so. Slade was suddenly at her side. He smiled pleasantly at Tristan. "You don't mind if I cut in, do you?"

Tristan looked as though he did mind, but stepped aside anyway. He nodded to Clarissa, and then gave her a long stare. "Thanks for the dance, Mrs. Hancock."

Despite her intentions to do otherwise, Clarissa blushed at his parting, which made it that much harder to look Slade in the eye.

The music started up, and Slade maneuvered her to where the floor was less crowded. She could tell by his expression he wasn't pleased with her, but she didn't say anything.

Finally he said, "Why did you dance with Tristan?"

"Because he asked me."

"Yes, but didn't you know what it meant when he asked you to dance?"

"Well, I supposed it meant he wanted to dance."

He shook his head at her, and when he spoke his words were clipped. "The two of you looked like you were a couple out here."

"We were dancing," she said. "Everyone looks like a couple when they're dancing."

His look was as intense as Tristan's, but without any of the warmth. "I don't swear anymore," he told her, "but you're tempting me."

She bit her lip, then forced herself to look at him. "Well, actually, you see, Tristan helped me out this morning and . . ." She hadn't meant to tell Slade like this. She had wanted to wait until he seemed to be in an understanding mood, but she couldn't really go any longer without telling him what had happened.

"Helped you how?" he asked, and he didn't sound at all understanding.

"This woman sat down next to me while I was watching the girls at the pool, and she asked me these sort of leading questions, and, well, it never occurred to me that she might be a reporter." She waited for Slade to break into some sort of lecture, or yell, but he simply stared at her with a cold expression.

"Tristan recognized her," she went on, "and told me who she was. Then he offered to give her an interview if she would forget she'd spoken with me."

"What did you say to her?"

"Not a lot really." She gulped, and her words tumbled out. "Just that I was a nanny and something to the effect that children could be challenging, and that my boss was nice."

His face showed no expression. "And what was all that business between you and Tristan earlier?"

"After his interview I ran into him in the hotel, and he asked me to the party, but I told him I was married, and that I had to watch Bella tonight." But not in that order.

Slade let out a slow breath and shook his head. "What we told you at the dinner table was the truth. Tristan is a womanizer."

"I know."

"But you danced with him anyway, and I could see you blushing from where I stood halfway across the floor."

He said this as though she had done something terribly wrong, and she felt her cheeks growing red all over again. "I'm one of those people who blushes easily." And then because she still felt the need to defend herself, she said, "It was just a dance. I was being polite to him."

"Well, stay away from him from now on. I'm not about to let you go and make fools of both of us."

She gasped and said, "How am I making a fool of you?" but she said it too loudly, and a few heads turned in their direction.

Slade rolled his eyes and moved even farther away from the main crowd.

Clarissa added more quietly, "You were the one who insisted I come tonight."

Slade swayed her to the left to avoid getting too close to

another couple, and as he did so, he pulled her nearer. "Exactly, so let's stick together. From here on out we'll sit out." Slade glanced across the floor, and his eyes stopped on Nataly. She stood in A.J.'s arms, flowing back and forth to the rhythm of the music, but as Slade watched her, she looked up and smiled at him.

Slade smiled back, then turned slightly away from her. "But first I think we'd better dance for a while."

Clarissa watched Nataly for another moment. The woman's smile returned to A.J., and she caressed the back of his neck with her hand. "I don't know why you're worried about Nataly," Clarissa said. "She seems absolutely devoted to A.J."

"It's called acting," Slade said, "and this is exactly the reason you have to trust me where Tristan is concerned. You're not used to being around actors. They're different."

Clarissa looked off into the crowd and not at Slade. "You can say that again."

Slade shook his head and then laughed. "Go ahead and be angry with me. You'll thank me someday."

She looked back up at Slade and saw the grin on his face. She hadn't expected it, but it totally disarmed her. And it seemed odd to her that one smile from him was more powerful than ten of Tristan's sultry stares. It suddenly became hard to dance with him, to not notice how close he stood or to feel his shoulder underneath her hand.

It was so true that she wasn't used to actors, to men who made your heart race when they glanced at you. She was going to have to learn to rein in these reactions, and rein them in fast.

She looked away from Slade and out at the crowd again, trying to think of anything but how near he was. She contemplated women's fashion, time-share condos, holiday gifts, and how many people were actually on that grassy knoll in Dallas.

Finally she said, "So what did you think of the paper today?"

"I didn't see it."

"Not even the picture of us?"

"Us?" he nearly spat out the word.

A lump suddenly formed in Clarissa's throat. Oh, no. He hadn't known about it, and she had just opened the floodgates for more criticism. Here it came. The loud angry voice. Repeatedly.

Slade stopped dancing, stopped breathing probably, and Clarissa quickly added, "I haven't seen it, either, but Tristan said there wasn't anything bad about it."

"Yes, well, Tristan's definition of 'bad' and mine are not exactly the same." Still holding onto her hand, he led her back across the dance floor.

7

Slade stopped only once, by A.J. and Nataly, and in a casual and unconcerned voice told them, "We've got to go, but we had a great time."

Nataly's blue eyes flashed with disappointment. "You're leaving so soon?"

"I'm afraid so," Slade said.

"Well, then we expect you to stay extra late at our next party, don't we A.J.?"

"Until the cows come home and the crew turns in," A.J. said.

Slade smiled at them easily. "I'll look forward to it." He gave them a parting wave, then pulled Clarissa toward the path leading to the resort entrance.

Once inside he let go of her and quickly strode across the lobby. She struggled to keep up to his pace without stumbling.

"You know, men don't seem to appreciate how hard it is to navigate on heels."

He slowed down a little but not much. With a backward glance he said, "You'd think after being liberated for so long, women would have done away with heels altogether."

"We were liberated from men," she said, "not from fashion."

He shook his head but didn't say anything, and his pace seemed to pick up again too.

"It's probably men who run the fashion industry anyway," Clarissa went on, "and they keep heels alive just to spite women for being liberated. It's revenge."

They reached the elevator. Slade pushed the button, and

Clarissa reached down to take off her shoes as they waited for the door to open.

"I was out of my room so quickly this morning I didn't even think to look at the paper," Slade said. "I hope the maid didn't throw it away."

Clarissa straightened, holding one shoe in each hand, and stretched her toes in an attempt to revive them. "I put mine in my beach bag. I thought I'd have a chance to look at it while the girls were swimming, but I never did."

"Then we'll go straight to your room."

The elevator door opened and Slade stepped inside. Clarissa followed him, then leaned against the back wall of the elevator, still trying to work the cramps out of her feet.

Slade glanced up at the numbers above the elevator door, watching as they slowly lit up. "What exactly did Tristan say about the picture?"

He'd said he'd have to be satisfied with having Clarissa's picture since she wouldn't go out with him, but she was not about to tell Slade this. "Just that it was in the paper."

Slade glanced over at her narrowly as though he knew she wasn't telling him everything.

So she quickly added, "And that you'd dropped in to visit the *Undercover Agents* cast." And even though she didn't mean to, she gulped. "Or something . . . like that."

Slade shook his head. "You're leaving out the part where he told you how stunning you looked, and how you ought to be a model, and how he knew people who could help you."

"He didn't say any of *that*," Clarissa said, and then stopped herself, because it implied he'd said something else.

The door opened and Slade stepped out without saying any more on the subject.

When they got to her room, she slid her card through the slot and opened the door. She wished she'd done a better job of arranging Elaina's things somewhere neatly instead of just piling them all on the furniture, but Slade didn't seem to notice the mess. He went straight for the plastic beach bag that sat on the couch and pulled out the newspaper. Clarissa couldn't see the picture because Slade held it in his hands, but she did see his jaw clench and knew he wasn't happy. He muttered several things, some of which may have broken his resolve not to swear, and then turned the paper over so she could see the page.

It was one of four pictures under the headline of "Agents Go Undercover in Hawaii." In the top corner was a photo of Tristan autographing a picture for a fan; below it were two pictures of the cast members mingling with the crowd, and in the bottom right-hand corner was a picture of Slade and Clarissa walking toward the hotel entrance.

It could have been worse, Clarissa decided. It could have been a picture of her trying to peel Bella off of Slade's leg while Bella screamed like a banshee. Instead they looked almost like normal people. Slade was smiling, and it didn't even look like a forced smile. He carried Bella with one arm and had his other hand on Clarissa's elbow. Clarissa looked a little dazed in the picture, but none of the frustration she'd felt at that moment showed on her face. Her hair was in place, and her mouth wasn't hanging open. All in all she could even consider it a good photo of herself.

"Look at this." Slade smacked the photo with the back of his hand. "Slade Jacobson and friend drop in at the Mahalo Regency. A friend," he repeated. "They called you a friend."

Only because they hadn't talked to her first.

He tossed the paper onto the bed. "I specifically told them you were Bella's nanny."

"Yes, and Bella told them that reporters are bad people and we weren't having an affair. All in all, 'friend' doesn't seem so bad."

"*Friend* makes it sound like there's something more to it. Anyone who sees this will wonder if there is. Next thing you know, *Hard Copy* will be here interviewing the maid service."

Clarissa glanced over at the paper and then back at him. "I

know you're a movie star and everything, but don't you think you're being a little paranoid about this? I mean, aren't there more interesting stories in Hollywood than what kind of relationship you have with your daughter's nanny?"

He turned, and for a moment Clarissa thought he would ignore her question altogether and walk out of the room. Instead he sat down on the couch and loosened his tie.

"It wouldn't have been a big deal to me before I joined the Church. I wouldn't have given any of this a second thought. But things are different now. You, of all people, ought to understand that."

"You want to avoid even the appearance of evil," she said.

"It's more than that." He leaned back against the couch, and for a moment he looked defeated, vulnerable. She suddenly had the urge to go and sit beside him and take his hand in hers to comfort him. Instead she walked to the chair across from the couch and sat down stiffly.

He didn't say anything for a moment and then in a weary voice said, "Most everyone I know puts someone who is religious in the same category as those nuts who believe they've been abducted by space aliens—except the space alien people have more interesting stories." He gripped his tie with one hand, then pulled it off altogether. "When I was baptized everybody thought it was a joke or a publicity stunt or something. I get the feeling the whole world is waiting for me to mess up so they can point fingers at me and say, 'See, he didn't mean it. He hasn't really changed.' They want to prove I'm a hypocrite, and that will prove that all religion is just hypocrisy."

She leaned toward him and was glad she was still too far away to reach out and take his hand. "I'm sorry, Slade."

"It's not your fault," he said. "Friend."

Friend. For the first time she felt like she was. She held her hand up in the form of a pledge. "From now on I'll try to make sure all my actions are beyond reproach."

"Thank you." They looked at each other, and for a moment

their gaze locked. His eyes were so dark, so warm. She knew they were only repeating the words, *thank you,* and yet she could read in them so much more.

She turned her gaze to the door. "I suppose we should go relieve Meredith."

"I suppose we should."

He got up and walked out the door and into the hallway. Clarissa followed and was glad she had to look only at the back of Slade's shirt. Looking at the back of his shirt was easier than looking into his face.

He knocked softly on Meredith's door, and after a few moments she opened it. She wore a navy blue silk robe, and the makeup was gone from her face, but her hair was still styled immaculately. "You're back early," she said.

Slade walked into her room and Clarissa followed. "We left when we found out our picture was in this morning's paper. I wanted to check it out."

Meredith nodded. "I noticed it after the girls fell asleep. I should have checked the papers first thing in the morning. I keep forgetting how fast they can run a story." She glanced to where it lay on the couch. "It's only a local story. It probably won't even be noticed by the larger press."

"Probably not," Slade said.

"And if it is, we'll just ask Clarissa's husband if he can be out here on the next flight and tell the press he's been here with us all along."

"And that Bella adores them both," Slade agreed.

Clarissa's mouth went suddenly dry.

Meredith turned toward Clarissa, "If the situation arose, you do think your husband could arrange that, don't you? It would be all expenses paid, of course."

"Oh, um, I mean, if he could get the time off work."

Slade's eyes narrowed slightly. "Couldn't he get the time off work if it meant saving your reputation from death by tabloids?"

"Well, I'm sure he'd try," Clarissa said.

Slade's voice took on an exasperated tone. "Tell him I'll personally make sure all the hangers in your hotel room are facing the right direction."

"I'll tell him," she said. She looked down at her skirt and pretended to brush away a piece of lint because she couldn't bear to look at Slade a moment longer. Her stomach felt as though it had turned to clay.

She should have told him at the beginning. Risking the job would have been better than perpetuating this lie. It would have been easier. Now she stood only one news article away from being revealed as a fraud, and that was the last thing she wanted for Slade or for herself.

Slade looked around the room. "You say the girls are asleep?"

"They're on my bed." Meredith walked over to her desk, where a computer sat. "I've something to show you," she told him, but Slade turned and went to check on the girls instead of following her. After a few moments he came back with a smile on his face. "They look like a pair of little angels in there sleeping."

"Yes, it's quite deceptive, isn't it?" Meredith sat down on the chair in front of the computer and with a few clicks of the mouse logged onto the Internet.

"They weren't good for you?" Clarissa asked.

"Oh, they were fine," Meredith said. "Just your normal, busy preschoolers, and I'm sure housekeeping will find a way to get that fingernail polish out of the carpet."

Slade raised a hand to his face and rubbed his forehead. "Remind me to tip the maids well."

"You always do," Meredith said, leaning back in her chair and surveying the screen. "Here we are. I have a piece of fan mail that should interest you. It's from your friend Kim."

Slade leaned over Meredith's shoulder and looked at the computer screen. He read out loud: "Slade, I can't believe you're in Oahu. For once our paths are going to cross. I'm going to be near the north shore to check out some plant species in a couple of days. We have to find a time to get together. I'm tired of seeing your face on the screen and never in real life. Besides, half of my roommates don't believe I'm really e-mailing you. I need proof. Pictures of us together and perhaps a notarized pair of finger-prints. Let's work something out. Love, Kim."

Meredith twisted in her chair to face him. "Isn't it perfect?"

He shrugged. "Sure. It's great. We'll have lunch somewhere."

"No," she said, "it's better than that. You bring her to the hotel the next time A.J. has one of his functions. She'll be your date. That way you'll be able to hold off Nataly and any rumors about you and Clarissa at the same time."

Slade nodded. "Sounds good. I'll ask A.J. when his next event is. It will give me an excuse to run into him tomorrow. Then I'll e-mail Kim back."

Clarissa watched them for a moment, then because her curiosity got the best of her, she asked, "Who's Kim?"

Slade smiled, a soft smile rich with inner meaning. "Eric Jones's little sister. Eric and I were best friends as kids when he lived in L.A. I hadn't seen him in something like twenty years and then about six months ago we ran into each other at Fashion Island Mall. Kim has e-mailed me off and on since then, but I haven't seen her since she was eight years old and their family moved to England." He smiled again and shook his head. "Eric and I used to tease her horribly back then. I'm surprised she's even forgiven me."

"Maybe she hasn't," Meredith said. "Maybe that's why she wants to see you. She wants to give you the 'what for,' for all those times you pulled her pigtails."

"We did worse than that," Slade said, rubbing his chin. "We used to torment her. I guess you could credit Kim for my first act-ing jobs. Once, we pretended we'd been hit by a car. We came staggering up the sidewalk, bleeding ketchup all over the place, just to hear her scream."

Meredith made a "tsking" sound with her tongue. "Now I

know where Bella gets her sense of humor. It's genetic, and it serves you right for having her."

"It certainly does," Slade said, "and I guess it's time I take my little angel home."

He turned and walked back to the bedroom and Clarissa followed. She watched as he gently picked up Bella and cradled her against his chest. He looked down at her with the same warm expression she'd seen on his face as he held her by the dining room table, and suddenly his words came to her mind. *Children just have a way of stripping off all the masks we wear.* She realized she was seeing him, for the moment, completely unmasked. In this setting, he wasn't the actor who smiled confidently for the camera, or even the slightly cynical man who had just walked her down the hall berating her for dancing with Tristan. This was who he was unmasked. A tender and gentle man who loved his daughter.

She looked down at Elaina and thought not of her, but of Alex. Perhaps he had also been unmasked by his daughter. To the rest of the world he was even-tempered, generous, and caring; but somehow all those things fell away when he was at home with his family.

Clarissa reached to pick Elaina up but paused for a moment to look down at her. She took in the shiny blonde hair, the pixie nose, and the soft brown lashes. Lying there bathed in the soft light from the open doorway, Elaina did look like an angel— except for the smudges of mauve fingernail polish smeared on her hands.

It was his loss. It was all Alex's loss.

She picked up Elaina, and the little girl nestled her head on Clarissa's shoulder and wrapped her arms around her neck. She smelled slightly of perfume and slightly of shampoo, and Clarissa held her for a moment, enjoying the softness of her body. "Come on, sweetheart," she murmured into Elaina's hair. "Let's go to our room."

Slade said softly, "I'll drop Bella off in the morning."

Clarissa simply nodded.

As she walked from the room he added, "Thanks for coming with me tonight."

"Sorry about my husband." Clarissa turned slightly to face Slade again. "I mean, I'm sorry about the stuff I said about my husband at dinner. You know, the hangers, and silverware tray, and womanizer stuff."

He nodded with a smile and an expression that seemed to look right through her. "I'll see you tomorrow."

Clarissa whispered a good-bye to Meredith, then walked out of the room.

After Clarissa was safely out of sight in the hallway, she shook her head. To think that Slade had asked her if she had any acting ambitions. She'd been here two days and could barely pull off acting like she was still married. She'd almost forgotten to tell Tristan about her husband altogether, and at dinner she had said all sorts of stupid stuff about Alex to Slade. And then there were all those racing pulse beats she'd had as she looked at Slade tonight. Had he noticed those?

She would have to be better.

And what if Slade actually asked her husband to join them? She shuddered as she balanced Elaina with one hand and fumbled to unlock the door with the other. She could barely even talk about Alex without mumbling incoherently. She'd never be able to come up with a believable excuse for his not being able to come to Hawaii to defend her honor.

Acting ambitions, indeed.

Clarissa pushed the door open, flipped on the light, and carried Elaina to her bed. After the little girl was settled, Clarissa tossed her shoes into the closet and peeled the lei from around her neck. She was tired, but not sleepy, so she wandered into the front room and sank into a chair.

The room was annoyingly quiet and empty. She supposed Slade Jacobson had that effect on rooms. Once he'd been in them and then left, they just naturally seemed duller. She glanced over at the couch he'd sat on and could still picture him there, his head tossed back, his brown hair smooth and shiny. His eyes dark and magnetic, looking into hers . . .

Clarissa immediately cut off the image. It was ridiculous to think about Slade like that. Even if he knew she was single, he still wouldn't be interested in her. She was the nanny. The hired help. He had beautiful and famous women like Nataly Granger after him. Why would he ever look twice at Clarissa? It was a good thing he thought she was married. That way she wouldn't have to face the humiliation of being unnoticed by him.

Clarissa picked up the paper from where it lay on the couch, looked down at the picture of Slade, and sighed.

A friend.

She carried the paper over to the table where her purse was, fumbled through it until she found a pair of small scissors, then carefully cut out the photo. She would put it in her journal—right after she color-copied a dozen prints to send to her friends and family. After all, what was the point of having fifteen minutes of fame if you couldn't share it with the people who actually knew you?

Her friends would all gasp at the caption and ask, "You're friends with Slade Jacobson?"

Then she'd have to say, "No, not really. Actually he hardly knew I was alive."

Perhaps she wouldn't make color copies of the photo after all.

Clarissa got up and went over to her own desk and flipped on the computer. She hadn't even thought about checking her e-mail until she'd seen Meredith do it, but it was a good idea. It would keep her mind off things she didn't want to think about. She could even e-mail her parents and let them know how she and Elaina were doing.

She logged on to the computer, then accessed her mailbox. The first thing she noticed was a message from Renea. Clarissa stared at it, tapping her fingers against the desk while she decided whether she was up to reading a message from her ex-sister-in-law. After a moment she clicked it open.

"Clarissa," it read. "I've called you twice and never got an answer back from you. I'm getting worried. I know how depressed you are, but it's important for you to get out and be with people. Don't hole up somewhere and spend your days crying. Especially not since I want to help you through this. I know how to deal with pain. I want to talk to you about Alex. I think you still have hope. Give me a call. Love, Renea."

Clarissa tapped her fingers against the keyboard a little harder than she needed to. Hope. She had hope. How nice to know.

She hit the reply button and typed: "Renea, I haven't returned your calls because, as I told you before, I'm in Hawaii. It's nice you're concerned about me, but I'm doing fine. In fact, just today Tristan McKellips asked me out. I turned him down though. He isn't my type." She hit the send button before she could change her mind about its contents.

And then to prove her point, she found the web page of the *Oahu Times* and copied the link to the picture of her and Slade and pasted it into another e-mail. A photo of Slade Jacobson dropping into the Mahalo Regency with a friend was just the right thing to send to Renea.

8

Slade woke up at 6:30 A.M. He wished he could sleep in later, especially since it was Saturday, but once he woke up he thought about calling A.J. and what he was going to say, and how he'd pitch the script, and then he couldn't get back to sleep even though he lay in bed for half an hour trying. He finally pulled himself out of bed and went to shower and shave.

A.J. had undoubtedly stayed up late last night, so Slade didn't dare call too early, but if he waited too long, A.J. might be off doing something. Perhaps 9:30 would be the best time.

Slade dressed, ordered room service for breakfast, then woke up Bella. She didn't want to get dressed in clothes—all she wanted to wear was her swimsuit.

While he was cutting up her pancakes she said, "Are you going to take me swimming today, Daddy?"

"We'll work something out," he told her. "I'm sure Clarissa wouldn't mind taking you."

"But I want *you* to do it," she said. "You throw me up in the air, and then I make big splashes."

Slade nodded seriously and took a sip of his orange juice. "Yes, I suppose that is important." For a moment he watched Bella trying to capture a piece of her pancake with her fork, then asked, "So, do you like Clarissa?"

Without looking up Bella shrugged and said, "She wouldn't take me to the beach yesterday, but she played with me in the pool. Your other girlfriends never play with me."

"She's not my girlfriend," Slade said. "She's your nanny, and she's supposed to play with you."

"Nuh-uh, Daddy." Bella's head bounced in a dramatic way with each word she spoke. "She's not old enough to be a nanny."

"She is too your nanny." It was vital Bella was clear on this topic, so Slade said it in his most serious tone. The last thing he wanted was for Bella to call Clarissa his girlfriend out in public. "I got you a young nanny this time because I thought she'd play better with you." And then almost under his breath he added, "She's stronger than the other ones. And sturdier and faster . . ."

Bella skewered a pancake piece, twirled it around, and then popped it in her mouth. "You'll make her leave though, if she's not nice to me, right?"

Slade raised an eyebrow at the question. Bella had never said much about his hiring practices, and now he wasn't sure how to answer the question. "Let's give Clarissa a try, and we'll talk about how you're getting along at the end of the week."

She didn't answer, just slid her fork into another pancake piece.

"I already explained why she jumped into the pool after you," he added and couldn't help but smile as he thought of Clarissa dripping on the pool deck. "She thought you were drowning. She wanted to help you."

Bella continued to look at her pancakes, but now she frowned. "When is Mommy coming back?"

Slade nearly toppled his juice glass over. Even now, after a year of being divorced, questions like this still pierced him. They let him see into the window that was Bella's mind and into a reality that existed only for her. In her mind her mother still loved her, and Evelyn's short visits every few months meant something.

"I don't know when she'll be by to see you again, honey."

"She has to be there for the first day of kindergarten," Bella said matter-of-factly. "Rachel said all the mothers come to school on the first day."

"I'll be there," Slade said.

"You're not a mother."

"They'll let you into kindergarten, even if it's your dad who drops you off."

Bella's brows knit together as though she didn't quite believe him.

"It's still a long time off," he said. "We'll make sure everything is all right."

"Okay." Bella went back to her breakfast, but Slade couldn't finish his. He put it back on the tray.

At nine-thirty he dropped Bella off at Clarissa's room, then went back to his room to make the phone call. It was imperative he had quiet—professional-sounding quiet—as he talked to A.J.

He made the call, but no one answered.

Could A.J. have left already? Maybe he was still asleep, or in the shower.

Slade went to his suitcase and pulled out the script for his part in an upcoming miniseries. Rehearsals didn't start for a couple of weeks, but he always tried to get as many lines learned in his free time as he could.

For twenty minutes he vehemently professed his innocence to the dresser, lamp, and nightstand, then he called A.J. again. Still no answer. Slade hung up the phone harder than he needed to. He must have missed A.J. The man was probably snorkeling off a reef somewhere, and Slade wouldn't be able to get hold of him all day.

He went back to his lines but couldn't concentrate on them.

Sometimes he hated this business. He hated the whole connections aspect of it—the way you had to be in the right place at the right time, and because those things rarely happened naturally, you had to force yourself to be in the right place at the right time and then fake that it was happening naturally. Slade had just gotten to the point in his career that he didn't have to hustle to get the right parts, and now he was starting on a whole new venture of hustling, hoping, and dealing with rejection. Who needed this?

Slade glanced over to his dresser at the manila envelope that held his screenplay.

He didn't need the money. He didn't need the recognition. It would be easy to let this project go.

Only he couldn't let it go.

It was an uplifting, wholesome story. It had a moral. In the larger collection of entertainment, it would be a voice for good in the world. You didn't hear too many of those voices these days, and if he didn't give this script his best shot, then every time he saw trailers for all the new inane movies of the season, he'd feel a pang of guilt and responsibility.

He tossed his lines onto the bed and headed out the door. He would go wake up Tristan and find out what the production schedule was like. That way he'd know when he had the greatest chance of getting hold of A.J.

Slade hadn't gone far down the hallway before he ran into the right place at the right time. A.J. and Nataly were standing in front of the elevator.

Slade sauntered up to them at an unconcerned pace. "A.J., you're just the man I was looking for."

Nataly took hold of A.J.'s arm possessively and smiled at Slade. "I say the same thing to him every day."

Slade laughed lightly at Nataly's joke, then turned his attention back to A.J. "I wanted to tell you again how much I enjoyed your party last night. I'm already looking forward to your next one."

"We're having one Halloween night," Nataly said. "It's going to be a masquerade."

"In the Iolani room at 7:00," A.J. added. "We'll count on seeing you there."

The elevator opened and all three stepped in. It was the right place, the right time, and it was only going to last for four floors.

"So," Slade put his hands in his pockets and donned a casual expression, "have you given any more thought as to when you'd be open to a pitch meeting?"

A.J. nodded. "Ah, yes, we were going to do that, weren't we?" He looked thoughtful for a moment, as though mentally reviewing his calendar, then said, "Why don't you join us for breakfast, and you can do it there."

"At breakfast? Right now?"

"Sure, there's nothing like hearing a good story over bacon and eggs," he smiled over at Nataly. "You don't mind, do you, sweetheart?"

"Of course not," she said, and her pink lips curled into a smile. "Join us."

They walked to the restaurant, and the hostess seated them in a corner booth. Slade waited until the waitress had taken their orders, then began his pitch.

"The story is called *Time Machine*. It's a love story with a sci-fi angle, but it's really a story about redemption." He paused for a moment to let the emphasis sink in. "People will relate to it because we all look back at our lives and at one point or another wish we could change things."

A.J. nodded and reached for his cup of coffee. "Yeah. I've wished for a time machine myself. Especially after divorce number two. If I had it to do over again, I would have skipped marrying Meagan altogether and just paid a large sum of money to her lawyer. It would have saved me all the hassle of working through the middle man that way."

Slade leaned forward a bit. "Well, that's the type of thing that happens in this story. The main character, Dalton Hammer, is a successful scientist and inventor. He's made millions, collected accolades, seen and done it all. But he's getting older—he's 65, retirement age, and he realizes he has nothing of real value. No wife, no family, not even a lot of friends. He's been a workaholic, a loner, and a lot of times a jerk. He wishes he'd done things differently in his life and so pours all his time and money into building this time machine that will permit him to go anywhere in time for 72 hours. Then he'll automatically come back to the present, and the time machine is used up, finished. He has one shot to change things.

"He decides the best way to repair his life is to go back in time to his college days and try to convince the young him to change his ways. You see, Dalton lost the love of his life, Kathleen, because he went to the right grad school instead of deciding to be with her. After he told her good-bye, they went their separate ways, and he never saw her again.

"Kathleen is the type of girl all guys want—beautiful, smart, sophisticated. Everything. Dalton figures if he'd only married her, his life would have had love in it, so everything would have been all right." Slade paused to see A.J.'s reaction.

A.J. nodded. "Typical leading lady role. Gwyneth Paltrow, Cameron Diaz—"

"Nataly Granger . . ." Nataly interjected.

"Right," Slade said, "and the reason Dalton thinks he has a chance of changing his life with Kathleen is that there was an incident back in college that almost made him stop and see the bigger picture of life. Kathleen's roommate, Sarah, was flying home for Christmas and was killed in a plane crash. It made an impression on the young Dalton, and for a few days after the accident, he realized how fragile life is. If he'd been more committed to Kathleen in the first place, if he'd had someone older and wiser to guide him, Dalton is sure he would have taken the leap and asked her to marry him.

"So the old Dalton uses the time machine to go back to right before the plane crash. He poses as a wealthy great uncle and tries to talk some sense into the young Dalton. The young Dalton is still a jerk, though, and the problem is, he won't listen to himself.

"The older Dalton has to think of more and more ways to convince him. He's bribing and setting things up; he even enlists Sarah's help. Then as he's creating all these scenarios, he realizes Kathleen isn't the right woman for him at all. She's just a female version of the young Dalton—a jerk. It's really Sarah who's the great catch. The only problem is, not only is she going to die, but the young Dalton isn't interested in her, either.

"The old Dalton realizes that he might not be able to change his own life at all but he might be able to save Sarah. He tries to convince her not to take the plane home because he knows it will crash. But you know kids, they never listen to anyone older than thirty, and she's still going.

"He can't let her go, so in the climactic scene the old Dalton dashes in front of her car to stop her from leaving. She tries to stop in time, but runs over him, and instead of catching her flight, has to rush him to the hospital.

"In the hospital all the doctors are afraid the old Dalton is going to die. The young Dalton comes to see him and is especially shaken about it. The old Dalton tries to tell him everything, but can't get out anything past the fact that he's Dalton from the future and has built a time machine to try to change his life. The young Dalton thinks the old man's delirious, but as the hospital people begin to prep him for surgery, the young Dalton notices some birthmarks on the old man's chest—the same birthmarks he has on his own chest.

"Sarah and the young Dalton are sent to a waiting room while the doctors try to save the old Dalton. And it's there she sees the news story about her plane going down. They're both in shock over this as well as what's happened with the old Dalton; and they talk about life, about what's important in life, and the audience can see a bond forming between them. Dalton starts trying to figure the whole thing out—starts wondering what kind of man he'll be at sixty-five and what all this time travel business means. Does he need to change his life? What will happen if he does?

"Just then the surgeon comes into the waiting room, very frustrated, and tells them they've lost the old Dalton. 'Lost?' Dalton says. 'You mean he's dead?'

"'No,' the surgeon says. 'I mean he's gone.'

"'Gone but not dead?' Dalton says.

"'He was there on the table one moment, and the next moment he was gone,' the surgeon says. 'We're searching the hospital for him.'

"The surgeon walks off, but Sarah understands. She takes hold of Dalton's arm and says, 'He went back to the future.'"

"'Or,' Dalton says, 'perhaps he changed the present so much that now I won't need to build a time machine in the future.'

"They look at one another, and Sarah says, 'I guess we'll never know.'

"But as they walk out of the hospital, Dalton takes her hand, and the audience knows." Slade held up his hands for emphasis. "The end. Everyone gets up from their seats, so moved they spill the remainder of their popcorn tubs on the floor."

Slade looked intently at A.J., trying to judge his reaction by the way he was chewing his hash browns. Finally A.J. said, "Interesting. Sounds like it might have potential."

"Then you'll look at the script?"

"Sure. Drop it by anytime."

Slade smiled. "You'll have it by the end of the day."

A.J. forked another bite of hash browns into his mouth. "I'm not sure how long it will take me to get to it though. Every minute we're not on the set, Nataly either has a sightseeing or a shopping trip planned." He looked at her. "Which is it this morning? I've forgotten already."

"Shopping," she said.

He nodded. "Of course."

Nataly glanced over at Slade, then folded her hands across her lap. "Still it doesn't seem right to make Slade wait so long when he's come all the way to Hawaii to give you his pitch." She slid one hand on A.J.'s arm and turned her attention completely to him. "I'll forgo my trip to Neiman Marcus if you want to spend the morning reading Slade's script."

"Really? You'd give up Neiman for the *Time Machine?*"

"I'll go swimming and work on my tan instead."

A.J. turned to Slade. "Well, I guess the story has one fan

already." He leaned a little closer to Slade. "I'm ready to green-light your script on the merit of how much money it just saved me at Neiman's alone."

"Great. I'll give it to you as soon as we finish here." Slade picked up his fork and looked down at his second breakfast for the first time. Finally, he felt like he had an appetite.

✦ ✦ ✦

The first thing out of Bella's mouth when she walked into Clarissa's room was, "Are you taking me to the ocean today?"

Leave it to a child to skip the small talk.

Clarissa turned her back on Elaina, who lay sprawled in front of the TV watching *Sesame Street*, and smiled down at Bella. While she smiled she wrestled between the pros and cons of giving in to a beach trip this morning.

Pro: No screaming right now.

Con: Screaming the next time Bella didn't get her way the first time she asked for something.

Pro: No screaming right now.

Con: Clarissa running around the beach after Bella because Bella never learned to obey Clarissa and wouldn't follow her instructions. Perhaps something dangerous could even happen, like losing Bella to an undercurrent—which would lead to a lot of other cons, like the heartbreaking funeral and a lifetime of therapy to deal with the guilt of Bella's death.

Clarissa bent down to be on Bella's eye level and kept her voice cheerfully upbeat. "I'm not comfortable taking you to the beach by myself, honey, but if you'd like, we can go put on our suits and go to the kiddy pool again."

Bella slouched her shoulders, tilted her face up, and let out a whiny, "Wh-y-y can-n-'t I g-o-o to the bea-ea-ch-ch n-ow-ow?"

"I'm not sure you can mind me well enough to follow the rules, and I don't want you to get hurt."

"I ca-an too-o ob-ey-ey the ru-u-u-les!"

Clarissa stared down at Bella, and all at once felt over-whelmed at the task ahead of her. How could she even think she

131

wanted a permanent position as this child's caregiver when she didn't know how she was going to make it through the next ten minutes with her sanity intact? Still, she continued to smile and tried again. "I'll see how well you obey at the pool, and then we'll talk about the beach."

Bella took a deep breath, and Clarissa braced herself for a bloodcurdling scream. Instead, Bella glanced over at the chair she had time-out in yesterday, and then let the breath out again. She frowned for a moment, as though considering her options, and then said, "Can we go to the pool right now?"

"Sure."

"And if I'm good, we'll go to the beach?"

"Right."

"And we can catch sharks?"

"Well, um, if they're very close to the beach."

"Okay."

Clarissa got the girls ready, and Bella reminded her, in two-minute increments, that she was being good. Which always made Elaina pipe in with, "I's being good, too, huh, Mommy?"

"Yes, you're both being very good," Clarissa answered. "I appreciate it." And she did. Still it was a relief when both girls finally splashed into the pool, bringing the constant performance review to an end.

Then Clarissa had time to think about her own performance review.

Yesterday had gone badly. In fact, thus far her career as Bella's nanny had—in Hollywood's terminology—been a one-star affair. If that. She needed today to be better. She needed to prove to Slade that she actually was competent and qualified to watch Bella. And for once it would be helpful if Bella could cooperate toward that end.

She looked out at the kiddy pool where Bella sat perched on the side of the pool, kicking her feet in the water.

Keep being good, she told her silently. *Keep being good until I can figure out how to handle you.*

❖ ❖ ❖

Slade stood at A.J.'s hotel room door, script in hand, and knocked lightly. As he waited for A.J. to answer the door, Slade said a silent prayer, *If this is the right thing then please let it happen. If not, then please help me know what I'm supposed to do with it.*

It was Nataly and not A.J. who answered the door. She wore a white bikini top, a short silky floral wraparound skirt, and a pair of white beaded sandals that looked as though they'd snap if she took more than two steps in them. "A.J.'s on the phone with California," she said in a hushed tone, "but I'll give your script to him. Just a second."

Leaving Slade standing in the hall, she took the envelope from his hands and disappeared into the room for a moment. When she came back she had a towel draped over her shoulder and was carrying a straw beach bag. She slipped out of the room and shut the door behind her.

Taking Slade's arm, she smiled and said, "Well, where are you taking me this morning? The beach, the pool, or somewhere else?"

"You want me to take you somewhere?"

"I got A.J. to read your script, didn't I?" She squeezed his arm and pressed against him. "You don't want me to get bored and change my mind about shopping, do you?"

Slade smiled at her warily. "All right then. I'll meet you at the pool in ten minutes. Just give me time to change into my swimsuit."

Her smile widened. It was probably the same smile the praying mantis used right before it devoured its mate. "I'll be waiting," she cooed, then turned and walked down the hallway, her skirt swaying softly as she went.

Slade walked back toward his room but stopped at Clarissa's instead. If she were still in her room, he could tell her to take the girls to the pool. With Bella around, climbing all over him and demanding to be tossed up into the air, Nataly wouldn't have a chance to implement whatever plans and plots she was concocting.

He knocked on the door. No one answered.

Plan number two. Meredith could show up at the pool and fake some sort of emergency. Anything that would require his immediate attention. He jogged down to her room and tried it. No one answered there, either.

Slade slapped his hand on the door one last time, then walked back to his own room. Women. How come they were never around when you needed them?

After he'd closed his door behind him, he took out his cell phone and punched in Clarissa's number. While it rang he unbuttoned his shirt as quickly as he could.

Clarissa picked up after a couple of rings. "Hello?"

Slade tossed his shirt on the dresser and balanced the phone against his shoulder while he worked on his pants. "Are you still at the hotel?"

"Yes."

"Okay. Stop doing whatever you're doing, and go to the pool with the girls."

"I'm already at the pool with the girls."

"Good. Then stay there." He dropped the phone as he tried to put one leg of his swimsuit on. He finished with his swimsuit, then picked up the phone from the floor and said, "Sorry about that. Look, I'll see you in a few minutes." He turned off the phone, dropped it onto a chair, and grabbed a towel and a bottle of suntan lotion. He had just slipped on his sandals when he heard a knock on the door. Shaking his head, he picked up his sunglasses and went to answer the door.

Somehow he'd known all along Nataly wouldn't wait to meet him at the pool. She had come to his room to wait for him while he finished getting dressed.

He opened the door, and she glanced over him casually. "I forgot to bring suntan lotion. Do you have any?"

He tossed his bottle to her. "You're in luck."

She caught it without even looking at the bottle. "I hope so."
He stepped out of the room and shut the door.
"You're ready, then?" she asked.
"I'm ready," he said, and they walked down the hall.

9

Clarissa slipped the phone back into her bag. Stay where you are? The man was absolutely cryptic. Maybe movie stars were just used to ordering people around without any explanations.

She lay back in a reclined position on the pool deck chair and watched the girls go down the boat slide. Bella went down waving her arms and squealing. Splash. Elaina followed. More squealing. Splash. Then both girls waded across the pool, up the steps, and dripped their way back to the slide. They never seemed to get tired of it.

That was fine though. When Slade came he'd see what a good time the girls were having, and he'd know that Clarissa was both competent and qualified. Perhaps with a little luck she might raise her rating to a three- or four-star nanny today.

"You were right. The blue suit does look the nicest on you."

Clarissa turned and saw Tristan, dressed in shorts and a tan polo shirt, standing behind her. His eyes scanned over her, taking in every detail.

She smiled at him, startled, and said, "Tristan, hello. Are you going swimming?" A stupid question. Of course he wasn't going swimming. He was fully dressed. Only people like, well, people like herself, went swimming in their clothes.

He didn't seem to notice, or at least didn't comment on the obvious. He pulled one of the pool chairs next to hers and sat down, his arms resting casually on the chair armrests. "I was passing by and noticed you sitting here. You've lured me to you again with your swimsuit."

Oh. This was just what she needed. Slade would be here in a few minutes, and he'd see her with Tristan and think she'd ignored everything Slade had told her last night. He'd think she was some sort of hopeless flirt. She could feel, as she sat stiffly smiling over at Tristan, her rating as a nanny fall to a dangerously low level.

"Well, it's nice of you to drop by and say hi. I mean, I'm sure you must be very busy working on your series. Swamped probably. In a rush to get somewhere . . ."

"I'll be busy come Monday. That's when the real work starts, but even then, my part is pretty light. It's mostly a chick story line this go-around. I only have a few scenes."

"Oh."

He glanced around the swimming pool and then back at her. "So what are your plans for the day?"

Clarissa watched Bella shriek into the pool. "I'm baby-sitting the girls."

"Today? On Saturday? Slade isn't even giving you the week-end off?"

"I watch Bella whenever he needs me to."

"Then I'll help you watch her." Tristan smiled over at Clarissa. "Which one is your daughter?"

"The one at the top of the slide."

Tristan glanced in that direction. "She's beautiful. Looks just like her mother. Same long blonde hair . . . same big blue eyes." Tristan turned his attention back to Clarissa, and his gaze felt heavy. She told herself she was absolutely not going to blush but wasn't sure how well she managed to achieve that goal.

"Um, thanks," she said. "But you don't want to sit around and tend children all day. They get to be quite a handful. I can't take my eyes off them for a minute."

"I'm great with kids," Tristan said, "and Bella is crazy about me." He leaned toward the pool and yelled, "Hi, Bella!"

She glanced at him, then turned away, splashing through the pool without saying anything.

"Bella!" he called to her again. "It's me, Uncle Tristan. Aren't you going to say hi to me?"

Without looking at him she yelled, "Hi!"

Tristan leaned back in his chair. "See. She loves me."

Clarissa heard footsteps behind her, and then a woman's voice said, "Who loves you, Tristan?"

She glanced over her shoulder and saw Nataly and Slade both dressed in swimming suits and carrying towels.

Tristan smiled widely at Nataly, then said, "Simply fill in the blank."

Nataly tossed her towel on the chair next to Tristan and undid the tie on her skirt, slowly peeling it away from her white bikini and tanned waist.

Tristan leaned farther back in his chair and continued to stare at her. "So, what brings you to the kiddy pool, Nataly?"

"Slade and I decided to spend the afternoon together while A.J. goes over Slade's manuscript. When we saw you all here, Slade had to come over and check on Bella."

Slade dropped his things on the chair next to Nataly's. He looked tense, though Clarissa couldn't tell whether this was from being with Nataly or whether it was the result of finding her with Tristan. Perhaps both. He said, "There's Bella now," and then walked into the kiddy pool without saying anything further to the group.

He was only a few steps into the water when Bella noticed him. She was halfway down the slide but tried to stand up anyway, and ended up falling face first into the water. Slade sloshed over to her as quickly as he could, but she popped back up out of the water with a smile on her face. "Daddy!" she yelled and held her arms up to him. He picked her up and swung her around.

Elaina slid down the slide next and then immediately splashed over to them. She held up her arms and said, "Swing me, too! Swing me, too!" Holding Bella in one arm, Slade reached with the other and scooped Elaina up, spun around, and

138

then fell down in the water. Both girls squealed with delight and chanted, "Again! Again!"

Clarissa hadn't even noticed she'd been gripping the armrests of her chair, but she found her grip slowly relaxing. Slade had picked up Elaina and held her along with his own daughter. There was no hesitancy, no sense of rejection—no sense that Slade considered Elaina a burden. It was a relief, but a bittersweet one. She couldn't help but ask: *Why couldn't Alex have been like that?* And then wondered if she'd always be asking herself that question.

"Do you mind rubbing some lotion on my back?" Nataly said. "I never can seem to reach there."

Clarissa glanced over at Nataly and saw her holding the sun lotion bottle out to Tristan.

He took the bottle with a grin. "I'm always willing to help."

Tristan poured a small amount of lotion into the palm of his hand and then rubbed it slowly across Nataly's shoulders, caressing the curves of her neck. She lifted her hair off her shoulders, then gazed back at Tristan through lowered lashes.

Completely obvious. Completely transparent. Next they'd be sending each other meaningful gazes and making guttural noises. Clarissa turned away, rolling her eyes as she did.

Had she and Tristan behaved this blatantly while dancing last night? She felt her cheeks redden in embarrassment at the thought. No wonder Slade thought she was foolish. You always looked foolish flirting with shallow people.

She wouldn't make that mistake again.

In fact, she was back to her resolve of swearing off men completely. Men just had a way of muddling your thinking and making you act in ways you regretted later.

No more men.

She glanced over at Tristan, and all at once his handsomeness diminished. His jawline, instead of square and masculine, seemed over-exaggerated. His eyes, so intense last night, now looked artificial, like costume jewelry.

Her gaze traveled to the pool again and to Slade. Slade was so different from Tristan. Slade had substance. Character. That's why he was avoiding Nataly, and that's why he would never look twice at Clarissa.

She watched him for another minute, wading backward in the shallow pool, grinning down at the girls as they splashed after him.

He would probably never come out of the pool. He'd stay there until dinnertime just to avoid Little Miss Coppertone's advances. In fact, if Slade ever did come back close enough so that he was in conversational range, he'd probably tell Clarissa she could have the rest of the day off, just so Bella could be his permanent chaperone.

On the downside, she would no longer have an excuse to avoid Tristan; but on the upside, Tristan was now so involved with Nataly he probably wouldn't care. They'd spend the day oiling each other and wouldn't even notice Clarissa's exit. Perhaps she could get some sightseeing done, or pick up some souvenirs.

"Clarissa, do you need lotion on your back?" Tristan asked. She turned to him and saw his smile was now aimed at her.

Oh. How nice. Tristan was an equal-opportunity flirter.

He wiggled his fingers. "My hands are already lotioned, so I might as well protect you from the sun, too."

"Um, that's okay. I put on sunscreen before I came out."

He swung his legs off his chair and faced Clarissa, then leaned over and put his hands on her shoulders. "You can never have too much sunscreen," he said as his hands caressed the lotion onto her shoulders. "You need to be careful, you know."

Careful. Yes. Clarissa quickly glanced over at Slade. He held one girl under each arm and was slowly spinning them through the water. He didn't seem to have noticed that his nanny was getting a massage from Tristan. Yet.

Clarissa glanced at Nataly, though she wasn't sure what help she'd get from that corner. Nataly wasn't even paying attention. She had lain back in her chair, stretched one arm above her head, and closed her eyes. Her pose looked as relaxed as it did seductive.

Clarissa swallowed and tried to appear casual about Tristan's touch. "Thanks. My shoulders are safe now."

With a gentle motion he swept her hair off of her back. "Here, lean forward, and I'll put some on your back."

"I don't think I need it," she said.

He shook his head, and his smile—though he tried to hide it—was tinged with mocking. "I think you do. You might be starting to burn already. You look a bit pink."

And they both knew why. Why did she have to blush when she really didn't want to?

Tristan's gaze ran over her in an appraising manner. "Do you feel like you're burning?"

Only with embarrassment.

"I'm fine," Clarissa said.

Tristan shook his head again. "Maybe you should go inside and get out of the sun."

"I've only been here for a little while," Clarissa said, "and Slade still needs me to baby-sit him. I mean, for him. He still needs me to baby-sit for him."

A smile tugged at the corners of Tristan's mouth. He seemed to think all of Clarissa's discomfort was a direct compliment to him, and he had no qualms about dragging more compliments out of her. "He looks like he's taking care of Bella just fine."

Nataly turned her head lazily toward Tristan. "If she says Slade wants her to baby-sit, then don't argue with her. You don't want to get her fired, do you?"

"Fired?" Tristan sat back in his chair, wiped his hands off on a towel, and looked out across the kiddy pool. "Slade isn't such a slave driver, is he? I mean, he's a religious man now. Firing you would break some commandment, wouldn't it?"

"Your religious knowledge is stunning," Nataly said.

"Thou shalt not let thy employees get sunburned," Tristan said. "It's in the book of Moses somewhere."

Clarissa pulled her towel up onto her legs. "I think I'll be fine now. Really."

"Slade isn't actually a religious man." Nataly's gaze zeroed in on Slade in the pool, and she sat up a bit in her chair. "It's just a phase he's going through. A midlife crisis. Most men go out and buy a sports car, but he already owns enough of those, so he had to do something different." She shrugged and closed her eyes as though the matter were decided. "In a few months the whole thing will be over. Sort of like Michael Jackson's marriages."

Clarissa hadn't planned on starting a religious discussion, but she suddenly felt the need to defend Slade, and she couldn't let Nataly's accusation stand.

Trying to match Nataly's casual tone, she said, "I would hope having faith is never just a phase. I think Slade joined the Church because he believes its teachings."

Now Nataly's gaze was back on Slade, and her smile was back too. "Well, I guess we'll see."

Despite the warmth of the sunshine on her, Clarissa felt a shiver run down her spine.

"Don't pay any attention to Nataly," Tristan said. "She's just not the religious type. As for me, I believe spirituality is an important part of a man's life."

Nataly rolled her eyes and snorted.

"Oh, really?" Clarissa asked. "What religion are you?"

"Well, I'm not exactly any particular religion. I'm just, you know, spiritual."

"If it suits your purpose," Nataly said.

Tristan leaned closer to Clarissa. "You see what I mean about her? Atheists are always such bitter, angry people."

"I'm not an atheist," Nataly said. "I just don't believe in organized religion. It isn't natural."

"Natural, meaning what?" Clarissa asked.

Nataly's shoulders heaved up and then down as she sighed. "God made the world, the plants, the animals, and us. The plants and animals live freely, as God intended them to, but religion subjects people to a lot of rules. It tells them what they can and can't do and how to live their lives. I'd rather live naturally."

"Like the animals?" Clarissa asked.

"Absolute freedom," Nataly said.

"Are you planning on devouring your young, too?"

Nataly's gaze snapped back over to Clarissa, and she grunted in disbelief.

"Well, you've obviously never watched a PBS documentary on nature," Clarissa said.

One of Nataly's immaculately formed eyebrows rose. "I'm too busy to watch PBS."

"The whole point of humanity is that we can act better than animals. We're not driven solely by instinct and self-preservation. We have agency. We choose how we will behave."

Nataly's eyes narrowed, and she looked at, and not just over at, Clarissa for perhaps the first time. Nataly tapped her long golden fingernails against the armrest of her pool chair with a calculating look. "And you choose to follow the rules."

"I try to," Clarissa said.

For a moment longer Nataly stared at her, dissecting her with her gaze. "Haven't you ever longed to be free from them?"

"Not really."

"Oh, come on, haven't you ever known you shouldn't do something, but you couldn't help yourself?" Nataly's voice turned smooth and lulling. She smiled, catlike. "The temptation, the lure of a few moments of ecstasy is just too much to resist, and you give in, even though you know you shouldn't?"

"Yes," Clarissa said, "I have those moments. They're called 'eating chocolate.'"

Nataly leaned back in her chair and closed her eyes with a huff. "You've never lived, Mrs. Hancock."

Clarissa also leaned back in her chair. "I had a fight once about rules with my father. I was fifteen years old, and we were driving on the freeway to get to my friend's house. I was complaining because my parents wouldn't let me date this boy at school. My father let me go on and on, and then I noticed he'd gone past the exit to my friend's house. When I pointed it out, my father just said, 'I don't have to follow the rules. I'm not going to let some exit sign tell me what to do.' We drove all over the city and were half an hour late getting to my friend's house, but I got the point. If you want the right destination, you have to follow the right rules."

Nataly stretched and then laid one tanned arm across her stomach. "Well, I guess I must have done something right then, because I've reached the right destination."

Clarissa wanted to contradict her but didn't. How did a divorced temporary nanny tell Nataly Granger that despite her fame, beauty, and wealth, something was missing in her life? Most women would have killed to be in Nataly's shoes; or in this instance, in her little white bikini. On the other hand, nobody would want to trade places with Clarissa.

She had chosen all the right roads, hadn't she? How had she ever managed to get so far off course? How had she ended up here?

Nataly watched her smugly. She was waiting for a response, and Clarissa didn't know what to say. Finally, because it seemed the only possible way to respond, Clarissa said, "I hope you're always so happy with your choices."

"And I hope one day you find someone so wonderful you won't care about breaking the rules." Nataly glanced over at Tristan then, and her eyes fixed on his with pointed meaning. Even from where Clarissa sat, she could tell Nataly had offered Tristan up a challenge. And Tristan, his eyes still on Nataly, gave her an easy smile.

A smile that meant what?

Nataly laughed slightly, stretched again, and settled back into her chair.

It would have been poetic justice if lightning had suddenly come from the sky and singed Nataly and her bikini, but lightning never struck when you wanted it to. Nataly would probably always be gorgeous, rich, and singe-free. She'd simply go through life amassing fans and collecting Oscars.

It was funny how you could talk about your beliefs—how you could profess Christianity in one breath, and then in the next one wish something horrible on a person.

It was definitely something Clarissa needed to repent of.

And she would. As soon as she stopped wishing something horrible on Nataly.

Perhaps because Slade was tired of tromping through the kiddy pool, or perhaps because he figured there was safety in numbers, he picked up Bella and carried her toward the group. Elaina watched them go for a moment, then headed quickly back to the slide.

Clarissa recognized the look on her daughter's face. She didn't want to leave the pool and didn't want to be close enough to her mother to hear, in case Clarissa called for her to come.

Slade grabbed a towel from his chair and, still holding Bella, wrapped it around her shoulders and back.

"Bella has a stomachache," he announced.

Clarissa sat up in her chair, perhaps a bit too eagerly. "Do you want me to take her back to the hotel?"

"No," he said, and to his credit he actually sounded as though he had debated the idea. "I'll hold her for a little while and see if she starts to feel better. I think Daddy just played too rough." He leaned his lounge chair back to a 45-degree angle, sat down, and cradled Bella in his arms.

Clarissa leaned a bit toward Slade and looked into Bella's face. "Bella was very good this morning. We'll have to go to the beach sometime soon."

Bella returned Clarissa's gaze without smiling. "I don't *want* to go to the beach."

It figured.

Clarissa spread her hands out as though offering up other possibilities. "We'll find something you do want to do then."

Slade bent down, gave the top of Bella's head a kiss, and said, "How's your stomach feeling now?"

She pushed one arm from underneath the towel and laid it on her father. "I feel good, but not gooder enough for you to leave me."

Slade couldn't have scripted a better line to keep Bella at his side, and as Clarissa thought about it, she wondered if Slade *had* scripted the line.

But if Slade wanted to be with Bella so he wouldn't have to be alone with Nataly, where did that leave Clarissa and her nanny duties? Was she supposed to stick around, or did Slade want her to leave so he'd be forced to keep Bella with him?

Clarissa wished she knew. She wished Slade would give her some hint. Perhaps she should ask in a roundabout way what his plans for the rest of the day were.

Clarissa glanced over at Tristan, now engrossed in a conversation with Nataly about the set, and decided against it. If Clarissa were to leave, Tristan might see it as an opportunity to join her.

As soon as this thought crossed her mind, Clarissa chided herself for it. Tristan, after all, had better things to do with his time than chase her around. True, he had flirted with her, but there were too many willing women around for him to concern himself with her.

Still, she hadn't imagined that challenging look Nataly had sent him. Nor had she imagined Tristan's smile when he seemed to accept it.

Clarissa sank a little farther into her chair. She'd stay here. After all, Elaina wanted to play in the pool. No sense in leaving now.

For the next hour Clarissa watched Elaina swim, splash, and plunge down the slide, sometimes going quickly, other times holding onto the side of the slide so she sat stopped, suspended above the water. Clarissa also listened while the others discussed reading lines, doing retakes, and wearing makeup in humid

146

locations. Nataly seemed intent on keeping the conversation on subjects Clarissa had no knowledge of. If ever one of the two men made a comment to Clarissa, Nataly quickly found a way to steal the dialogue back to herself.

Clarissa accepted this without resistance. If Nataly aimed to keep Clarissa in her place as a paid servant by ignoring her, that was fine with Clarissa. That sort of treatment just reflected poorly on Nataly. And besides, it was easier to say nothing.

Bella stayed with the adults, and her stomach must have felt better, because she took fishy crackers from Clarissa's bag, climbed back on her father's chair, and ate the entire school. Then she fell asleep in the crook of Slade's arm.

Finally Nataly allowed the conversation to drift from talking shop, and she began discussing social events. Specifically, her next party. She eyed Slade with Tristan-like subtlety and said, "Have you decided on a costume for our masquerade?"

"I haven't even thought about it yet."

Nataly's gaze lingered on Slade's physique. "You'd look great as Tarzan."

Slade shook his head and grimaced. "I don't think so."

"I know," Tristan said. "Go as a monk—it will fit in with your new image."

"I'll go as Shakespeare," Slade said. "Then maybe it will be easier to convince people I'm a writer."

Tristan turned to Clarissa. "What are you going as?"

"A nanny. I'll have to baby-sit." She glanced at Slade and for a moment wished he'd protest, but he didn't.

Of course he didn't. She was here to be a nanny. That's what she wanted. She wished differently only for a moment because she was so tired of the way Nataly pointedly left her out of the conversation.

Tristan tilted his chin down, staring over at his friend in a silent appeal. "Come on, Slade. Let Clarissa go. You're working her to death."

"Of course," Nataly added. "Just look at her, she's withering away under the strain of her workload."

"It's all right," Clarissa told Tristan quickly. "I'm here to work."

Slade grinned over at Tristan. "He doesn't understand. Work is a foreign concept to Tristan."

Tristan looked down at his watch. "Actually it's not." He glanced at Clarissa, then the others. "I had better get going. I've still got some lines to work on before rehearsal."

Clarissa waited until Tristan had returned to the hotel and then motioned to Elaina to come out of the pool. As the little girl trotted up to her, Clarissa said, "I think you've had enough sun for the day." She held open a towel, wrapped it around Elaina's dripping body, and glanced over at Slade. "I'm going to take Elaina inside. Do you want me to take Bella, too?"

"No." He said the word a bit too quickly, but then recovered his casual manner. He looked down at Bella and fluffed her damp curls with his hand. "If we try to move her, she'll wake up, and she probably needs the extra sleep, what with her stomachache and all."

Uh-huh.

Clarissa smiled as she took Elaina's hand and stood up. Nataly might have fame, fortune, and a figure that looked stunning in a white bikini, but she didn't have Slade. Not even his friendship or respect. All the conniving and flirting in the world couldn't bring her those.

And somehow, while Clarissa walked back up to her room, she felt better about the afternoon.

10

Slade stayed at the pool talking with Nataly for another hour, carefully measuring the minutes to give A.J. enough time to read his manuscript. He draped his towel carefully over Bella so she wouldn't burn, and kept the conversation focused on Nataly. As long as Nataly was talking about herself, she wouldn't talk about subjects he wanted to avoid: specifically he and she together in any way beyond sitting here by the pool.

It was easy to contain the conversation. He just kept asking Nataly about her goals and projects, and she happily ate away the time. She complained about her agent, the director of her last movie, and the media coverage of her career.

"Someday I'll get a role where I'm not just another pretty face. You know, a role with meat to it." She pulled her legs up on the lounge chair and leaned forward, wrapping her arms around her knees. "That's the problem with being beautiful. No one takes you seriously."

Poor thing. He could tell by the way she preened and postured how her beauty troubled her.

"You'll find something," he said.

He glanced down at his watch then. Surely A.J. had had enough time by now to not only read the manuscript but to assign parts. Sitting forward in his chair, he said, "I really ought to take Bella inside. Should we go check in with your boyfriend?"

She picked up her skirt and towel from the side of her chair and stretched her arms. "Sure. We can drop Bella off at your nanny's room first."

He walked slowly back to the hotel, carrying Bella against his shoulder and trying not to jostle her too much. Nataly walked beside them, wrapping her skirt back around her waist as she went.

"Do I look tanner?" she asked.

Slade glanced at her. "Sure."

She waited for a moment and then said, "I don't know how you can tell. You haven't looked at me all day."

They came to the hotel, and Slade opened the door for Nataly but didn't respond to her statement. They walked without speaking across the lobby to the elevator. As Slade pushed the button Nataly said, "Your nanny seems quite dedicated."

"I think so," Slade replied. He could feel Nataly's gaze on him as he watched for the elevator doors.

"She's a little stuffy, though."

"She's responsible," he said.

"And her fashion sense is appalling."

"Her fashion sense is normal. Not everyone lives on Rodeo Drive, you know."

"But she is quite pretty."

Although he knew it was pointless, Slade pushed the lighted elevator button again. "You don't suppose this is broken, do you?"

"I noticed you didn't disagree with me about that last statement," Nataly said.

"What? About Clarissa being pretty? It would be pointless to disagree with the obvious."

The elevator door opened, and Slade stepped inside and pushed the button for the fourth floor. Nataly followed him in and leaned up against the elevator wall. "Your tastes have changed since I knew you."

"A lot about me has changed since you knew me."

"Oh, yes, you were born again."

"Wrong religion," he said, "same concept."

As the elevator rose, Bella stirred, slightly lifting her head and then putting it back down on Slade's shoulder. Nataly watched Bella for a moment, then moved from the elevator wall and walked around Slade. At first he had no idea why she was circling him, but then he saw her look into Bella's face.

"She's still asleep," Nataly said.

"She was playing hard."

"Just like her father." Nataly smiled at him. "He's been playing hard to get all day."

"Nataly—" he began, but she cut him off.

"I know what you must think of me, I mean, being here with A.J. and talking to you like this. But the truth is things haven't gone well between A.J. and me for quite some time. I just haven't gotten around to breaking it off with him. I haven't had a reason to until now." She tilted her head and looked up at Slade, her lips slightly parted. "But seeing you again—Slade, you're one of the few men I've ever really cared about, and here you are with me again. That can't be coincidence. Don't you believe in fate?"

He sighed and in a low voice said, "Nataly, you're as beautiful and as persistent as ever. But it would never work out between us."

"Why not?"

Because he wanted someone he could respect—a woman he could trust. Because of a dozen other reasons, all of which he couldn't tell her without the risk of being slapped before they reached the fourth floor. "I'm seeing someone right now."

"Oh," her voice suddenly sounded tight and crisp. She inhaled sharply and said, "And to think I just heard on *Entertainment Tonight* that you are a confirmed bachelor."

"Well, you know how accurate those shows are." He cleared his throat nervously. "Her name is Kim, and she's flying in from England to see me on Wednesday."

"England. How lovely." She drew her lips into something that was half smile and half scowl. "Such a warm, passionate people, the English." The elevator door opened and they stepped out. "Is she an actress?"

"No, actually, she's a botanist," and then because Nataly was

151

staring at him in disbelief, he added, "She's finishing up her Ph.D. in botany at the University of Sheffield."

"A botanist and a doctor," Nataly said. "You can't be serious."

He wasn't. "I am," he said, and hoped Kim would understand when he told her of these new developments in their relationship.

Nataly's voice was all sharp edges. "Well, it's become suddenly clear to me why no one knows you're dating her. I'd hide something like that, too."

They'd reached Clarissa's room, and Slade knocked lightly on the door. "Kim's a lovely person," he said. "And I'm not hiding her. In fact, I plan on bringing her to your costume party."

"Well, I can hardly wait to meet her. She can put on a lab coat and come as herself."

Clarissa answered the door. She'd changed into a denim jumper and put on just enough makeup to emphasize her large eyes. Her hair was out of the ponytail and brushed into soft blonde waves that lay on her shoulders. She looked both wholesome and beautiful.

Slade said, "Do you mind watching Bella for a bit? I'm going to go check in with A.J."

Clarissa opened her door all the way and smiled at him. "You know the way to the toys." Her eyes, though not as blue as Nataly's, were brighter, clearer. And suddenly it struck him exactly how alike and yet how contrasted the two women with him were. It was as if someone had created Clarissa purely to make a point—not all beautiful women were like Nataly.

"Bella is asleep," Slade said, but as soon as the words came out of his mouth, he felt her little arms tighten around his neck. Stepping into the room, he tried to lay her down on the couch, but she wouldn't let go of his neck.

"I want to stay with you," she mumbled into his shirt.

"I'll be back in a few minutes," he told her.

She still didn't let go of his neck, and now she started to wail, "Noooo!"

Clarissa came and helped peel Bella's arms off him, all the time repeating, "It's all right, Bella, we'll order some lunch, and then you'll feel better."

At last Clarissa was able to drag her from her father's arms. "She'll be fine in a minute," Clarissa told Slade over the wailing. "Just go."

Slade hesitated for a moment, then turned and went with Nataly. The wailing was still audible, though faint, all the way down the hall.

Slade would have liked to change out of his swimming things before he talked to A.J., but he didn't want to suggest it to Nataly. It was better to limit his time with her as much as possible.

As they came to the room, Nataly put her hand on Slade's arm and said, "You're just walking me back to A.J.'s room, and while you're here we decided to check and see if he's read the script."

"Right," Slade said, wondering why she felt the need to give him an alibi. After all, he *was* simply walking her to the room, and the whole point of the walk was to find out if A.J. had read the script.

Nataly knocked and a moment later A.J. answered. He stood in the doorway, his cell phone still pressed to one ear, looking exactly how Slade had seen him hours before. Nataly walked past Slade into the room and plopped down on the couch without saying anything. Slade stood in the doorway, though, watching A.J. continue to nod and mutter things into the phone.

At last A.J. said into the phone, "Hold on a minute," and then held it away from his face.

He shook his head at Slade. "I'm sorry, but I haven't had a chance to even look at your story. The production people messed up the props, and now I have a crate full of fake diamond necklaces somewhere in California, which no one can seem to locate, and nothing here. I've spent half the morning calling jewelers on the island, trying to figure out whether it would be easier to track down necklaces here or get more in California and have the studio fly them over. Then when I suggested to the writer that we just change the script to cut out the necklaces, he got all defensive about it and brought up every grievance he's ever had during his entire career. He told me he wants to renegotiate his contract. I spent the last half of the morning trying to convince our lawyer to kill him." He shook his head again, looked at the phone, and muttered, "Writers. They're worse than actors, and that's saying something."

Well, yes, especially if you were both a writer and and an actor. Slade decided not to bring up this point. Instead, he said, "It's all right. I understand how crazy things can get in this business."

"I'll try to find some time this weekend to go over it though. At the latest Monday—maybe Tuesday. I'll give you a call as soon as I've had a chance to look at it."

"Great," Slade said. "I'll talk with you then."

He turned around and walked back to his room, only realizing when he was halfway down the hallway that he'd forgotten to say good-bye to Nataly. But then, perhaps that was for the best.

✦ ✦ ✦

He continued around the corner, and as he approached Clarissa's room he was glad to note that he couldn't hear Bella wailing. He knocked on the door, and after a moment Elaina, not Clarissa, answered the door. He didn't have to ask where everyone else was, though, because he could see Bella, standing sullenly on the couch, and Clarissa on her hands and knees picking up chunks of a broken lamp.

"Bella," he said sternly, "you didn't."

Bella turned, looked at her father, and then let out a forlorn and desolate sob, which made her entire body shake.

Despite his chastisement he walked over to the couch and picked her up to comfort her. She buried her face into his shoulder and continued to cry as though her heart was at this very moment bleeding from deep wounds.

Clarissa looked up at them while she dumped lamp parts into a nearby waste basket. "It was an accident," she said. "I was ordering room service, and Bella was jumping up and down behind me, making sure I didn't forget anything. I should have known it was a doomed venture." Clarissa dropped the last of the pieces of glass into the waste basket and then surveyed the floor. "I suppose we should have the maid service come up and vacuum up the little pieces. You did say you were tipping them well, didn't you?"

Slade ignored Clarissa and rubbed Bella's back. "I'm sorry I snapped at you, sweetheart."

She mumbled something unintelligible into his neck.

"Daddy will be with you for the rest of the day. In fact, right after lunch we'll take a drive. Okay?"

This time she looked up and nodded, and although tears still made wet smudges on her cheeks, a smile also grew on her face. "And Elaina's coming, too?"

"Of course," Slade said. "It wouldn't be any fun if Clarissa and Elaina didn't come along." He looked over at Clarissa for a sign of agreement.

She smiled back at him, which meant she wasn't angry with him. It was just one more area in which she was the opposite of Nataly.

❖ ❖ ❖

After lunch, Slade, Clarissa, and the two girls drove to the Polynesian Cultural Center in Laie. As they wandered through the exhibits and watched the performances, Slade was impressed by the way Clarissa balanced enjoying the shows with watching the children. Even though he was there, she kept an eye on Bella, making sure she never wandered too far away, and every once in a while said things such as, "Yes, that man is very talented, but you'll never try to climb a tree with a knife in your mouth to retrieve coconuts, will you, Bella?"

And Bella, for the most part, was well-behaved. Aside from a couple of incidents where she ran close to the water to "see if there were fish in there," she alternated between being carried by

Slade and holding Clarissa's hand. She also enjoyed being a tour guide for Elaina. "The reason they wear grass skirts," she told her friend in a serious voice, "is because pants don't grow here."

It was a relaxing outing, made all the more enjoyable by the fact that no one came up to Slade to ask for his autograph or chat with him about any and every movie he'd done. It might have been the sunglasses and baseball cap that hid his identity, but it was more probable that it was because he was hauling two little girls around. He looked like a family man, a tourist dad, and people didn't equate those with movie stars.

Once this idea came into his mind, it wouldn't leave. Throughout the day he kept glancing at Clarissa. People probably thought she was his wife. It was, after all, the natural conclusion. She was walking close beside him and holding his daughter's hand. As they walked around the grounds talking and looking at things, it almost felt as though she was his wife, like it would have been perfectly natural for him to reach over and put his arm around her shoulder and natural that she would turn and smile back at him, happy he'd done it.

He wished, periodically, that she *was* his wife, that this was a typical family excursion and that afterward they would go back to their home, tuck the girls into bed, and sit together on the sofa discussing the day's events. And then perhaps not discuss the day's events.

Each time these thoughts came, he dismissed them. Clarissa was a married woman. He wasn't attracted to her; he was simply attracted to the qualities she had, qualities he would most certainly find sometime down the road in another woman. He just had to keep going down the right road.

❖ ❖ ❖

At eight-thirty, Clarissa buckled two tired little girls into the backseat of the car. They'd left before the show and dancing ended because Elaina kept falling asleep and Bella, during the Maori dancers' routine, kept yelling, "It's not polite to make faces!" Rather than take her out, Slade suggested they all leave.

Clarissa didn't argue. She was afraid if she got separated from Slade, she'd never find him again, and then she and Elaina would have to take up residence in the grass hut display.

They had barely pulled out of the parking lot before Bella's head nodded against the car seat, and she joined Elaina in slumber. Neither Slade nor Clarissa spoke for a few moments as they drove, and then Clarissa asked, "Where do you keep the matches at your house?"

Even though he was still looking straight forward, she could see an eyebrow raise. "In the kitchen cupboard. Why?"

"Well, I'm not sure if Bella was paying attention during the fire dance or not, but you might want to lock up all your flammable devices just to be on the safe side."

He laughed and said, "You have an uncanny knack for understanding my daughter."

Clarissa stared out at the dark forms of the foliage growing along the road and debated whether or not she should pursue this subject. On one hand she was Bella's nanny, the person he was paying to take care of her—Clarrisa was supposed to be looking out for Bella's welfare and voicing any concerns about his daughter. On the other hand, Clarissa knew that parents rarely looked at their children objectively, and Slade wasn't likely to listen to anything she said on that subject. Alex had never listened to her when it came to parenting.

But then Slade wasn't Alex.

She glanced over at him, at the form of his profile. Even in the dark his jawline looked strong, his cheekbones, nose, and forehead all perfectly proportioned.

What had she been thinking about?

Oh, yes, Alex. How Slade wasn't Alex. How Slade was so . . . Slade.

She turned her gaze back toward the window and tried to think of Bella instead of Bella's father. She weighed the pros and cons of speaking, but in the end the issue was decided by one thing. She honestly cared about the little girl. "On one level I think I understand Bella," Clarissa said, "but on another, I don't think I've even begun to understand her."

Slade smiled. "Well, that's normal isn't it? After all she is a female."

"I'm serious," Clarissa said.

"So am I. Women are the ultimate mysteries, followed closely by quantum mechanics and Dick Clark's real age."

"She's a delightful child," Clarissa said, "confident, charming, and extremely precocious—"

"She takes after her father."

"But do you think it's normal for a child to go from one scrape to another like she does?"

Here Slade shrugged. "She's a kid. Kids get into scrapes. I'm sure you had your share of them when you were little."

"Meredith says you have your own parking spot at the emergency room."

"Only figuratively speaking." Slade glanced over at her nonchalantly. "Bella's just accident-prone. She'll grow out of it."

Once again Clarissa debated keeping silent. Once again she didn't. "Haven't you ever noticed there's a pattern to her accidents?"

"Yes, most of them involve damage to expensive items."

"No, I mean she's the most accident-prone when you're not paying attention to her."

"Well, of course. If I were paying attention to her, I could stop her from doing whatever it is she's not supposed to do."

Clarissa shook her head. "I was paying attention to her on the first night we came here, and Bella ran off to find you. I was paying attention to her when she jumped into the pool and when she broke the lamp. Meredith was paying attention when she decorated the carpet with fingernail polish. It isn't that she's unsupervised, it's that when you're not around, she's fast."

"You're saying she does everything on purpose?" His eyebrows furrowed together in disbelief. "She's not even five years old yet.

Trust me, she has neither the planning nor acting abilities to pull that off."

Clarissa could hear the edge in his voice, but went on anyway. "I'm not saying it's necessarily a conscious decision on her part, but doesn't it seem peculiar that when you're around, when you're around and paying attention to her, she's no longer accident-prone?"

"So you're saying you think I don't give her enough attention?"

"No, I'm saying that's what *she* thinks."

He tightened his grip on the steering wheel. "I give her a lot of attention. I give her everything a kid could ever want. She has more toys than Mattel."

"Indulgence isn't the same as attention."

"Oh, now I'm indulgent."

Clarissa sighed and didn't say anything else.

Maybe it wasn't Alex after all. Maybe it was just men. Maybe they never listened to your opinions, never cared what you thought, and never thought you were smart enough to have any real insights. Maybe men always criticized you and twisted everything so it seemed like it was your fault and then always demanded more and more until you locked yourself in a room and spent the night crying.

And there she was, back in her marriage with Alex again. How many times did she have to divorce herself from him before she finally left him completely?

Slade sighed. When he spoke next his voice was soft and conciliatory. "Okay, maybe I am a little indulgent." He held up one hand for a moment to concede the point. "But Bella lost her mother. She deserves something to make up for that."

"Bella doesn't see her mother often?"

"Nope."

"Was it a painful divorce?"

Slade glanced over at her, surprise registered on his face. "I thought everyone knew about my divorce. It was in the tabloids for long enough."

"I never read them."

"I'll fill you in then." He leaned back against his seat and held onto the steering wheel with only one hand, as though it wasn't a stressful thing to describe the breakup of his marriage. The edge in his voice, however, betrayed his nonchalance. "First there were all the pictures of Evelyn out with Brad Nash. He was the opposite lead in her soap opera, so I didn't think much of it; I mean, she assured me it was all business.

"Then there were the pictures of them kissing. That was harder to pass off as business, but she still tried. I mean, after all, she kissed him a lot for her show. For all I knew, those pictures were taken on the set." He shook his head. "Isn't acting a peculiar profession? It must be the only one in the world where you can see photographs of your wife kissing another man and still not know whether she's being unfaithful to you."

"So how did you find out?"

"I followed her. You'd think after two run-ins with the tabloids, she'd have been more careful, but she wasn't. And come to think of it, neither was I. There was an ugly scene at a restaurant, you know, a sort of yelling, screaming, punching Brad across the salad bar type of thing—the tabloids fully documented the event for posterity. It hit all the newsstands the next day."

"I'm sorry. That must have been awful." Without thinking about it, Clarissa reached over and put her hand on Slade's arm. And then a second later, when she realized what she'd done, she removed it just as quickly.

Slade seemed not to have noticed either her gesture or her quick end to it. He simply shrugged and said, "You don't need to be sorry for me. I'm better off without Evelyn."

"Probably. But Bella got a whole new set of issues to deal with. Issues you need to be aware of and address."

Slade shrugged his shoulders. "Bella is fine. She just needs more time to adjust."

Well, so much for thinking Slade would listen to her.

Clarissa folded her arms and stared unseeing at the night scenery. "It's all well and fine if you want to let her continue to break things. I'm sure you can afford it, but one day she might actually hurt herself, you know."

"Bella is fine," he said again, and then added under his breath. "And to think I thought getting a nanny with a family science background was a *good* thing. Next you'll be telling me I discipline all wrong, too."

"I wouldn't know," Clarissa said. "I have yet to see you discipline Bella."

"Well, I do," he said. "Sometimes."

She pressed the point. "Children need limitations. They need to know where the boundaries are. They'll keep pushing until they find them. I know you'd rather be nurturing than be a disciplinarian, but Bella needs you to be both. If you don't teach her there are consequences for her actions, who will?"

She saw his jaw clench and heard him mutter, "It's easy enough for you to dispense parenting advice. Your family is intact. Every time I punish Bella, she cries for her mother. I feel like I'm wounding her all over again. You wouldn't be much of a disciplinarian either if you had to go through that."

They were only a short distance away from the resort, but even that was suddenly exhaustingly far away.

For several moments she didn't respond; she just sat watching the black ribbon of road in front of them. *I know what your life is like. I know how hard it was to sit down and divide your possessions with someone who hurt you, to divide things that couldn't be divided, so you ripped them apart. You ripped your whole life apart and then had to find some way to tell your child the fabric of her life had been torn, inexorably tattered, and there was nothing she could do about it.*

The truth lay on her lips, waiting to be spoken. In another moment she would have told him everything, but he spoke instead.

"You seem to have a way of making me say things I regret later," he told her. "I know you mean well, and I apologize for snapping."

"I like Bella," she said. "It's just that she needs a father and not a Santa Claus to take care of her. Will you just promise me you'll think about what I've said?"

"Sure. I'll think about it."

She knew he wouldn't. His words were said simply to brush her off.

Still, she had tried.

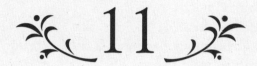

11

Slade pulled up to the front of the hotel, gave the car keys to the valet, and opened the back door of the car. Clarissa stood by as he lifted Elaina out of the backseat and placed her in Clarissa's arms. Then he lifted Bella into his own, and they walked into the hotel, across the lobby, and toward the elevator.

An overflow crowd from one of the meeting rooms was mingling in the hallway, and dance music drifted into the lobby. A party. And by the looks of the people in the hallway, another not-so-undercover cast party. Clarissa pushed through the crowd without stopping, but a middle-aged woman waylaid Slade and insisted he come say hello to her daughter.

He glanced over the top of Bella's head at Clarissa and said, "I'll be a few minutes," then followed the woman into the room.

A few minutes? Did that mean he expected her to wait for him, or was he giving her permission to leave? She stood in the lobby holding Elaina and debated the question. Then, because Elaina was growing increasingly heavy, she decided he'd given her permission to leave and headed toward the elevator. Besides, if she was wrong, he knew where to find her.

Reaching awkwardly to push the elevator call button without bumping Elaina's head against the wall, Clarissa heard a man's voice say, "That's a heavy load you're carrying."

Clarissa turned to see Tristan walking toward her. She smiled at him and said, "I'm used to it."

"It looks like you're about to fall over." He reached out his hands to take Elaina. "Here, let me help you."

"That's all right. You don't—" but before she could get out anymore, he lifted the little girl out of her arms.

"See, isn't that much better?"

"Thanks," she said stiffly.

The elevator door opened, and Tristan stepped inside. She followed after him, a bit too quickly, as though she didn't want to lose them.

He pushed the four button, but before the doors closed all the way, she caught a glimpse of Slade walking across the lobby. He didn't look happy. Which meant he'd seen her and Tristan get into the elevator together. Which meant she was going to hear all about it later. She sighed out loud.

"Long day?" Tristan asked.

"I guess."

"You need more time to relax."

"Don't we all?"

"Why don't you put your daughter to bed and come join our party?"

She shook her head. "I couldn't leave Elaina alone like that. She might wake up and need something."

He gave her a long, appraising look, then nodded slowly as though he'd figured her out. "You're one of those women who worries too much, aren't you?"

"Maybe."

The elevator door opened and they stepped out. "What's your room number?"

She hesitated, and then told herself she was being paranoid. It wouldn't hurt to let Tristan know which room she was staying in. "Four-twenty-one," she said.

They headed in that direction, walking slowly in the brightly lit hallway. "You could check in on your daughter every once in a while, you know."

"Thanks, anyway," she said.

He shook his head and made a "tsk"ing sound with his tongue. "There you go again, worrying too much."

They walked the rest of the way to her room in silence. When they reached the door she said, "Thanks for carrying Elaina for me" and reached out her arms to retrieve her daughter.

He nodded at the lock. "You might want to open the door while your hands are free."

It seemed silly to protest. After all, it would have been hard to retrieve her card from her purse, run it through the lock, and open the door while trying not to drop Elaina on the floor.

Clarissa dug through her purse until she found her key card, then opened the door. Instead of handing Elaina to her, Tristan pushed the door open farther and walked into the room.

"Where do you want me to put her?"

She bit back the response, *In my arms, back out in the hallway* and followed him into the room. "How about on the couch?"

He laid her down gently, pausing to gaze at her as he did. "She really does look just like you."

"Thanks."

"It must be hard taking care of her all by yourself."

At that moment every struggle, problem, and worry she'd had since the divorce flashed through her mind. She stood before Tristan still and breathless, wondering how he'd known she was a single parent. And more important, what was he going to do with that information? Would he tell Slade?

Or perhaps he was only guessing, and she'd just confirmed his suspicions by standing here wide-eyed and gaping.

In a voice as casual as she could feign she said, "What makes you think I'm raising Elaina by myself?"

Tristan tilted his head sideways and bit back a smile. "I didn't say 'raising,' I said 'taking care of.'" And then because he must have seen that she still didn't understand, he added, "I meant here in Hawaii, on your trip . . . away from your husband."

He walked over until he stood close to her. His gaze felt penetrating. "*Are* you raising her by yourself?"

She held up her chin and wished she were a better liar. "No."

"Are you sure you're not just using that husband story to scare men off?"

"If I were single, why would I want to scare men off?"

He smiled at her, but it wasn't this smile she saw. It was the one he'd given Nataly while they all sat at the pool that Clarissa saw on his lips.

He took a step nearer to her. Hardly any room separated them, and he leaned toward her to diminish that. "Maybe you're afraid to let anyone get close to you." His gaze went from her eyes to her lips, and she knew he was about to kiss her. She turned her head and walked a few steps away.

"See," he held one hand out to her as though showing her something. "You're afraid to let anyone get close to you."

"Thanks for helping me with Elaina," she said firmly. "But I'd like to be alone now."

"You still owe me a favor."

"Well, I'm not paying it now."

He walked toward her again. "You're worrying about nothing again."

She didn't have to reply. A sharp knock came on the door, followed by, "Clarissa, open up. It's me, Slade."

"She wants to be alone now," Tristan called back.

Clarissa glared at him and went to open the door. Slade stood in the hallway without Bella and with his hands on his hips.

"Hello, Slade," she said in what she hoped was a calm voice.

He walked past her into the room and stopped in front of Tristan. "Tristan," he said flatly, "people down at the party are asking where you disappeared to."

"Is that what you came up here for? To tell me I've been missed?"

"Actually, I came to talk to Clarissa about the schedule for tomorrow."

"Oh," Tristan nodded slowly. "Well, then, I'll let you get on with business." He looked back at Clarissa for a moment with a wry smile, then said, "I'll see you later."

166

"Thanks again for your help," she said.

Slade held the door open for Tristan and shut it behind him as he left. Then he turned back to Clarissa. His expression was cold. "What was that all about?"

"He helped me carry Elaina up here."

Now Slade came and stood close to her, anger emphasizing his movements as much as seductiveness had emphasized Tristan's. "You *let* Tristan into your room?"

"I didn't *let* him into my room. He just sort of pushed his way in here. But he was just leaving when you knocked. I had everything under control."

"You had everything under control? You were the one that let him push his way into your room in the first place."

"I asked him to leave, and he was leaving. You're acting like you think Tristan is dangerous."

Slade stared at her, tight-lipped, and didn't speak.

"He's not dangerous, is he?"

"Only to those people who insist on being naïve. A group in which, I'm afraid, you have a membership."

"I'm not naïve," she said. "I'm a married woman with a child."

"And that's another thing. Your husband is either as naïve as you are, or he's a fool to let you out of his sight. I can't believe he agreed to let you come on this trip, and I can't believe that suddenly *I'm* in charge of defending your honor." He walked to the chair and sat down in it as though he were exhausted. "What a family man I've become."

"You are not in charge of defending my honor," Clarissa protested.

Slade held up one hand. "We're not arguing about this anymore. I want you to listen to me for a minute, Clarissa. Can you do that?"

Clarissa folded her arms. "I'm listening."

"I want you to avoid Tristan from now on."

"I *am*."

"Well, I want you to do a better job then. You need to avoid him *outside* your hotel room."

She almost argued the point but bit her lip instead.

"You might think you're just being friendly, but he's bound to see it as encouragement. So from now on, don't let anyone into your room. Anyone. Do you understand?"

"Perfectly. Get out of my room."

He glared at her but got up and slowly moved to the door. "I'm glad you're finally taking my words to heart."

"And don't expect me to be friendly to you, either. I wouldn't want to encourage you."

He opened the door, but before he stepped out, he turned back to her and said, "By the way, church starts at ten o'clock. I'll be by to pick you up at nine-thirty."

"Great," she said. "I'll be ready." But as she shut the door she felt anything but spiritual.

✦ ✦ ✦

Instead of going back to Meredith's room, where he had dropped off Bella, Slade went to the elevator and back down to the party. He surveyed the room until he spotted Tristan by the bar. The blond actor had a drink in one hand and the other resting on Brandy's arm. Tristan couldn't have been with her very long, but still the two were leaning toward one another, laughing, as though they were on a date. As Slade walked toward them, Tristan lifted his hand and began caressing Brandy's long red hair. Typical.

Slade moved next to Tristan, who ignored him. After a moment, Slade called over the music, "Tristan, can I talk to you for a minute?"

Tristan looked away from Brandy with a twinge of annoyance. Then he sighed. "Sure." He gave Brandy's arm another pat. "Catch you later, babe."

Then the two men walked silently from the room and into the lobby—Tristan in a slow saunter, the drink still in his hand, Slade more quickly, with his jaw clenched. As they went out the front door of the resort Slade turned to Tristan and shook his head. "Why in the world do you call women 'babe'? It's the most irritating way you could possibly address a person."

Tristan gave a small cough and rolled his eyes. "I could think of a few more irritating ways to address someone. How about hauling someone away from a beautiful woman"—he glanced down at his watch—"twice within the space of ten minutes?"

"That is exactly what I want to talk to you about."

They walked away from the hotel entrance onto a path leading into the garden, until they were far enough away from the entrance that Slade felt they could talk without being overheard.

"Look, Tristan, I'm going to come right out and say this. I want you to stay away from Clarissa."

There was no embarrassment, only amusement on Tristan's features. "Why? Am I bothering her?"

"You're bothering me."

"I see." He nodded knowingly. "I'm encroaching on your territory and apparently making more progress than you are. That's what's bothering you, isn't it?"

Slade spoke very slowly. "She's a married woman, Tristan. Since when did you take up homewrecking?"

Tristan rolled not only his eyes but his whole head. He stared up at the sky for a moment and then back at Slade skeptically. "Oh, give up the married woman routine. She's no more married than I am."

"And how did you come to that conclusion?"

Tristan shrugged and took a sip of his drink. "You can tell when a woman is married. At least, I can." When Slade didn't comment, Tristan added, "It's in all those subtle signals they send out. That chummy body language. The way they carry themselves. The way they smile. The way they look at you and blush. Clarissa can barely remember her husband exists. Married women don't act that way. At least not happily married women. One way or the other, her marriage is a sham."

For a moment Slade considered the idea, but only for a

moment. It was much more likely that Tristan had misread the cues. Clarissa was no doubt star-struck with Tristan's attention and had simply smiled and blushed and done the other things that he was interpreting as interest. This explanation made sense, but in the next instant made him uneasy. If Clarissa was that enamored with Tristan's stardom, then she might be tempted to do something she'd regret later.

Slade let out a slow breath and looked directly into Tristan's eyes. "Regardless of your thoughts on her marriage, you don't need to be chasing Clarissa around. You don't seem to be suffering from lack of companionship while you're here."

Tristan shrugged. "You mean Brandy back at the party? She's just a friend." He took another sip of his drink, then waved his glass in the air a bit to help make the point. "Just someone to help ease the sting of rejection and the embarrassment of having a friend order me out of the room."

"Don't worry. You'll recover from the loss somehow."

Tristan grinned in a reminiscing sort of way. "I helped Clarissa pick out that swimsuit she wore today. I made a good choice, don't you think?"

"I think your choices have all been questionable lately."

Tristan swirled the contents of his drink around in his glass and looked at it instead of at Slade. "Clarissa is so different from all the women around here."

"Exactly. She turned you down."

Tristan smiled, still looking at his drink. "Perhaps that's part of it."

Slade had seen Tristan take up this attitude before—this pursue-the-woman-at-all-costs attitude—and it had never particularly bothered Slade. With his carefree, fun-loving approach to life, Tristan was a likeable guy, and he and Slade had always gotten along well. Previously, Slade had viewed Tristan's attitude about women as just an egocentric quirk of Tristan's personality. A machismo thing. They had joked about it. Several times Slade had laughingly told Tristan that one day he'd lay a snare for someone and get caught in it himself.

Now Slade didn't feel like joking at all. He felt like strangling the machismo right out of Tristan. This was Clarissa they were talking about, and Slade was not about to stand idly by while she got hurt. He thrust his hands in his pockets to keep them away from Tristan's neck. "Look," he snapped, "if you want a challenge, take up hunting. That way you can stuff and mount your trophy's head on the wall afterwards."

Tristan ignored him. "I don't know why you're making this your concern, anyway. I mean, it's not like you're giving your chauffeur marriage counseling, are you? You're not checking up on your secretary to see who she dates. If Clarissa is interested in me, why don't you let her make her own choices and keep out of it?"

"She's not interested in you."

"She must be, or we wouldn't be here having this talk, would we? No point in saying all these things to me if you know she's just going to shoot me down anyway."

"She's going to shoot you down, Tristan. I'm just trying to spare you the smoke inhalation."

Tristan smiled and finished off the last of his drink. "Have you ever noticed that her eyes glow when she smiles?"

"No," he said slowly, "I haven't."

"Well, maybe it only happens when she smiles at me." Tristan flexed his shoulders, then glanced over at Slade. "Thanks for the fresh air, but I'm going back to the party."

Slade didn't follow him back. Instead, he stayed outside, hands still shoved in his pockets, and gazed across the resort grounds to the beach and the churning waves below.

He knew he'd just made things worse, and it bothered him how things always seemed to turn out that way lately. Every good goal of his had backfired. He wrote a script with a moral, and was having to chase halfway around the world to try to sell it. He brought his daughter with him instead of leaving her home, and the newspaper reported a questionable relationship between him and Bella's nanny. He tried to keep Clarissa from making mistakes, and she got angry at him. And now, he'd tried to put an end to Tristan's pursuit of Clarissa, and had only thrown fuel on the fire instead.

In retrospect he could see his mistake. He should have said, "Her brother is a high-powered harassment lawyer," or "She's a college grad student writing her thesis on egomania in Hollywood," or better yet, "Only some of her multiple personalities like you." But no, he'd upped the challenge. He'd said, "She'll shoot you down," absolutely ensuring Tristan would try to see to it that she didn't.

Well, there was no way to undo the damage now.

Perhaps the best thing to do would be to call Clarissa's husband and see if he wanted to come to Hawaii for the rest of the trip.

Slade let this thought sit with him for a minute, but any way he thought about it, he didn't like the idea. He intensely didn't like it and spent the next few moments searching hard for a reason to reject the idea.

Clarissa had just told Slade she'd be more careful about encouraging Tristan. That should take care of things, shouldn't it? And besides, it would create all sorts of problems between Clarissa and her husband if he thought she was acting inappropriately while she was here. The last thing Slade wanted to do was create more problems for Clarissa.

So for now the husband stayed put, and Slade would just have to make extra sure he kept watch over Clarissa. It was a much better idea than calling her husband.

❖ ❖ ❖

On Sunday morning Slade picked up Clarissa and Elaina, and they drove to a nearby LDS chapel. They left after the sacrament meeting though. Both Bella and Elaina vehemently refused to go to a strange Primary, and it seemed pointless to try to go to any other meetings with bored, wiggling, loud children.

"Well, consider it money saved, anyway," Clarissa said

brightly as she buckled Elaina into the backseat of the car. "At least this way you didn't have to pay for any broken pews. I hear those are on the expensive side."

Slade rolled his eyes but didn't respond to her comment. He finished snapping Bella's seatbelt on and said, "At least I didn't have to recount my conversion story. Whenever I meet a new set of Mormons they make me tell it to them. They enjoy seeing me eat my words all over again." He shut the back door, then walked around to the front of the car. "Somewhere there's a list of the stupidest things ever said, and at the top of it are the comments Slade Jacobson made on *The Tonight Show* about religion."

Clarissa smiled but didn't say anything. She got into the front seat and waited for Slade. He sat down, turned on the ignition, and slowly pulled the car out of the parking lot.

"Tell me your conversion story," Clarissa said. "I want to see you eat your words."

He pressed his lips together as though he were trying to suppress a smile. "No. I've avoided it once today, and you're not going to force it out of me now."

"Please."

"No."

This time Clarissa batted her eyelashes innocently. "*Please.*"

"Your wiles won't work on me, Mrs. Hancock. I'm immune to them."

So, she was back to being Mrs. Hancock. She would have loved to have come up with some reasonable way to tell him she never wanted to hear that name again but couldn't think of any.

It was about this time Clarissa noticed they weren't headed back to the hotel. "Where are we going?"

"To see the temple, and then to have a picnic lunch on the beach, and then to whatever location I can think of where Tristan isn't likely to be."

"Oh? Why are you avoiding Tristan?"

"I'm not avoiding him, you are. I'm just driving." He glanced at her. "And your husband owes me a big favor for all this."

Clarissa rolled her eyes.

"You think I'm kidding, but I talked to Tristan last night, and he thinks your marriage is a sham."

"Really?" Clarissa half choked out the word.

"He said you've been sending him signals that you're interested in him." Without giving her a chance to answer he said, "Did he really help you pick out a bathing suit?"

"Well, sort of. I mean, not because I asked him to. I ran into him while I was trying them on."

"You ran into him in the dressing room?"

Clarissa laughed. "No, I was wearing one out on the sales floor."

It sounded perfectly legitimate to Clarissa, but Slade shook his head. "Clarissa, I don't think you understand what I'm trying to tell you about men, so I'll just put it this way: don't talk to Tristan, don't look at him, don't blush at him, and absolutely don't use any chummy body language around him."

She didn't say anything, just tapped her foot against the car floor.

"Which reminds me, let me see you smile."

"What?"

He looked at her. "Smile for me."

She gave him a smile that felt more like she was baring her teeth than being pleasant.

"Hmm," he said. "I didn't see your eyes glow."

She folded her arms tightly. "Was this in my job contract? Because I don't remember anyone warning me about interrogations."

His glance left the road and trained on her face again. This time his voice was completely serious. "Just promise me you'll think carefully about what you're doing from now on."

"I promise," she said.

It was a promise she had to remind herself of over and over again throughout the day. Not that Tristan was anywhere around.

He didn't even make an appearance in her thoughts. It was Slade's presence that was plaguing her now.

Had someone asked her what attracted her most in a man, Clarissa wouldn't have thought "a good father" would be the first trait on her list. And yet somehow watching Slade with the girls, Clarissa couldn't think of anything more attractive than the attention he paid to Bella and Elaina. That had to be the reason all her frustrations with him melted, and in their place she felt a strange ache and a quickened heartbeat.

As they walked on the temple grounds, Slade took each girl by the hand and told them in hushed tones why they needed to be reverent. At the beach he took off his shoes and rolled up the legs of his suit pants so he could look for shells with the girls at the shoreline. He was so down-to-earth. So openly casual. So horribly good-looking.

It was this last thought that plagued Clarissa the most.

If she didn't think carefully about what she was doing, she was bound to make a fool of herself by doing something rash— like, say, throwing herself into his arms.

Well, so much for swearing off men.

She had to tell him the truth. She knew that now. She had to find some way to tell him she was divorced, to tell him she was free if he was interested.

But would he be interested?

The thought brought a sharp pain to her stomach.

Of course not.

It wasn't even in the realm of possibilities. After all, at the employment center practically the first thing Mr. Peterson had told her was that Slade wanted to hire a married woman. Slade wasn't looking to find a love interest in his nanny.

So she had to squelch these feelings, which kept popping up every time she noticed how deeply brown his eyes were. And how perfectly rugged his jawline was. And how broad and muscular his shoulders were.

If he had ever shown any hint he was attracted to her, she

could have perhaps mustered the courage to tell him everything, but as she thought over their time together, she could think of no solid evidence on that matter.

Instead of attraction, he'd only shown annoyance that she was young and pretty. He couldn't give her a compliment without calling her Mrs. Hancock, and he wanted her to talk about her husband in sweet and loving tones. True, he'd shown her friendship, but she was not about to pretend it was anything more.

And besides, he would be terribly angry at being deceived. She didn't want that, and she couldn't afford it either. So she would go on pretending to be married. In fact, if Slade extended the nanny position after they got back to California, she'd go out and invent a husband just to continue the facade. Maybe some time in the years to come, after she knew Slade well enough to feel secure in her position, she'd tell him one day that her husband had been inadvertently killed in a freak manhole accident. But only after she felt really secure with the position.

12

On Monday morning Slade dropped Bella off at Clarissa's room so he could stop by the set of *Undercover Agents* to find A.J.

This time Bella didn't scream at all. She just looked around the room, sat down beside Elaina, and said, "Where are we going today?"

"Do you think you can mind well enough to go to the beach?"

Bella's brows knit together as though she was actually taking time to consider the question. After a moment she said, "Yeah."

"Okay, then, to the beach it is." Clarissa pointed out the window behind the couch and said, "We'll go right down there. Not far away from the hotel at all. That way, if we need something we can come right back." She stopped this line of dialogue when she realized she was trying to reassure herself and not Bella.

They packed the beach bag, put on their sunscreen, and then walked, holding hands, down to the beach.

For a time, the three of them played in the water, edging toward the ocean as the water pulled back, then trying to outrun the waves as they came surging onto the shore. Several times the waves won, crashing into their legs and backs—once or twice toppling the little girls in the foamy water.

Clarissa was quick to pick them up and set them right. She brushed wet sand from their faces, looking for tears, but never finding any. Bella thought her face plants were especially funny. "Look 'Laina," she said opening her mouth. "I got sand on my tongue!"

After a while the girls settled down to the less dangerous pastime of building sandcastles, and Clarissa returned to her towel. She tugged at the back of her swimming suit as she sat down, wishing it weren't so French cut.

She hadn't even noticed this about the suit when she bought it. All that business with Tristan had distracted her, and she hadn't really looked closely at the suit until the next morning. And then it was too late to wear anything else. She'd already thrown out her old blue suit, and housekeeping had disposed of it along with the empty soap wrappers and used towelettes.

Clarissa stretched out her legs, glad the beach was relatively deserted. Swimsuits were awful things, anyway you looked at it. In fact, swimsuits beat out high heels when it came to the most annoying article of women's clothing.

She watched the girls throwing sand over their shoulders and pondered all the ways women had tortured themselves over fashion during the years. Corsets seemed like a particularly bad idea. Binding feet was worse. And what were those heavy rings African women used to wear around their necks called?

She was just considering the place of liposuction in the catalog of tortures when Sylvia set a folding beach chair down beside her.

Sylvia wore a different swimsuit than she had at the pool, a black one-piece with bright pink lines running from the shoulder to the waist. Her dark hair was still pulled back in a bun, but this time was wrapped in a pink scarf, in a shade that exactly matched her lipstick. She wore the same dark sunglasses and surveyed the sky with a smile. "It's another beautiful day in paradise, isn't it?"

Clarissa folded her arms across her chest. "No comment."

"Oh, you're not mad about Friday, are you?"

"Slade is the perfect boss, and Bella is an angel."

Sylvia laughed, but it held no humor. "Oh, you don't have to worry about me, dear. As far as reporters go, I'm one of the good kind. I never make things up. I just try to get to the truth. That's why I'm respected and believed. It's why I'm the top columnist at

The Scoop." Sylvia took off her glasses and nodded down the beach. "See that man walking over there—the tall, blond one with the yellow towel—*he's* the one you have to worry about."

The man she referred to walked along the shoreline, hands in his pockets, surveying the people on the beach. He wore regular glasses, not sunglasses, and reminded Clarissa of a science teacher she once had. Stuffy and proper. "Why would I worry about him?"

"He's Grant Rockwell, a reporter from the *Celebrity Buzz,* and he doesn't share my respect for the truth." As Sylvia looked over at him, her eyes narrowed, and she shook her head slowly. "Inside sources, my foot. I'll tell you what his inside sources are: his wishful thinking, his wild imagination, and his delusions of grandeur." She slipped her sunglasses back over her eyes with a humph. "You know that article he ran last week on Britney Spears? Pure fiction. It wouldn't surprise me if he had never even talked to Britney. Just look at him." She shook her head again. "He's over there scouting for some big name out on the beach, and that, my dear, is why I will always be a better journalist. I don't just wait for the stories to come to me—I dig, and I never overlook the small details." Her attention was suddenly back on Clarissa, and the pink lips curled into a smile. "You're probably wondering why I'm telling you all of this, aren't you?"

Actually Clarissa wasn't. She was simply letting Sylvia go on in the hope she'd talk herself out and leave.

"I'm telling you because you are one of those small details of which stories are made."

"I really don't have anything to tell you, and—"

"Oh, but you do," Sylvia interrupted. "Some of my best sources are the worker bees around the great hive of the superstars. You're the ones who see things as they really are."

"My employment contract says I can't talk to journalists, and even if it didn't, I still wouldn't. Slade has a right to keep his private life private."

The pink smile didn't falter, even for a moment. "Pity. Then

I'll just have to go with my other story. The one about the nanny who is an old friend of Tristan McKellips, the nanny who works for Slade Jacobson, and who isn't happily married at all."

Clarissa simply stared at Sylvia and felt her stomach tighten into knots. This wasn't supposed to happen. Hadn't Sylvia promised Tristan she'd leave Clarissa alone if he gave her an interview?

Sylvia leaned toward Clarissa. "I did a little research and called your ex-husband. He wasn't at all hesitant to talk to me. In fact, he had a lot to say about you. For example, he didn't even know you were a friend of Tristan's, but it didn't surprise him. He said you were always meeting men in your last job at the fitness center."

"I handed them towels. That's different than meeting men."

"He said the reason you taught aerobics was you enjoyed prancing around in a skimpy leotard."

"I taught aerobics because I could make more money that way than just checking people in at the front desk."

"So you put on the skimpy leotard for money?"

This wasn't happening. She absolutely wasn't sitting here talking to a reporter about her divorce and discussing the skimpiness of her aerobics outfits.

"You're twisting my words," Clarissa said. "You're probably twisting Alex's, too." But the truth was, Clarissa wasn't sure if Sylvia needed to twist Alex's words. He had a way of twisting reality all by himself. Since the time things had gotten bad in their marriage, he'd made a habit of taking minor incidents, blowing them up, and throwing them back at her. Or rather, he'd thrown them at the marriage counselor. It was at counselling that Clarissa had learned she couldn't keep a budget, was a hopeless flirt, an incurable slob, and that the calls she placed to her parents on major holidays constituted "running up a huge phone bill every month."

Sylvia smiled, catlike, surveying her mouse. "I'm not twisting Alex's words at all. Actually I've softened them a bit to save your feelings. Men can be such cads, you know."

Clarissa bit back her first response and tried to focus her attention on the girls and their sand heaps. "I don't think your readers will really care about some unknown nanny's divorce."

"They will if Tristan is in the middle of it."

Clarissa's gaze swung back to Sylvia. "He's not in the middle of it. I didn't even meet Tristan until after my divorce."

Sylvia tilted her head back in a relaxed fashion. "Then why would he tell me the two of you were old friends?"

Because he was trying to do Slade a favor. But Clarissa couldn't tell Sylvia that. The last thing she wanted to do was bring up Slade's name in front of this reporter.

Or maybe not. Maybe the best thing to do would be to come clean with the whole story. If she just explained the whole situation to Sylvia, then certainly the woman would understand that nothing untoward was going on.

Or maybe it would just give Sylvia more information she could pounce on.

"You and Tristan made quite the couple on the dance floor Friday night," Sylvia went on. "It was certainly nice of Slade to bring you to the party and leave someone else to watch his daughter, wasn't it?"

"How do you know what went on at the luau?"

"Sources, dear. I have my sources."

Yes, sources. The thing that was making the cast so edgy. And now whoever was dishing the dirt was aiming his or her shovel at Clarissa.

She clenched her fists so tight her fingernails dug into her palms. "Slade only took me because . . ." but Clarissa didn't finish the sentence. Instead she said, "I thought you told Tristan if he gave you an interview you'd leave me alone."

"I said I wouldn't quote you on your opinions about Slade and his daughter, and I won't. Once you're working for me, I won't mention your name at all. You'll simply be another one of my sources." Sylvia lifted one leg up and rested it against her knee so that her sandal dangled from her foot. "So, is it a deal? You give me a more interesting story, and I'll never use the one about you and Tristan."

Clarissa tried to match Sylvia's conversational tone. "That's blackmail."

"No, dear, blackmail is when you pay me money to bury a story. Reporting is when the magazine pays me to uncover a story. I'm just reporting." She smiled at Clarissa for a moment longer, then stood up and collapsed her beach chair. She held one hand up in what appeared to be a weak wave. "Think about your story, but don't try to contact me. It wouldn't do, you know, to have people see us talking together. *I'll* contact you later." With that, she turned on her heel and walked away.

Clarissa didn't watch to see where Sylvia went, but wouldn't have been surprised if she had slithered under some nearby rock. Instead, Clarissa leaned forward and rubbed her temples. Her head was pounding in dull aching throbs that matched the cadence of the waves hitting the shore.

All she had wanted was a job where she could spend more time with Elaina, and now she was reporter fodder, eyed over by Sylvia like she was destined to be her next meal.

Clarissa let out a slow, jagged breath. She would just have to tell Slade everything. There was nothing else to do. Then he'd order her to leave Hawaii on the next flight out, which all in all might not be such a bad idea.

And when the news story broke that Tristan McKellips had somehow facilitated the breakup of her marriage, she'd just have a good laugh about it with her friends. And hope that no one in her ward believed it. And hope that Elaina never read those news clips when she got older. And hope that Alex wouldn't get any ideas about making her life more miserable because of them. And hope that Sylvia would keep her word and leave Slade completely out of everything. *Sylvia,* she thought bitterly, *one of the good kind of reporters.* What did the bad kind of reporters do? Take hostages?

Clarissa let out a small groan. She knew Sylvia would drag Slade into this. And she couldn't let that happen.

Would it really hurt to give Sylvia some sort of story? After all, she could think of one rightoff hand: "Nataly Granger finally pulls off an Oscar-winning performance—that of devoted girl-friend." Or perhaps: "Nataly Granger thinks her boyfriend should change his initials from A.J. to H.C. As in, He's Clueless."

It was all true.

And Nataly deserved it.

Clarissa stared out over the ocean, the story forming in her mind. It would be so easy. The article almost printed itself, and she could see the headlines on the covers of millions of maga-zines, lining the shelves in grocery store checkout lines.

And she knew she couldn't do it.

Not to Nataly.

Not to anyone.

Clarissa sighed heavily. So it was a trip home, an existence filled with endless explanations to everyone she knew, and good-bye to the chance of ever seeing Slade again.

There had to be another way.

Maybe she could find a nice story for Sylvia, a story that wouldn't upset anyone. Maybe she'd get lucky and Slade would rescue someone from a burning building. She was ready to set the fire herself if it would help.

She swallowed hard, feeling like it was she and not Bella who had got a mouthful of sand. *I don't have to think about it right now,* she told herself. Sylvia said she'd check back with her later. Maybe Clarissa could put her off indefinitely. Maybe Clarissa could figure a way out of this. Maybe she really would stumble onto an upbeat story.

Maybe.

Maybe.

✦ ✦ ✦

After milling around with Tristan and Brandy as they went over their marks for an office scene, Slade did in fact run into A.J.

The producer pulled Slade aside and apologized for not getting back in touch with him. "I haven't had time to read your script yet," he said. "But I'll get to it soon. I promise."

Which could mean anything.

Slade went back to his room and spent some time running over the lines for his miniseries, but after a half hour of listless recitation, he tossed the script down. He just couldn't muster the enthusiasm for work. He was in Hawaii. He wanted to be on vacation. Besides, hadn't Clarissa told him he needed to give Bella more attention? He would. And he'd take Clarissa along, too, but of course, only to prove the point.

He walked to Clarissa's room, knocked, and when she answered the door he said, "*Time Machine*'s reading is still set in the future. Let's take the kids and go to Hanauma Bay. No point in sticking around here when we can go grind sand into our clothes."

"Oh," she flushed and looked uneasy. "I took the girls to the beach this morning—"

She didn't get to finish. Bella grabbed Slade's pant leg, looked up to his face, and said, "We get to go to the beach again?" as though she'd just won the preschool jackpot.

And so they went. Meredith came, too. Her Idahoan banker had left the night before, and she didn't want to be by herself. While Slade and Clarissa sat on the blanket watching the girls scavenge the beach for shells, Meredith languished nearby on a low beach chair. She wore an oversized straw hat and sunglasses, and as she ran her fingers through the sand, she sighed a lot.

"It isn't as though Idaho is that far away from California," Slade told her. "I can give you the time off to fly over and see him."

"Oh, I know," Meredith said, "but everything is so difficult when you have a long-distance relationship. You have to decide whether you really want to work at it. You have to figure out if it's worth the commitment up front." She picked up her hand and let another stream of sand pour through her fingers. "Speaking of long-distance relationships, your new girlfriend, Kim, e-mailed back."

"She's not my girlfriend yet," Slade said. "At least she doesn't know she's going to the party as my girlfriend yet, so don't mention it to her over the Internet."

Clarissa raised an eyebrow at him. "And when were you planning on telling her that she's your girlfriend?"

"Don't you start on me, too," he said. "I'm not being egotistical; I'm being cautious. It's just better to explain these things in person. I'll tell her on the way to the party."

Clarissa looked over at Meredith and mouthed the word *egotistical* to her.

Meredith nodded in agreement. "You're far too sure of yourself, Slade, and it would serve you right if she's as ugly as a troll underneath her Cat Woman costume."

"Her Cat Woman costume?" Slade asked.

"Yes, she wrote back that she'll bring her Cat Woman costume to Hawaii. On the night of the masquerade, she'll be in the lobby of the Sunset Park Motel purring for you."

"I bet she's gorgeous," Clarissa said. "Gorgeous women are the only ones brave enough to purr."

Meredith nodded again. "She's probably tall, blonde, and stunning—and in that case I hope she's eight months pregnant and Slade has to explain to everyone at the party that she's not *really* his girlfriend."

"She's brunette," Slade said, "and I'm sorry to disappoint you two, but I don't think they make Cat Woman maternity wear."

Clarissa leaned toward Meredith. "He's not at all worried. I bet they've been sending pictures of one another over the net. She's tall, brunette, stunning, *and* skinny."

Slade had heard women use the same tone of voice that Clarissa was now using, and it always meant one thing. Jealousy.

Part of him knew Clarissa wasn't really jealous of Kim, but another part of him sat back and enjoyed the feeling anyway.

"I've never seen a picture of Kim, and I wouldn't know her if

I walked past her on the street," he told them. "In my mind's eye she is still eight years old." Then he smiled graciously at Clarissa and Meredith. "Some people, those who aren't catlike—or catty, as the case may be—are aware there are more important things about people than their looks."

"Oh, right," Meredith said.

"Meow," Clarissa answered. "I think it's time for me to go check on the kittens."

She stood up and walked across the sand to where the girls were stockpiling their beach findings. Slade watched her go, her sundress billowing and blowing around her knees, her long legs eating up the distance on the beach. She sat down on the sand by the girls, and they both chattered up at her happily. She smiled back at them, exclaiming over each of their treasures.

"You're staring," Meredith said.

Slade turned to her. "What?"

"You're staring at Clarissa," she said. "And smiling."

"I'm just happy I chose her. She's a good nanny for Bella."

Meredith nodded. "And Bella must like her because she hasn't run her off yet."

"Of course Bella likes her," he said. "She's kind, intelligent, and beautiful. She's the type of person who's fun to be around . . . and she's patient . . . and beautiful . . ."

"You already said beautiful," Meredith said.

"What?"

"You said beautiful twice."

His eyes settled back on Clarissa. "I guess I did, didn't I?"

Meredith sat up a bit in her beach chair and turned to look at him. "Slade, this would be a good time to stop and think about what you're doing."

"I'm not doing anything." He pulled his gaze from Clarissa and looked at Meredith squarely. She wore a skeptical expression. "I was just thinking it's another reason I'm glad I joined the Mormon Church. It encourages women to develop the important qualities. I admire Clarissa only as a type—there are thousands of women like her out there, and in the future I'm sure I'll meet quite a few of them." He looked back over to where Clarissa was sitting with the girls. "Someone who's caring and wholesome and . . ."

"Beautiful?" asked Meredith.

"Yeah," he said, "beautiful."

Meredith nodded and pulled a newspaper from her beach bag. "I guess I'd better familiarize myself with the paper's format," she said. "That way it will be easier to spot the reports on your latest scandals."

"There aren't going to be any scandals." He honestly meant it and felt much better having analyzed his impressions of Clarissa out loud. All those feelings of guilt over being attracted to a married woman were pointless—because he wasn't actually *attracted* to Clarissa. He simply admired her many fine traits. Just like he admired Steffi Graf's serve and Celine Dion's vocal range. He wasn't planning on making advances toward either of those women, just like he would never think of making an advance on Clarissa. He was simply appreciating her good qualities.

It was all completely sin-free.

He reminded himself of this several times as the day went on. Like when he found himself watching Clarissa with the girls and daydreaming about how nice it would be if she were to be there for Bella all the time. And when he was appreciating Clarissa's legs. They were fine, fine qualities.

They drove back to the resort after eating dinner at a fish and chips place next to the beach. The girls were dirty and tired by then, and Clarissa held their hands, guiding them as they walked into the lobby. "Don't touch anything," she said, steering them around the couch. "And don't bump into anything, either."

The clerk at the front desk watched them come in and then called over. "Ms. Hancock?"

Clarissa looked up. "Yes?"

"Some flowers came for you. You weren't in your room, so the delivery man left them here." She pointed to a vase containing a dozen red roses.

"Oh." For a moment Clarissa simply stared at them.

Slade took Bella's and Elaina's hands. "I've got the girls," he said. "You carry your flowers."

Clarissa went to the counter, but before she picked up the vase she took the envelope from the flowers and opened it.

"Are they from your husband?" Slade tried to make the question sound casual, but even to him it had a sort of pointed sharpness to it.

Clarissa read the card silently, and Slade noticed a blush creep into her face as she did. Instead of answering his question, she handed him the card. He read out loud, "Clarissa, I'm sure you're working like Cinderella, but somehow I doubt your fairy godmother will show up on the night of the ball. Expect a visit from Zorro instead."

"I don't think my husband sent the flowers," Clarissa said.

Slade gave her the card and a glare. "Have you been encouraging Zorro again?"

"I haven't even talked to Zorro since you chased him out of my room."

Slade folded his arms. "Well, you had better keep your door locked Halloween night. And for that matter, you'd better keep it locked every night."

Meredith folded her arms as well. Then she shook her head listlessly. "I never get flowers anymore. You'd think Bill might have sent me some. But no. Only Zorro sends flowers. How can I have a long-distance relationship with a man like that?"

Clarissa handed Meredith the vase. "Here, on behalf of the Bills of the world, let me give you these flowers. The friendship of one sincere man is better than all the attention in the world from a Zorro."

Meredith held the flowers to her face and inhaled the fragrance of the roses. "Yes, well, I suppose you have a point." She smiled and said, "Still, flowers are lovely. I have half a mind to go after Tristan myself." She turned to Slade. "Do you think he's my type?"

"No." Slade started herding Bella and Elaina across the lobby and toward the elevator.

Meredith followed after him slowly. "I don't see why not. Some men appreciate the maturity and grace of an older woman." She took another whiff of the flowers as she walked. "Besides, you work me like a Cinderella too."

"That's not true. I've barely seen you this whole trip," Slade said.

"That's because you've had Clarissa to abuse." She looked over at Clarissa. "You know, dear, if you'd like to go do something tonight, I'll watch Elaina for you."

Clarissa smiled at her. "Thank you, Meredith. I'd like that."

Slade didn't like it but couldn't say why. Perhaps it was because he had visions of Clarissa taking a solitary, relaxed walk around the resort and Tristan suddenly intercepting her. Tristan and his charm . . . and his ulterior motives. It didn't matter that Clarissa had been warned about him. That was the thing about Tristan. Women knew he was a womanizer and still succumbed to him anyway.

It would be better if they all stayed in and watched something on pay per view. Or played charades. Or Chutes and Ladders. He would have suggested it, but by this time Clarissa and Meredith were busily engaged in a conversation about masquerade costumes. At least he thought they were talking about masquerade costumes. When he heard two women using terms like "period clothing" he just didn't want to ask.

13

Clarissa decided on a late-night swim as her free-time activity. Swimming was healthy, free, and best done under the cover of darkness anyway. And it would give her time to think things over. She was sure that if she only racked her brain long enough, she could find some way out of this mess with Sylvia. Besides, she'd been in Hawaii for five days and hadn't ever actually gone swimming. Every time she'd gone near the water during this trip, she'd been watching the girls.

At eight o' clock she dropped Elaina off at Meredith's room and then went back to her own room to change.

Clarissa was standing in the bedroom, her suit only halfway on, when she heard a knock at the door. She jumped, feeling awkward, and tried to shake the fear that whoever it was might have x-ray vision. "Who is it?"

"It's me, Slade."

Slipping the last strap over her shoulders she called, "Just a minute." Then she walked into the living room, grabbing her bathrobe as she went. She put it on, haphazardly tying the sash, then stepped to the door. She paused for a moment to smooth down her hair and then opened it. "Come in."

He walked past her with only a glance, his arms folded across his chest. "This is just the sort of thing I came to talk to you about."

"What?"

He held out one hand to her in an accusatory manner. "This."

"What?" she said again.

"Haven't you listened to anything I've told you over the last few days? You just invited a man into your hotel room, and you're wearing only a robe."

Her mouth fell open momentarily. "But it was only you."

"Thanks. You don't know what these little commentaries of yours do for my ego."

She twisted one of the robe ties around her finger and tried to defend herself. "It's not as though you haven't seen me in this robe before. I wore it half of Friday afternoon—nobody seemed to think it was particularly seductive then."

His eyes took her in, from the polish on her toenails to the way her hair refused to be completely smoothed down. "The difference is that when a man sees a woman in a robe sitting by a swimming pool, he thinks she's covering up. When a man walks into a woman's hotel room and she's wearing a robe, he thinks about what she's wearing underneath, which is probably some skimpy little negligee thing. It's almost an invitation."

"But you're wrong again. I'm wearing exactly the same thing I was on Friday." She undid the tie and held open the sides of her robe. "See, no negligee. I was on my way swim—"

Before she even finished her sentence he was standing in front of her. "Would you stop that!" He took hold of the sides of her robe and pulled them together. "I can't believe you just did that. You really don't listen to anything I say, do you?"

"But it's my swimming suit."

"That's exactly my point. You don't flash a man your swimming suit while you're alone in a hotel room." He pulled the robe even tighter closed until nothing below the top of her neck was visible. "You need to button this thing up."

"It doesn't have buttons."

"Then use safety pins."

She laughed. She hadn't meant to, and she tried to stop herself, but was unsuccessful.

He still held the front of her robe closed. "You can find this all very funny now, but I'm warning you, you can't afford to be so lax. Especially not here. If I were a different sort of man . . . in fact, if I were the man I was five months ago . . . " He suddenly let go of her robe. "Well, never mind about that. You just need to be more careful."

She nodded, and although she tried to look serious, she knew she didn't reach the desired effect. "May I go swimming now?"

"No. Not by yourself." And then after giving her another harsh stare, "And not in that suit."

"What's wrong with my swimming suit?"

"You obviously haven't noticed all the attention it's gotten you."

"The only attention I got was when I jumped into the pool wearing my robe to save your daughter, who could already swim."

She walked to where her sandals lay on the floor and slipped them on.

His gaze followed her. "I came over to suggest we all stay in and watch something on television."

"Sorry, I want to get at least one swim in while I'm here."

"Cards? Monopoly?"

She took her key card from the dresser and slipped it into her bag. "I'm going now."

"All right, all right, you can go swimming." He walked to the door and put his hand on the knob. "But I'm going with you. Just give me a minute to tell Meredith I need her to watch Bella for the rest of the evening."

He opened the door and walked out while she picked up a towel and checked to make sure it was big enough to use at the pool.

She had just finished gathering everything she thought she might need for an evening swim when Slade knocked on her door and called, "We can go now."

Clarissa walked out of her room and was surprised to see him still dressed in his clothes. "Aren't you going to swim?" she asked.

"No, I'm going to sit by the pool, read, and chase off any scoundrels when necessary."

She rolled her eyes, then walked down the hallway. "Suit yourself. Literally in this case."

He didn't say anything else and so neither did she until they stood in the elevator. It was then she looked over and noticed the book that he carried.

"You're going to read the Book of Mormon?"

"It's the perfect book for a trip to the pool with you. It's fortification for me and big enough to make a useful weapon in case I have to throw something at Tristan."

"Fortification?"

His gaze took her in for a moment, and then he shook his head and looked back at the elevator doors. "Bathsheba probably didn't have such nice legs."

Clarissa looked down at her legs, then back at him skeptically. "Oh, right, and I thought Tristan was one for handing out lines. If you're going to use flattery, you could at least pick a believable feature."

"Mrs. Hancock, not only is your husband a fool, but apparently he's also very negligent in the compliments department. If you were my wife, there would be no doubt in your mind as to the appeal of your legs." He looked quickly away from her again. "But you're not my wife, so I'll be reading the Book of Mormon while you swim."

She blushed and once again had the urge to blurt out that she wasn't married. But she couldn't do it. At this time, at this moment, it would be as good as just blatantly telling him she wanted a relationship with him. That was such a big step, such a huge risk to take, all because he'd made an offhand comment about her legs.

He probably thought Nataly had nice legs, too. But when Nataly had told Slade she was interested in him, he'd immediately done everything possible to avoid even being in her proximity.

What would he do if he thought his nanny was after him, too?

Clarissa shifted her weight around uncomfortably in the elevator and clutched her beach bag closer to her. How much rejection did she need in life? Wasn't Alex enough? Did she really need to go out and look for extra opportunities for men to shred her ego?

Slade was just one of those men who spoke his mind. Even Meredith said so. It didn't mean he was flirting, let alone actually interested in her.

They got off the elevator and walked silently to the pool. No one else was there, and Slade pulled a deck chair over next to one of the decorative lightposts that lighted the area. It must not have thrown off enough light, however, because he held the book up close to his face.

Clarissa took off her robe, threw it onto a chair, then walked to the deep end of the pool. Without hesitating, she dove in. The water was colder than she had expected, but it felt good as it slid over her skin. It felt cleansing, as if she could wash away all her thoughts. She swam a dozen laps, and when she tired of that, she floated on her back, gazing up at the stars.

Nothing occurred to her about her predicament with Sylvia. In fact, it was hard to think of Sylvia at all when she knew Slade sat just a little way away watching her. At least he *said* he'd be watching her. She never actually saw him look at anything except his book. And she checked often enough.

She peered over at him again. His elbows rested on his knees, and his dark eyes were completely engrossed in the scriptures.

Handsome *and* spiritual.

Perhaps her husband's freak manhole accident could happen very soon.

Finally she swam over to where Slade sat and hung onto the side of the pool while she looked up at him. After a moment he glanced down at her.

"What part are you reading?" she asked.

"Jacob," he said. "I'm on my second time around. I didn't catch it all the first time through."

"I don't think you ever do. I can't tell you how many times I've read it, and I'm always finding something new."

"You're probably right," he said, without looking at her.

She watched him silently for another moment.

"Tell me your conversion story."

He smiled, but still didn't look up. "It's nothing dramatic."

"Well, you eat your words somewhere in it. That's pretty dramatic."

"And probably the only time you figure you'll hear me admit I was wrong. Is that it?"

"Exactly," she said.

He put the book down in his lap, leaned forward, and looked down at her. "Okay, this is my conversion story. I went home to my parents' house all prepared with a bunch of arguments about how they'd been brainwashed into joining a cult, and I found the most amazing thing had happened to them. They weren't fighting anymore." He held up one hand to emphasize the point. "All the time I was growing up, they used to fight. Not about anything major, mind you, just about stupid little things like how long you were supposed to cook the chicken or whose turn it was to walk the dog. They'd pick at each other endlessly.

"Over the years they tried different techniques to improve their marriage, but they always fizzled out. The contention got so bad that my sister and I could hardly stand to be around them.

"So I went home prepared to argue in the best Jacobson fashion, but the amazing thing was, they were different people. Both of them. They weren't fighting at all. I asked them what had happened, and they told me the gospel had happened, and then they handed me a Book of Mormon. I didn't know what it was, but I read it anyway, because I was trying to get to the part where it told people how to solve their marital problems.

"I was in about 3 Nephi by the time it hit me. There were no passages on how to fix marriages. The book was all about letting

Christ change your heart. Once that happens a lot of problems are bound to fix themselves."

He smiled in a reminiscing sort of way. "By the time I realized that, it was too late to go back to my old life. I'd been changed myself." He looked down at her, but the smile was still on his lips. "There. Did I eat my words well enough for you?"

She nodded.

"You're lucky to have always had the gospel," he said. "Sometimes I think about how different my life would have been if I'd been raised in the Church. I'd probably have married some nice LDS girl, and we'd still be married."

Clarissa felt a weight pressing against her chest. Now she was not only going to look like a liar if Slade found out the truth—she was also going to make her entire religion look bad. She'd had the gospel, and so had Alex, and they'd still gotten divorced.

It would have been easier if Alex had shown up with some bimbo at a salad bar, and then she at least would have had an easy and understandable excuse for explaining to people why they'd broken up. But how did she explain to Slade what her marriage to Alex had been like?

Alex had lived a charmed life, a perfect life. All through school he'd been popular, sought after, and revered. He'd played football in college and had often been recognized around campus. When he and Clarissa had married during their last year of college, things were good for a while. It was when he took his first job that everything changed.

Alex suddenly became just a junior accountant in a big firm that didn't care how popular he'd been in high school or whether he could catch a football. He wasn't surrounded by adoring women. He had only Clarissa, and she'd grown less glamorous every day with a new pregnancy.

Clarissa could see the transformation in him happen, could almost see his dissatisfaction becoming tangible. He complained about everything Clarissa did. She was supposed to be always beautiful, organized, and cheerful. The house was supposed to be

196

spotlessly clean, dinner always ready, and Elaina completely under control.

That way, at least part of Alex's perfect life could continue. But no matter how hard she tried, Clarissa hadn't been able to meet his expectations.

She stayed with Alex much longer than she wanted to, trying to work things out, and hoping Alex would someday find a way to be happy. She stayed and felt her joy for life corroding on a daily basis, but she stayed nonetheless. On the day they married, she'd made a commitment to Alex, and she felt bound by it. Perhaps she would still be with him if it weren't for Elaina.

As Elaina grew older, Alex turned his unrealistic expectations on her as well. And although Clarissa had been willing to put up with Alex, she was not about to let him drain the joy from her daughter's life. She gave him an ultimatum: he needed to change, or both she and Elaina would leave. He chose the latter. And he chose it without much struggle or regret. That part still stung.

Clarissa looked up at Slade and tried to tell him the truth without telling him the truth. "The gospel doesn't ensure happiness," she said. "It just gives people the chance."

"I know," he shrugged casually. "I guess there are always exceptions to the rule."

Now I've become an exception, Clarissa thought.

"Are you happy?" he asked her.

She paused for a moment, perhaps too long. "Yes, for the most part."

"Good. Then your husband is very lucky. Even if he is a fool."

She hadn't realized Slade had been asking about her marital happiness, but she didn't correct him. She just stared off at all the empty chairs surrounding the pool.

Slade said, "I think you're very good with Bella."

"Thank you."

"Meredith probably told you I start work on a miniseries in a few weeks. I'll need someone to care for Bella then. Would you be interested?"

Clarissa ran her hand along the tile on the edge of the pool and considered how to respond. She couldn't accept the offer without first telling him the truth, without telling him Sylvia had a warped version of the truth she was threatening to print.

He said, "You're hesitating. That's not a good sign."

She glanced up at his face, found his gaze heavy, and looked back at the tile. "I'm not sure that I'm, I mean . . ." She didn't know how to come out and say it. "I've made a lot of mistakes on this trip."

"Listen, I'm sorry about the way I yelled at you that first night. I really am. I've been meaning to tell you that. I know it wasn't your fault that Bella ran away."

"I wasn't talking about the first night. I've made mistakes since then—"

He didn't let her finish. "You're the best nanny Bella's had. You're doing great."

His praise made it that much harder. "I'm glad you think so. I mean, I want you to know that I really do care about Bella."

"And Bella likes you. That's what matters. Say yes, and I'll have Meredith make up a new contract."

"That's not all that matters. You said so yourself. Remember back when you told me how I didn't understand Hollywood?"

He left his chair and sat on the pool deck next to her. His response came quickly, overlapping her words, not really listening to what she'd just said, and yet there was a softness in his voice and an urgency in the way he spoke. "I don't want to let you go after this trip. That matters, too."

She pulled herself closer to the pool's edge and looked up into his eyes. His gaze was warm and intense, and she completely forgot about her explanation.

Perhaps she'd been wrong to remain silent in the elevator.

Perhaps none of Sylvia's threats to expose her mattered because perhaps Slade wouldn't care when he found out she was single. Perhaps he'd even be glad.

"All right," she said.

He smiled, and she could see him relax a bit. "If my work schedule picks up, I'll need you a lot; if not, then maybe just a few times a week. Maybe a couple of evenings here and there, if I have a date or something."

"Oh." The inside of her mouth suddenly felt like dust. She'd been right to remain silent, she'd been right the first time when she told herself not to read anything into his compliments. She hoped her voice sounded normal as she spoke. "Of course. You probably have a girlfriend, don't you?"

"No, but I think I need to get one." He looked out across the pool and sighed. "I mean, I can always hope."

"Oh, right," she forced herself to smile, even though it felt like her lips couldn't maintain the position. "I'm sure it's terribly hard for you to find interested women."

"It isn't finding women that is the problem. It's finding the right kind of women."

"Maybe you're not looking in the right place."

"Probably not." He looked down at her with his eyebrows slightly wrinkled together. "Where did you say you came from?"

"Woodland Hills."

"Well, there you have it. I've never looked in Woodland Hills." He took his gaze from her and looked at something beyond her in the darkness. "It's a pity, too."

Her racing pulse and pounding heartbeat were instantly back. *Say something more*, she thought. *Say something—anything that will give me a reason to tell you I'm single.*

"Well," he said, "are you finished with your swim?"

"I guess so." She pulled herself out of the pool, wiped as much water off as she could with the towel, then slipped into her robe. But even so, the night air was uncommonly cold against her wet skin, and as they walked back to the hotel, she began shivering.

✦ ✦ ✦

Clarissa held Elaina's sleeping figure against her shoulder and walked into her hotel room. When she flipped on the lights she noticed a pale green envelope lying on the floor just inside the entryway, as though it had been slipped under the door. After she tucked Elaina into her bed, she went back to retrieve it.

The envelope bore no writing, and the piece of pale green stationery folded inside was also empty.

Strange.

She turned it over in her hands a couple of times and then looked back on the floor to see if she'd missed something. Nope. The floor was empty, too.

She was about to toss it on the desk with the hotel stationery when the phone rang. She picked up the phone by the couch and heard Sylvia's voice on the other end of the line.

"I noticed your lights come on and knew you had come home."

Clarissa's gaze flew to her open windows, and she suddenly wished she had closed all the drapes before going for a swim. Out there, somewhere, Sylvia sat watching her hotel room.

"What do you want?" Clarissa said the words angrily, half tempted to hang up. Not only was the woman blackmailing her, now she'd turned into a stalker.

"I'm just telling you about my system, dear, now that you've had a chance to think about some stories."

"I don't have any stories for you."

"By your door, you'll find a green envelope and paper on the floor. Write what you have to tell me on it. I'll call you back in a day or two and tell you where to leave it for me."

A click followed, and Clarissa knew Sylvia had hung up. She slammed her own receiver back down on the cradle and stormed to the windows. After yanking the curtains closed, she turned, threw the envelope on the floor, and sank into the couch.

She rubbed one hand over her eyes, then stared at the envelope.

The woman was absolutely insane.

Pushing things underneath her door? Watching her hotel room? Telling her where to leave her information as though it was all some sort of cloak-and-dagger affair? Sylvia didn't think she was a reporter; she thought she was an underworld operative. Next she'd be asking Clarissa to murmur passwords to strangers on park benches: *The sly dog howls at the full moon. . . . I have a delivery for you, comrade.*

She wasn't going to do this. She'd tell Slade everything first chance tomorrow. So just let Sylvia call back. Clarissa would tell her where she could put her envelope.

But instead of throwing it away, as she meant to do, Clarissa picked up the envelope and put it in her purse.

14

Slade woke to the shrill ringing of the phone beside his bed. He reached for it, still half asleep, and knocked it off the nightstand. He felt around the floor for a moment until he'd retrieved it and said a sleepy "Hello?" into the receiver.

"Hi, Slade," a lush voice said back. "Did I wake you?"

"No, it's only—" He glanced at the digital clock on the nightstand. "12:15. Why would I be asleep, Nataly?"

"Don't be mad at me. A.J. finally read your script, and I wanted to talk to you about it."

Slade pulled himself up on one elbow and tried to shake off the remaining sleep that muddled his mind. "Okay, shoot."

She gave a throaty laugh. "Wouldn't it be wonderful to hear A.J. say those words?"

It took Slade a moment to understand what she meant. "Are you telling me he's interested?"

"I'm not telling you anything right now. I want you to meet me out on the restaurant terrace, so we can talk about it."

He glanced over at Bella's small form in the other bed. "Can't this wait until morning?"

"No. Definitely not. I need to talk to you before A.J. talks to you."

So that was it. The news about his script wasn't good, or at least not entirely good, or Nataly wouldn't be scheduling meetings with him in the middle of the night.

He rubbed one hand across his forehead and glanced back over at Bella. He nearly said, "I can't leave my daughter. Why don't you come up here?" But it was better to meet with Nataly out in public—someplace where she'd be more inclined to show up in clothing instead of seashells.

"Okay," he said. "Give me ten minutes to get there."

He hung up the phone, slipped from bed, and groped around his dresser in the dark until he found a pair of jeans. Then he felt around for something that resembled a shirt and put it on.

He glanced back at Bella one more time before he left. He didn't like the idea of leaving her alone, especially since she occasionally woke in the night, but he didn't see any alternative. Clarissa and Meredith would certainly be asleep by this time.

Slade quietly closed the door behind him and walked to the elevator. He would just make sure his meeting with Nataly was short and hope he didn't come back to his room to find Bella wailing in her bed.

When Slade walked onto the terrace he immediately spotted Nataly. The restaurant was empty, except for her. She was sitting at a table, leaning back with her feet up on a neighboring chair, sipping a drink. She wore a tank top and jeans and had a sweatshirt wrapped loosely around her shoulders, but somehow still managed to look elegant in the moonlight.

As Slade approached, Nataly moved her legs to the floor and pointed to a glass on the table. With a patronizing smirk she said, "I didn't know what you wanted to drink, so I ordered you a lemonade. You can still have that, can't you?"

"Yes." He sat down but didn't touch his drink. "So what news do you have about my script?"

She sighed and ran her finger around the outside of her glass. "A.J. read it this afternoon. He said there wasn't enough action."

"Action? It's a story about relationships."

"And parts of it were unrealistic."

"It's science fiction. It's supposed to be unrealistic."

Nataly held up one hand to silence him. "Not the time machine, the people. You have a scene at a frat party where nobody swears. Have you ever actually been to a frat party?"

Slade ran one hand quickly across his hair. "All right, that may have been taking artistic liberties, but do moviegoers really need to hear more cursing and bathroom humor?"

Nataly leaned toward him and laid one of her hands softly on his arm. "I understand why you wrote it that way."

"You do?"

"Sure. A lot of actors reach a point in their careers where they want to do a movie they can take their children to. Then they start endorsing kids' products and showing up on *Sesame Street.* There's nothing wrong with that." Nataly gently ran her hand back and forth across Slade's arm. "I think it's sweet."

"But A.J. doesn't see it that way."

"A.J. only thinks about marketing and dollars," she said slowly, "and me." Her manicured hand moved down his arm until it rested on the back of his hand. "I could change his mind."

"How could you do that?"

"I could tell him I read it and loved it. I cried, in fact. I could tell him I think it will appeal to women. He trusts my judgment where women are concerned."

Slade looked down at her hand, which still rested on his. "Yes, well, heaven knows *he's* not the best judge of women."

She took her hand off his and reached for her drink. "Don't be mean, Slade, I'm trying to help you."

"You're trying to make a deal with me."

She brought her drink to her mouth, caressing the rim of the glass with her lips. "Deals are what this industry is all about. You know that."

Deals. And compromises. Was there someway to take Nataly's help without betraying the cause he'd written the story for? He knew the answer to that question, and yet he hesitated for a moment anyway. She probably *could* convince A.J. to take the script. It was the best shot he'd had so far of turning his goal into a reality, and at this moment he could almost envision the people lined up in front of the theaters. Once his movie was made, it would sell, he was confident of that. And after that, producers would be more willing to try similar projects.

He glanced over at Nataly. She had pushed her drink aside and was leaning forward, her elbows resting on the table, her chin supported by her fists. "You know," she said, "I'm not so sure you're the best judge of women, either. I've never met anyone with a Ph.D. in botany, but I can tell you, they aren't your type. I mean, honestly Slade, could you possibly have found a more boring person?" She put her hand back over Slade's, gently teasing his fingertips with hers. "I can't believe you would rather spend time with some stuffy little scientist than with me."

This time he took her hand and placed it back on the table. "I think I'd better go now."

"Slade," she said, "I won't give you my help unless you ask for it. Nicely."

Slade paused only for a moment before he stood up. He looked into her face, and as he did her mouth curled back into a smile. She thought she'd won.

He shook his head. "Go back to A.J., Nataly. If he cares for you half as much as you say, you need to stop doing things to risk losing him." Then he turned and walked through the maze of empty tables across the terrace. But instead of going back into the hotel, he turned toward the beach.

At this late hour, the beach fronting the hotel was deserted. Illuminated by the moon, long lines of waves rolled toward the shore, each mounding up until it broke, flooding the white sand with its foam. Slade didn't notice the beauty though. He noticed the darkness.

With every step he took, he considered his manuscript. What had A.J. said about it? Not enough action and unrealistic. The words stung, but even worse was the thought that A.J. might be right. After all, his agent had given his script to half a dozen producers. If it was a good script, then certainly someone would have taken an interest.

When it was rejected before, Slade had told himself it was

because it hadn't been given the proper attention. That it had most likely been passed off to overworked, underpaid, indifferent readers who had barely done more than glance at it before rejecting it.

But this time he'd put the story into the hands of the producer himself.

So perhaps it just wasn't any good.

Perhaps it was a blessing it had been rejected. Perhaps if it were made, it would turn out to be one of those cinematic bombs that would be derided by movie critics all year and end up crippling his acting career.

So maybe this was a blessing.

Only it didn't feel like a blessing. It felt like a kick in the stomach.

He'd put a good distance between the hotel and himself but didn't slow his pace. His muscles were still charged with anger. He was angry at A.J. for not liking his script. And angry with all the other producers for not liking his script. And angry at himself for not being a good enough writer to find a way to write around their objections.

Did one really need car chases and shoot-outs to make a successful movie? Would the audience refuse to come if there wasn't a set number of love scenes and explicit dialogue?

Was that realistic?

Realistic, realistic. He said the word in his mind over and over again with each step. Didn't he want something more uplifting than reality? Wasn't the whole point of his writing to encourage a better reality?

So how could he ever write around that?

Maybe he was doomed as a writer. Maybe the time for his kind of writing was over, and now all the people who went to movies just wanted to watch naked women and exploding cars.

He wasn't sure how long he walked and didn't even remember retracing his steps back to the hotel. But now he was climbing into the elevator and pushing the four button.

He still wasn't tired and doubted he'd be able to sleep. Perhaps he could turn on the TV and catch a late-night movie. Instead of counting sheep he could count exploding cars.

When the elevator door reopened, he trudged down the hallway. As he neared his room he suddenly remembered that Bella was by herself, and he felt a sense of panic. He should have hurried back to her. Still, he didn't hear any wailing emanating from the room, so she must not have wakened.

He slipped his card through the lock and opened the door. He walked into the room slowly, silently kicking his shoes off while he let his eyes adjust to the dark. Then as he pulled off his shirt, he walked into the bedroom to check on Bella. The covers on her bed were rumpled and wadded as they always were, but when he looked among the blanket and the stuffed animals, he couldn't find her. The bed was empty.

He looked on the floor first, to see if she'd rolled off. No Bella. He went back into the living room, pulling his shirt back over his head as he walked.

Bella had awakened, seen he wasn't there, and had gone out to find him. Even now she was wandering around the hotel in her nightgown, sobbing uncontrollably.

He'd go find her.

No, he'd call security first, then go find her.

It was during this moment of indecision between the door and the telephone that he noticed in the darkness the shape in the recliner by the door.

He first saw Clarissa, and then noticed Bella in her lap, and both were fast asleep.

How they had both gotten there was a question that only briefly occupied his mind. Relief was his first reaction, and then staring at them quickly took precedence. Bella's delicate head and wild curls lay nestled on Clarissa's chest, and Clarissa's head rested softly against the back of the chair. In the dim light he studied Clarissa's every feature—her dark lashes, her half-parted lips, her hair cascading everywhere.

It didn't matter how many times he told himself otherwise, he wanted Clarissa, and not just someone like her.

He sat down on the couch, still staring at her, and tried to digest this information. His first thought was that he would simply take what he wanted. Divorces happened, didn't they? And it would just be too bad for Clarissa's husband that one was in store for him. The guy seemed like a jerk, anyway. He deserved it.

And then, pained that he'd even thought about it, Slade rejected the idea. How could he think of tearing apart a family simply because he'd fallen in love with someone he shouldn't have? That would be his gift to the woman he loved? He'd destroy her marriage and the home life of her daughter? Of course he couldn't do it.

Still he stared at Clarissa. It would be hard. It would be horribly hard, but he'd never let her know how he felt. He'd never do anything to jeopardize their professional relationship. He would stay as far away from her as propriety and good judgment required.

After convincing himself of these things, he got up from the couch and went to the recliner to retrieve Bella. He would put her back to bed and then awaken Clarissa. He leaned forward, but before reaching for his daughter, he paused, contemplating Clarissa. *I'm so close to her*, he thought. *I'm close enough to her that I could easily lean over a little more and let my lips brush across her cheek. She'd never know. No one would ever know—except for the devil, that is, and he'd immediately make reservations in hell under my name.*

Stepping back, Slade called softly, "Clarissa."

She didn't move.

He said her name again, this time more loudly. When she still didn't respond, he reached out and touched her lightly on the shoulder.

Her eyes blinked open, and she stared blankly at him for a moment. "What are you doing in here?"

"This is my room," he told her.

She looked around in confusion, and then seemed to remember.

"Let me have Bella," Slade said, reaching for his daughter, "and I'll go put her back in bed."

Still seated, Clarissa helped lift the sleeping girl into his arms. He took her into the other room, laid her on the bed, and pulled the blankets around her.

When Slade returned to the living room, he walked to one of the lamps and switched it on. Clarissa was standing by the door, looking beautifully disheveled and holding her robe closely about her.

"Bella woke up and you weren't here, so she came and pounded on my door. I figured if I kept her in my room you'd worry, and since I had your key . . . I was only going to sit with her until she went back to sleep. I guess I fell asleep instead."

"I guess so."

She pulled the tie to her robe tight and looked up at him questioningly. "Is something wrong?"

"No, nothing's wrong." Except for everything.

"Where did you go off to at midnight?"

He nearly sat down on the couch, then decided against it. Sitting down would encourage more conversation. He remained standing and thrust his hands in his pockets instead. "It was another one of Nataly's stupid ploys. Apparently making my life difficult during the day is no longer enough."

"I'm sorry, Slade. I hope it was nothing too terrible."

"Nothing I couldn't handle."

She looked at him, her head tilted in a thoughtful way. "You know, for all the lectures you've given me about Tristan, you'd think you'd be the last one to jaunt off for a midnight rendezvous with a woman of questionable moral character."

"Oh, there's no question about Nataly's moral character," he said. "That's already been established."

"The point is," she continued, "you need to be careful, too. Temptation can pop up even when you think you're impervious."

"Oh, really?"

"I'm serious."

"So am I."

He must have said the words too harshly, because the expression on her face changed. She shook her head slightly and said, "You're impossible."

"So you've told me."

"Yes, well, I was right then, too."

Go ahead and be mad at me, he thought. *I've just saved you from a broken marriage and myself from hell.* But as he watched her leave the room, he still wasn't sure he had made the best choice.

✢ ✢ ✢

On Tuesday morning Slade brought Bella over to Clarissa's room. His face looked pale, and the lines on his face too sharp. Probably from lack of sleep. "I'll only be an hour or so," he told her at the door. "I need to call my agent, go over some things with Meredith . . ."

He seemed to be in a hurry, and so she didn't try to talk to him.

After he left, she took the girls to breakfast at the hotel restaurant. She was getting tired of being in her room and wanted to be someplace different, even if it meant having to enforce restaurant etiquette on two preschoolers.

Thankfully, the service was fast. The girls had eaten half a waffle each before they grew restless. Clarissa hurried to finish her own, wiped off two pairs of sticky hands, left a tip, and then led the girls out of the restaurant.

"Can we go swimming?" Bella asked.

"I don't think we have enough time before your dad comes for you," Clarissa said.

Elaina took her mother's hand, swinging it back and forth,

but Bella hung back, shuffling her feet as she walked. "Can we play hide-and-seek then?"

"Sure. We can play hide-and-seek in our room."

Bella hurried her pace at this, skipping across the lobby past Clarissa. She stopped in front of the elevator and pushed the button. "I get to hide first."

"Okay."

"You'll never find me."

Clarissa smiled down at her. "We'll see."

The elevator door opened and Meredith stepped out, looking crisp and professional in a business suit and heels. "Oh, hello," she said with surprise.

Clarissa reached over to stop Bella from going into the elevator, and the door slid closed.

She turned to Meredith. "Is Slade done with his business already?" Perhaps she should just take Bella to his room instead of starting new games.

"Just his business with me," Meredith said. Then she leaned toward Clarissa and lowered her voice. "And I don't know when I've seen him in such a bad mood. Trust me, steer clear of him today."

Okay. So maybe this wasn't a good time to tell him about Sylvia.

"I don't think he got a lot of sleep last night," Clarissa said.

Meredith shook her head. "He just worries too much. Honestly, the man needs to work on his vacationing skills."

Clarissa repushed the elevator button. "I'll let *you* suggest that to him."

It was then she noticed that Bella was gone.

Clarissa glanced around the lobby, looking for some sign of her, but saw nothing. "Did you see where Bella went?" she asked.

Meredith shook her head and joined Clarissa in casting glances in every direction.

"Bella?" Clarissa tried to quell the panic that gripped her. Not this. Not again. Not when Slade was already in a bad mood.

"Bella, come out here right now. We're not playing hide-and-seek yet."

"Hide-and-seek?" Meredith asked. She shook her head sadly. "Oh, no. You'll never find her."

Clarissa looked down at Elaina. "Did you see which way Bella went?"

Elaina nodded silently and pointed down the hallway where the conference rooms were. Clarissa gave Elaina's hand to Meredith, and with a sickening feeling that she was reliving her first night at the resort, ran toward the conference rooms. Her feet felt heavy, and her purse thunked wildly against her side as she went.

The hallway was empty. She peered into a couple of open rooms, saw nothing, and then ran to the end of the hallway and pushed open the door to the stairwell. She looked both up and down. Bella wouldn't have gone up there, would she? She listened to hear the echo of little feet against the steps. Nothing.

She turned and hurried back to the conference rooms, this time opening the doors that were closed. The first was filled with businessmen, a few of whom turned to stare at her as she stood in the doorway.

Okay, Bella probably wasn't in that one.

The second was filled with rows of empty chairs, but she could see under them all. No four-year-old. She called out, "Bella!" and checked behind the podium anyway. Where was that moppy little dog when she needed him?

When she came out of the room, she saw Meredith walking down the hallway with Elaina in her arms. "I'll check up the stairwell."

"Thanks."

"We'll find her."

Clarissa didn't answer. An assortment of frightening scenarios had entered her mind. What if Bella had been abducted? What if Elaina had been wrong about where Bella went? After all, Clarissa was taking the word of a three-year-old to determine her search area, and what did Elaina know about directions? She couldn't even find her way home from the mailbox yet.

Clarissa tried to push these thought away. No one had taken Bella. She was here, somewhere, playing hide-and-seek and proving the point that no one could find her.

Clarissa darted into the third room, and found it full of tables and chairs. A few silk plants lined the wall. She hadn't noticed those the first time she glanced in the room. Now she checked behind each of them, feeling her heart pound more intensely with each moment that passed.

She pushed open the door to the fourth room. It looked as though it was set up for some sort of luncheon. Round tables stood around the room, surrounded by chairs on all sides. Two long buffet tables sat side to side in the back, with bird-of-paradise centerpieces on them. As she circled around the tables in the middle of the room Clarissa called out, "Bella, I need you to come out now."

She got no answer.

She felt tears stinging the back of her eyes.

On her trip around the third table, she stopped and looked at the long tables more closely. They were draped with long table-cloths, just like Bella's dining room table back home.

Clarissa walked to one, saying a silent prayer as she went, and lifted one edge of the tablecloth. In the far corner, Bella sat huddled against the wall. She let out a shriek of laughter when she saw her nanny but didn't move.

Neither did Clarissa. She just stood holding up the cloth and wrestling with the desire to pull Bella out by her feet and spank her, and the desire to cry.

"Come here, right now, Bella!"

It sounded harsh, even in Clarissa's ears, and the smile immediately dropped from Bella's face. She stared up at Clarissa, wide-eyed, and still didn't move.

Clarissa looked down at Bella for another moment, and suddenly the relief outweighed the anger.

"Listen, Bella," she said more softly, but knew it wouldn't have any effect. She sighed, got down on her hands and knees, and crawled underneath the table, dragging her purse clumsily across the floor as she went. Once she was close to Bella, she lay down on her stomach and looked over at the little girl. "Listen," she said again, this time so softly it was no more than a whisper. "I was very worried about you. I was afraid you might get hurt."

Bella gulped and blinked up at Clarissa. "Just like when you jumped into the pool?"

"Just like at the pool."

And then without thinking about it, Clarissa gathered Bella into her arms and held her close. Bella hugged her back, burying her head into Clarissa's shoulder.

They remained like this for several moments, Clarissa afraid to let the moment end, not wanting it to end, enjoying this moment of love she felt.

Then she heard the conference room door open and quick footsteps crossing the floor.

Meredith.

Clarissa reached over to the tablecloth, lifting it in order to call out to her, but then dropped the tablecloth back down again just as quickly.

It wasn't Meredith. It was Brandy, looking tentatively around the room, but thankfully, not under the tables. Clarissa had no idea why Brandy had come into the room but could tell she was headed to the back wall, back toward Clarissa and Bella.

Exactly how do you explain to a near-stranger why you are hiding under a buffet table in an empty room?

Wasn't it bad enough that the woman had already seen her jump into a pool wearing a robe?

Clarissa turned to Bella and held one finger against her lips. "Shhh," she whispered. "We're playing spies now."

A smile lit up Bella's face, and she slipped one of her hands into Clarissa's, clearly pleased to be a coconspirator in this new game.

Please don't come near this table, Clarissa thought. *Please be just passing by and on your way out.*

Brandy's heels stopped at the far end of the table.

Even worse. Every moment this was getting harder to explain. *Well, you see, Brandy, I was giving Bella an educational lesson on how tables work. And we study in silence, otherwise we would have of course said something to you when you walked in . . .*

The corner of the tablecloth next to Brandy's heels was momentarily lifted. Next—although Clarissa wasn't sure why—Brandy would look under the table and discover them.

Clarissa hoped Brandy wasn't the type who screamed loudly when startled.

Holding her breath, Clarissa looked toward Brandy, with what she hoped was a casual expression, and willed a plausible explanation of her situation to come to her lips. But only Brandy's hand came under the table. She thrust it under the cloth and pressed a pale green envelope onto the underside of the table. It stuck there. The next moment the tablecloth dropped back down, and the sound of Brandy's heels clicked away from the table and back across the room.

Clarissa stared at the envelope, too surprised to even be relieved that they hadn't been discovered. When she heard the conference room door close, she crawled to the envelope and peeled it off the table.

So Brandy was one of Sylvia's sources.

As she ripped the envelope open, Clarissa wondered what sort of horrible story Sylvia had on Brandy that would make her turn over information about her own cast.

She pulled out a pale green piece of stationery and unfolded it.

"Is it a clue?" Bella whispered.

"I think so," Clarissa said. "Let me read it, and then I'll tell you."

Written in a hurried scrawl were the words:

Parker Wentworth came to the set with such a big hangover on

Monday that had he been carrying a real gun, he would have shot half the cast. Crew members are beginning to grumble about his unprofessionalism on the set.

Nataly Granger is on another of her odd diets. For the third day in a row she's eaten only lettuce and raw fish for lunch.

Tristan McKellips and Brandy Reynolds spent a good portion of the evening together on Saturday at a party, fueling talk of an offscreen romance between the two.

Nice of her, Clarissa thought, *to include herself in all this muckraking.* She wondered if what Brandy had written was true, or just wishful thinking on her part.

The last entry she read more carefully. *Tristan's trademark carefree attitude may soon be changing. Rumor has it that Tristan's father has fallen off the wagon and is drinking heavily again. Tristan may ask for a leave from the show to help get his father treatment for alcoholism.*

Clarissa took a sharp inward breath.

Apparently Tristan shouldn't have spent so much time with Brandy on Saturday. She was not the woman to discuss your life with.

Clarissa held the paper in her hand and reread the last entry. Was it true? She supposed it didn't matter, not to Sylvia, not to Brandy, not to all the millions of people who would read it. It mattered only to Tristan and his family, to those who would be further wounded by such a report.

I hope for your sake, she told Tristan silently, *that the talk of a romance with Brandy is just a red herring. You deserve much better than that in a girlfriend.*

Without even realizing she'd done it, Clarissa ripped up the letter. Then she looked at the ragged strips of pale green paper lying on the floor and wondered what to do next. If Sylvia didn't get her report from Brandy now, she'd just get it in a different way later.

So Clarissa would march right up to Brandy and tell her she knew Brandy was feeding Sylvia information and that if Brandy ever told Sylvia anything again, Clarissa would let the entire cast of *Undercover Agents* know who was turning over their personal information to the tabloids.

And the cast would, of course, take the word of some unknown temporary nanny over one of their own.

Clarissa sighed and ran one hand through her hair.

Besides, even if Clarissa did stop Brandy, it would take only one of Sylvia's sources away from her.

Plus Sylvia would be so mad at Clarissa, who knew what type of story she'd print about her.

Well, she could at least warn Tristan about what type of person Brandy was. Although, now that Clarissa thought about it, she realized she didn't even know Tristan's room number. And that wasn't information the front desk was likely to pass out. How could she get hold of him?

She tapped one finger nervously against the floor. Slade would know how, but it wasn't as though she could ask him for Tristan's phone number without some really good explanation. A really, really good explanation.

Nope.

After the way Slade had insisted Clarissa avoid Tristan, there wasn't an explanation good enough to get Slade's help. She would just have to wait until she saw Tristan again. He had said he would show up Halloween night—tomorrow night—she could tell him then.

"What did the clue say?" Bella asked.

Clarissa had almost forgotten Bella was lying beside her. Now, just to put Bella off, she said numbly, "I'm not sure."

Clarissa still needed time to think, to run through all the possible solutions and find the best one.

"Why don't you write back?" Bella asked.

Clarissa looked down at Bella, about to put her off again, and then realized she had given Clarissa the perfect answer.

"I think I will."

She opened her purse, pulled out the green envelope of her own, and smoothed out the folds in the stationery. As she did so, she noticed the cell phone next to her wallet. It was only then she remembered Meredith in the stairwell, still searching for Bella. By this point Meredith had probably reached the fourth floor, told Slade, and enlisted him in the search. Most likely they were both half panicked and about to call security.

Clarissa punched in the numbers to Slade's cell phone and listened while it rang.

"Hello?" He sounded sharp and impatient.

"Hello, Slade," she whispered, "I just wanted to call to let you know I found Bella."

"Found Bella?" he asked. "Was she lost?"

Oops. He didn't know, and now she had just admitted to losing his daughter again.

"We were playing hide-and-seek."

There was a pause and then Slade's voice, sounding tight. "Clarissa, my agent is on the other line, and you're calling to report the results of your game of hide-and-seek?"

Clarissa gulped. This was not getting any better. "Well, she was playing really well, and we were afraid she might be lost. Sorry to bother you though."

"Clarissa, why are you whispering?"

Because I'm hiding under a banquet table in a conference room about to do the most devious thing I've ever done in my life, and I couldn't find my normal voice if I tried. "Bella and I are playing spies now."

"Great," he said slowly, and then, "I'll talk to you later."

He hung up, and she gratefully put the phone back into her purse. She'd just have to hurry and hope that wherever Meredith was, she wasn't overly worried.

She took a pen from her purse and tried to match Brandy's skinny scrawl as well as she could. She thought for a moment, then wrote:

Mob activity is suspected among the cast of Undercover Agents. *Several of the cast members wondered why A.J. insisted on spending the time, money, and effort to take the cast and crew to a remote*

Hawaiian location. Now suspicions have been answered. The crate full of assault rifles marked props—the one A.J. hasn't let cast or crew near—are all real. They're apparently part of an illegal weapons ring, waiting for mob operatives to pick them up.

Clarissa folded the stationery, put it into her envelope, then used the tape from Brandy's envelope to stick it back on the underside of the table. She smiled. She wasn't sure who would face the greater consequence for this story, Brandy or Sylvia, but somebody's credibility was about to crumble.

Clarissa quickly gathered up the shreds of torn paper and stuffed them into her purse. Stretching to relieve the cramps in her legs, she took hold of Bella's hand and whispered, "Come on, Bella. It's time to report back to spy headquarters."

15

Slade had just hung up with his agent when he got a call from A.J. "Let's meet in the restaurant for dinner and talk about your manuscript."

Slade agreed but did so with only forced enthusiasm. It was hard to be enthusiastic about a dinner-long rejection.

He then walked to Clarissa's room to pick up Bella. She didn't want to leave. She, Clarissa, and Elaina had made a tent in the bathroom and the three of them were sitting together in the tub discussing spy strategy.

It figured.

He was trying to take Clarissa's advice to spend more time with Bella, and now Bella didn't want to be with him.

Still, he dragged her from the room and drove her to the Sea Life Park. He tried to get into the spirit of the thing—buying her dolphin-shaped balloons and a starfish hat—but found himself poor company. He'd purposely planned time away from Clarissa but longed for an adult to talk to. An adult who would under-stand the frustrations of trying to convince Goliath to give David a chance. An adult who could offer consolation. An adult who had clear blue eyes and the face of an angel.

Instead he escorted his daughter around and grew crosser as the day wore on. By midafternoon he was snapping at Bella and feeling horrible for not being able to control his temper.

Finally he decided to call it a day and drove back to the resort. On the way there Bella folded her arms, scowled at the window, and said, "I want to go home."

"We are going home."

"I want to go home to my *bedroom*," she emphasized.

Slade grunted, then considered the idea. "I suppose it would be better if we cut this trip a couple of days short," he said. "There isn't much point in sticking around." He started mentally arranging the details of leaving the next morning and then remembered Kim.

Kim.

He couldn't very well leave on the day she arrived. Not after he'd already made plans with her. They were supposed to go to that stupid costume party.

So it was one more day. He'd endure one more day of this vacation and then go back to California.

✦ ✦ ✦

Slade dropped Bella off at Clarissa's room, told her of his dinner plans with A.J., his plans to leave Hawaii early, and then left before he could spend any time talking with her. She had stood in the doorway of her room, leaning up against the door frame, looking very much like she wanted to talk to him, but he'd said a curt good-bye and walked quickly back to his room. The time for conversations with Clarissa was over. Conversations led to familiarity, to intimacy, to all sorts of things he had to be on guard against now.

He went back to his room to work on his lines. He memorized them quickly but couldn't say them with the right degree of emotion. They all came out sounding angry.

At six o'clock he went down to the restaurant to meet with A.J. and Nataly. Slade donned a pair of casual slacks, a Christian Dior shirt, and his best acting style. He was acting like a man who didn't know the outcome of this meeting, who hadn't had a midnight rendezvous with A.J.'s girlfriend, and who wasn't in love with a woman he couldn't have. In short, he was acting like the man he was yesterday.

The hostess showed him to the table where A.J. and Nataly were already seated. A.J. wore alligator skin cowboy boots and another western shirt. Nataly wore a tight red dress spangled with sequins. The two of them greeted him warmly.

After they'd ordered, just so they'd have something else to talk about, Slade asked A.J. how the *Undercover Agents* shooting was going. A.J. recounted the show's many problems and the trials of a producer in general, until the waitress came with their orders.

They all ate silently for a few minutes, and then A.J. brought up the subject at hand. "Well, Slade, you have more writing talent than I ever expected. Good characters, good dialogue, and a decent plot. However, the script has two major deficiencies. First of all, it's a nice story, but it doesn't have enough action to be a major motion picture. It reads more like a made-for-TV property."

"But that's the point," Slade broke in. "You don't see anything on the screen anymore unless it's about lust or carnage. A lot of people would like to be able to go to movies without worrying they're going to be shocked and offended in five-minute increments."

"Yes," A.J. said, "and those shows are called cartoons. Disney has done a pretty good job covering that market."

Slade looked intently at A.J. as though he could make him understand by pure will. "It's not just children who want G-rated films. Believe it or not some people in this country still have morals. They have money to spend, they like entertainment, and there's nothing on the screen for them."

"Which brings me to my second problem with the script," A.J. said. "It's too preachy."

"Too preachy?"

"For example, when the hero realizes he loves the girl, he has this great epiphany. They're all alone in the waiting room, and what do they do? They talk about life. No way. In real life he takes her in his arms and gives her a kiss that makes the entire audience blush." A.J. reached into his briefcase and handed the script back to Slade. "I'm sorry. I really am. If you can hype up the story a bit, I might reconsider."

Slade took the manuscript and laid it beside him at the table. "Thanks for your time, A.J."

"And a shoot-out scene at the end couldn't hurt."

"I'll keep that in mind." Slade picked up his water glass to take a drink. It was then he noticed Clarissa standing at the front of the restaurant. She held Bella by one hand and Elaina by the other and was talking to the hostess.

Which meant at any moment Bella would see him, insist on joining him, and inevitably turn the rest of dinner into a zoo.

Slade clenched the water glass and returned it to the table with a thud. Why in the world had Clarissa brought the girls to the restaurant when he had specifically told her he would be here?

And then he remembered he hadn't. He'd only told her he was going out to dinner with A.J. In his haste to get away from her room, he hadn't told her where. She must have thought he meant "out" as in out of the resort.

The hostess had picked up menus and was escorting Clarissa and the kids into the dining room. It was then that Clarissa glanced up and saw him. A look of surprise and then apprehension crossed her face. In that moment he could tell Clarissa had also anticipated the outcome of dinner and was now rethinking the situation. She called to the hostess, shook her head, and said something while trying to redirect the little girls back out the way they had come.

They were almost to the door when Bella noticed Slade. Over the clink of dishes and hum of conversation, he heard the word, "Daddy!" but pretended he hadn't. And a moment later they were gone. He couldn't hear the subsequent wailing, but he could imagine what it sounded like as Clarissa dragged Bella across the lobby.

He took another drink of water.

"Did you decide on your costume yet?" Nataly smiled over at him, and he tried to bring his concentration back to the table. "What mask will you be wearing tomorrow night?"

"Batman," Slade said.

"Oh? Thinking of vying for that part?" she asked.

"No, Kim wanted to be Cat Woman, and the costume store was all out of Riddler wear."

Nataly still smiled. "Well, with a doctor of botany on your arm, I would think you'd go for the Joker costume."

A.J. shot her a look. "Now, Nataly, just because a woman is a scientist doesn't mean she can't also be charming." And then with a wink he added, "Although it certainly raises the probability."

Slade picked up his fork but paused before taking a bite of his fish. "Some men find intelligence a charming quality."

A.J. waved his hand in a shooing motion. "We're just teasing you. I'm sure she's a lovely woman, and we can hardly wait to meet her."

"Oh, yes," Nataly said. "I'm dying to meet her."

It was then that Slade heard Bella. She called out, "Daddy!" and when he turned, he saw her small legs hurrying toward him. She climbed onto his lap and threw her arms tightly around his neck. "I knew you were in here," she said breathlessly.

Slade looked behind Bella, expecting to see Clarissa coming in for the recapture, but she was nowhere in sight.

"Bella," he said sternly. "Did you run away from Clarissa again?"

She shook her head slowly. "No, Daddy. I didn't run. I just got out of the elevator."

"And where are Clarissa and Elaina?"

"Still in the elevator," Bella said.

Slade tilted his head back, looked at the ceiling, and sighed. He could suddenly envision the entire scenario. Clarissa took both girls into the elevator in an attempt to go back to their room. Bella, in her usual stealth fashion, pulled away from Clarissa's grasp and stepped off the elevator just before the doors closed. He could almost imagine the look on Clarissa's face as she had to decide whether to stay on the elevator with Elaina and leave Bella by herself, or pursue Bella and leave Elaina alone on an elevator that was headed to the fourth floor.

"Isabel Jacobson," he said slowly, "that was a very naughty thing to do."

Her bottom lip quivered, and he could tell she was on the verge of another wail. In order to salvage dinner he added, "And we will discuss it as soon as we go back to our room."

Bella laid her head against Slade's chest. "I wanted to be with you," she said sadly.

Slade looked across the table. "A.J., this is my daughter, Bella. And of course Nataly has already been introduced." Slade then glanced down at Bella. "Do you remember Nataly from the pool?"

Bella nodded solemnly and kept her face pressed against her father's chest.

A.J. bent over a little to be closer to Bella's eye level. "I've heard about you, Bella Jacobson," he said. "You seem to be in the habit of breaking sets."

"You break things, too," Bella said.

A.J.'s eyebrows rose. "Is that so?"

Bella nodded. "I heard Nataly say she was going to break something with you."

"What are you talking about?" Slade asked. "Nataly never talked about breaking things."

He realized his mistake too late. Before he could stop her, Bella said, "She did too. She said she was going to break it off with A.J."

A silence, the kind that isn't really silent at all, but is loud with the sound of your heart collapsing, descended on the table.

Slade opened his mouth to speak, to say something about his daughter's last statement, but no words came to his tongue. It probably wouldn't have mattered anyway. Neither A.J. nor Nataly were listening to him. They were staring at each other—one turning red, the other turning pale.

A.J. said, "What did you say?"

"I was just joking," Nataly said.

"You were joking with a four-year-old about breaking up with me?"

"Yes," she said, and Slade could see her acting persona suddenly spring to life. "I was telling her I had the perfect boyfriend and teasing about her stealing him away from me. It was all a joke."

A.J. looked over at Bella. Slade could tell he was trying to keep his voice light, but it still came out sounding pointed. "So, Nataly was trying to set you up with a boyfriend, huh, kid?"

"She thought I was asleep," Bella said. "But I was pretending."

Another awful moment of silence ensued, and Nataly's paleness crept back into her face.

Thankfully, no one had to say anything else. Clarissa had pushed her way through the tables and now, still holding onto Elaina's hand, stood before them. Her jaw was clenched, and she said sharply, "Bella, it's time for you to come with me."

Under any other circumstances Slade would have handed Bella to her nanny and simply put up with the ensuing scene. Now he saw Bella's resistance as the perfect excuse for him to exit the restaurant. He started to rise and was about to say, "I think I'd better take her back to our room," but he never got the chance. Apparently Bella thought he was going to transfer her into Clarissa's arms, and she yelled, "No!" then grabbed onto the tablecloth with both hands. As Slade stood, the tablecloth came up with him.

Plates, glasses, and the rest of Nataly's lobster tail all migrated to the other side of the table and then tumbled to the floor.

A.J. jumped out of the way in time to miss most of the food, but a glass of wine and a plateful of salad splattered all over Nataly's sequined dress. She stood up, gasping, and tried to wipe bits of salad dressing from her sequins.

"I'm so sorry," Slade said, and then couldn't say anything else because Bella's wailing had begun.

16

When Slade got back to his room, the girls were wearing their pajamas and sitting on the floor in front of the TV. He looked at them, looked at Clarissa who sat behind them combing through Bella's wet hair, and then took off his jacket and threw it over a chair. He collapsed on the couch, leaned his head back until it touched the wall, and stared at the ceiling.

Clarissa left the floor and sat next to him so they could talk without disturbing the girls. "Did the restaurant manager accept your check?" she asked.

"They're going to take account of everything and send me a bill."

Clarissa nodded, then glanced back at Bella. Neither of them said anything for a moment, and then she said, "I think your big mistake was letting go of Bella's hand to help Nataly wipe off her dress."

Slade dropped his gaze from the ceiling and looked at Clarissa. "Well, how was I supposed to know Bella was going to run off crying underneath the salad bar table?"

"Experience."

"You'd think they'd use a sturdier table for all of that salad stuff."

Clarissa shook her head sadly. "It probably would have held up fine if I hadn't crawled under there to retrieve Bella. But, you know, I was just so afraid she was going to bump it and send everything crashing to the floor."

"Yes, well, that's irony for you." The beginning of a smile

tugged at the corners of Slade's mouth. "How is your head doing now?"

"Don't smirk at me." She crossed her arms tightly. "I'd like to see you wrestle with a five-year-old under a table and see if you can keep it from toppling over."

"She's only four," he said.

"She's nearly five, and she's as strong as a wildcat." Clarissa ran her hand over the top of her head, where a small bump had formed from ramming it into the underside of the table. "Besides, my head is the least of my wounds."

"Oh, did you sustain other injuries when the seafood platter fell on you?"

"I'm talking about my pride," she said. "I was covered with cocktail sauce, and by the way, I noticed you didn't jump over to wipe off *my* dress like you did Nataly's."

"I was holding onto Bella," he said and then added more quietly, "besides, the way you were hopping around, I would have been hard pressed to catch you, let alone wipe off anything."

Clarissa tilted her head and gave him an aloof stare. "You would have jumped around, too, if you'd just gotten seafood down your dress."

The smile was back on Slade's lips, but he tried to suppress it. "It was only shrimp."

"It was dead fish, and it was stuck down my back and in my bra." She gave an involuntary shiver. "I'll probably smell like a wharf for days."

He reached out and patted her hand as though she were a child. "Well, it's over now, and if the restaurant staff works hard, I'm sure they'll have the place cleaned up by the breakfast shift."

Clarissa glanced over to where Bella and Elaina lay staring up at the TV. "At least the girls don't seem any worse for the trauma, although I think I'll always remember the sight of Elaina standing there, crying in the middle of the Jell-O salad remains." She shook her head again. "Poor thing. I think all of the people screaming frightened her."

"It's amazing what will make people scream," Slade said. "Most of them only got a little splattered when the table tipped over."

"Except for that one lady," Clarissa said with a wince. "She got the full brunt of the potato salad."

Slade stared back at the ceiling and sighed. "You know, about the time the condiments went up in the air, I started having flashbacks to the whole Evelyn-and-Brad-Nash affair." He ran both hands through his hair as if to shake off the memory. "Man, I hope no one there had any connection with the tabloids. That would be all I need. Another restaurant scandal."

Clarissa reached over and rested her hand on top of his. "Did it ruin your deal with A.J.?"

"No, that was ruined before Bella even walked into the restaurant. Which, of course, now seems like a blessing since it saves me the humiliation of being officially banned from all of A.J.'s sets."

"But none of the mess was really your fault," Clarissa said. "Surely A.J. won't hold it against you."

Slade tilted his head and lifted one eyebrow. "I still haven't lived down the tropical fish fiasco from *Mermaid Island*."

"Oh? What happened there?"

"A Tonka truck and a fifteen-hundred-gallon aquarium. Suffice it to say, it was at that point I began encouraging Bella to play with Barbie dolls, because no matter how hard you throw one of them, it won't break glass."

Now Clarissa smiled and tried to hide it.

Slade sighed again and rested his head back against the wall. "What am I going to do with her, Clarissa?"

Clarissa glanced at Bella and then back at Slade. "Was that a rhetorical question, or do you really want my opinion?"

He leaned toward her and lowered his voice. "If Bella is doing this all on purpose, then I need to know how to help her."

It wasn't something Clarissa had thought about in clinical terms, and yet she knew exactly what Bella was feeling. She knew it because she felt it herself. She knew it because she'd seen the shadows of the same emotions flicker around her own daughter. Now she struggled to explain it to Slade.

"I don't think Bella necessarily plans it. She's just frightened and angry. She lost control of her world, so she's trying to control what's left of it the only way she knows how. With every scrape she gets into, she gets more attention and love from you."

"I wasn't very loving to her tonight," he said.

"Well, you weren't when you were barking out new rules. And by the way, I don't think she even heard rule 22 or 23; but after that, you held her in your arms like you always do. That's what she wants. I might rip off a tablecloth or down Miracle Grow if I knew it would get me more love."

"So I'm supposed to comfort her less?"

"Less after her accidents and more beforehand. Reward good behavior positively and enforce consequences for negative behavior."

He didn't say anything, but she went on anyway. "And be grateful Bella still wants love. Some people cope with divorce by turning off their emotions altogether. They refuse to open up or trust anyone because they don't want to be hurt again. It's easy to turn off the trust, but it's hard to turn off the anger. That stays with you." Clarissa suddenly stopped because she realized she was talking about herself and didn't want Slade to realize it, too.

Perhaps he already did. He was looking at her intently, as though he were trying to figure something out.

"Well, I guess I'd better go back to my room and take a shower—you know, make sure I'm rid of all the dead fish."

"Wait a minute." He turned toward the girls and called, "Bella, come here."

She trotted over and looked up at him.

"I've been thinking about it," he told his daughter. "And I've decided we ought to go downstairs and help clean up in the restaurant."

"But I'm not allowed to touch broken glass," she said.

"We'll clean something besides the glass," he said.

Her brows furrowed together, and she glanced over at Elaina. "But I want to stay here."

He took hold of her chin and turned her face so she was looking at him again. "When you made that big mess, you made a lot of people unhappy. Now we've got to try and set it right."

The brows were still furrowed, but she didn't say anything. Instead she pulled away from Slade and looked at the floor.

"The restaurant manager was very sad that so many of his things got broken," Slade went on, "and all the people who were trying to have a nice dinner and got showered with salad fixings were sad. Clarissa got a bump on her head. I think that made her sad, too."

Bella's lip began to quiver, then the tears came, but she went and threw her arms around Clarissa, and not her father.

With her face pressed into Clarissa's dress she said, "I'm sorry I ran under the table!"

Clarissa picked her up, held her close, and rubbed the little girl's back while she sobbed. She suddenly understood Slade's dilemma much better. It took everything she had not to completely absolve Bella of all wrongdoing. Instead she simply said, "I still love you, Bella. I just hope next time you'll make a better choice."

Bella took a shaky breath and nodded. With her arms still around Clarissa's neck she said, "Are you going away?"

Clarissa hesitated, but only for only a moment. "No, of course not."

"Not even if I'm naughty?"

"You've already been naughty," Clarissa said, "and I'm still here."

Bella seemed to consider this for a moment. "Then will you take me to kindergarten when I'm big enough?"

Clarissa smiled at the odd request. "If that's what you and your daddy want." She looked over at Slade, expecting he'd also be smiling, or wearing a puzzled expression, but instead his features were stern, and his face looked pale.

So perhaps she had overstepped her bounds. Perhaps Slade didn't expect she would still be working for him by the time Bella went to kindergarten. Perhaps he regretted already that he'd asked her to continue on as Bella's nanny when they got back to California.

Clarissa held Bella for another minute and then reluctantly gave her to Slade. He put her back on her feet but kept hold of her hand. "Let's go down to the restaurant and see what we can do."

She nodded, and then the two of them left the room, hand in hand.

✦ ✦ ✦

The next morning Slade called Clarissa's room and said he'd decided to spend the day alone with Bella. "I figure we could use some more father-daughter time together."

Clarissa commended him and said she hoped they'd have a good time and then felt very sorry for herself as she hung up the phone. It was their last full day in Hawaii, and she would spend it without Slade.

She and Elaina went for a walk along the beach, went to the pool, had lunch, then went back to their hotel room. While Elaina took a nap, Clarissa straightened up the room, repacking what she could. Then because she decided it was time she did something educational with her daughter, Clarissa used the hotel stationery to cut out the letters of Elaina's name. When the little girl woke up, Clarissa would give them to her to color. She was trimming the top of the letter *I* when Meredith dropped by.

She looked over Clarissa's shoulder into the room. "Is Slade with you?"

"No, he decided to spend the day alone with Bella. They're out at the Aloha Tower."

Meredith walked into the room and sat down on the couch dejectedly. "I just had a phone call from Kim. She's in Mexico."

Clarissa picked up the scissors and started on an N. "In Mexico? Why?"

"There was an algae bloom off the gulf, and she went to examine it."

"Oh," Clarissa could muster only mild disappointment. "Slade won't be happy about that."

"Well, he's going to look like a fool in front of Nataly and the *Undercover Agents* cast, but I suppose he'll find a way out of it. He can just say her plane went down, or something of the sort." And then Meredith looked over at Clarissa with a peculiar expression.

"What?" Clarissa asked.

"You could go as Kim."

"What?" Clarissa said again.

"You'll be in a Cat Woman costume. No one will even know it's you."

"Well, not unless I also pretend I'm mute. I mean, they have heard my voice."

"You could fake an English accent, couldn't you?"

Clarissa looked around the room as though it would provide an excuse for her. "But I'm watching the girls."

"I'll watch them."

Clarissa shook her head. "It would never work."

"Why not?" Meredith said, growing happier by the moment.

"I don't know why not. I just know it won't, and then Slade and I will both look like fools." She held up one hand as though trying to show the reasonableness of her argument. "Besides, Slade won't want me to try a stunt like that. He'd rather use the airplane disaster story."

Meredith sighed and seemed to concede the point. "I suppose you're right. It's just that I hate to think of Nataly Granger being smug about the whole thing." She stood up then, as though her visit were finished. "I suppose it doesn't really matter. Slade has lived down worse things. Last night's dinner, for example."

Meredith moved to the door and then as though it were an

afterthought said, "You've told your husband we're coming home early, right?"

"Of course," Clarissa said.

"Good. I got the impression he was feeling neglected when he called."

Clarissa felt, very quickly, that her blood had turned to stone. "He called?"

"Oh, that's right! I never told you. He called the night when you were at the pool. I was in your room getting Elaina's stuffed dog when the call came in."

He called? How did he get her phone number? He didn't even know where she was. And then with a sudden rush of dread, Clarissa realized he did. She had sent that information to Renea by e-mail, and Renea had undoubtedly given it to her brother. It would have been easy for him to look up the phone number of the Mahalo Regency Resort.

Clarissa could barely speak but somehow managed to ask, "What did he say?"

"Not much. He just asked if you were in, and I said you were out. Then he said to tell you that Alex called. I said, 'Oh yes, you're her husband.' And he said, 'Her ex-husband.' So you see, I think he's feeling a little put out." Meredith turned to give Clarissa a smile, but it immediately dropped from her face. A look of concern replaced it. "Clarissa, you're as white as a sheet."

"Am I?" Why couldn't she pull off a laugh? A laugh would have made everything all right. A laugh would have hidden everything. She should have been able to say, "Yes, he likes to threaten when he's in a bad mood," but she just sat on the couch trying to control her shaky hands.

"Is something wrong?"

"No. Nothing's wrong." Clarissa turned to her scissors and busily started cutting paper again.

Meredith was silent for a moment, and then when she spoke her voice was even and serious. "Alex is your husband, isn't he?"

The paper fell from her hands and with it her whole facade.

Had she wanted to, she couldn't have forced any sort of fabrication from her lips. Instead she shook her head. "Not anymore. We're divorced."

Meredith came back to the couch and sat down heavily on it. "Why on earth did you lie about it?"

"I didn't mean to. I mean, at first it was just an oversight at the employment agency, but I needed the job, and I didn't think it would really matter."

"I think it will matter a great deal to Slade."

She hung her head and sighed. "I know. Dishonesty in an employee is the last thing he wants."

"Is that how you think he thinks about you? As an employee?"

Clarissa slumped down farther on the couch. "No. I mean, he also thinks of me as a friend—and that's even worse—to deceive a friend."

Meredith opened her mouth to say something, then shut it instead. She surveyed Clarissa with narrowed eyes, then said, "Let me ask you a question. How do you think of Slade?"

"I think he's wonderful. One of the most wonderful people I've ever met."

"And?"

"What can I say beyond wonderful?"

"How does he make you feel when you look at him?"

Clarissa didn't answer, but she felt her face flush bright red.

Meredith nodded. "I thought so."

"Please don't tell him."

"I wouldn't dream of it. That's your job."

Clarissa shifted uneasily on the couch. "I'm not going to tell him."

"And why not?"

"Because it wouldn't matter to him. I'm just his nanny. He doesn't see me as anything more than that."

Meredith tilted her head with a thoughtful expression. "Well, you're wrong, of course, but I'm not sure how to prove it to you."

"I know he's flirted with me a little in the past, but that's simply because he felt safe doing it. He knew I was never going to reciprocate. If he knew I was unmarried, he'd just feel awkward and uncomfortable around me."

Meredith tapped the couch with her fingertips and didn't answer.

Clarissa leaned back into the couch in a big mournful lump. "Slade could have his pick of anyone he wanted. He wouldn't choose me. He's going to choose some leggy supermodel or Nobel Peace Prize winner or something."

Meredith still didn't answer.

"Why should I put myself through any more pain and rejection? It's easier to let him go on believing I'm married. At least that way he won't be afraid to be my friend."

Meredith nodded solemnly, as though agreeing to a conversation she held within herself. "I think I *will* go rent a Cat Woman outfit," she said. "The shop still had a couple when I went to pick up the Batman suit. You'll put it on and meet Slade at the Sunset Park Motel at seven o'clock."

"What good would that do?"

"Well, you want to know if he likes the real you, and you want to do it in such a manner as to guarantee you won't be hurt. What better way to find out than to be costumed as someone else? While you're talking just ask him . . ." Here Meredith faltered for a moment, rolling her hand in the air as though not even she knew how to phrase it. "Ask him what type of thing he looks for in a woman. Ask him what he thinks of his nanny. That way if he doesn't like you, you can return to being Clarissa Hancock, his nanny, and he's none the wiser. But if he does like you, then you pull off your mask and tell him the complete truth." She smiled triumphantly and waved a hand in Clarissa's direction. "Cinderella, you're going to the ball after all."

"As an English botanist dressed in a Cat Woman suit? I don't think so."

Meredith stood up and looked down at her watch. "Speaking

of that suit, I'd better get a move on to the costume store. I'm not sure when it closes."

"Wait." Clarissa stood up but didn't follow her to the door. "I really don't think I can do this."

"Nonsense," Meredith said. "You'll be fine. Simply drop your H's and remember to complain about the royal family every once in a while."

"You just want me to do this because of Nataly," Clarissa said, but it was no use. Meredith left the room with a cheery wave and called out, "I'll be right back."

Clarissa sank back to the couch, exhausted. "It will never work," she said again.

✥ ✥ ✥

Clarissa didn't move from the couch for a good twenty minutes. She sat watching the waves from her window and feeling her stomach churn. Now that Meredith had found out the truth, Clarissa knew one way or the other, she had to tell Slade everything. Tonight. She couldn't ask Meredith to pretend she was unaware of Clarissa's deceit. It wouldn't be right to put her in that position.

The churning grew, and Clarissa wished for the thousandth time she had told Slade the truth at the beginning.

Would he still want her to be Bella's nanny after he found out she'd lied to him? Could he ever trust her again? The thought of losing the job was hard. The thought of never seeing Slade again, never talking with him, never feeling his gaze rest on her, was even harder. Perhaps if she didn't tell him how she felt now, she'd never have the chance.

And then again, perhaps that was for the best.

She tapped her foot nervously against the side of the couch.

Well, at least if she went out as Cat Woman she'd go out in a big way.

Still, she didn't think she could do it.

If she was going to lose Slade, she ought to lose him with as much of her dignity as she could preserve intact. If he didn't know how much she cared about him, it would hurt less when he fired her.

And after this was all over, she'd make sure nothing like it ever happened again. She'd never lie under any circumstances; and more important, she'd never care again about anyone enough to be hurt when she lost them.

This thought left her cold.

Could she do that? Could she really cut herself off from the good emotions in order to escape the bad?

Instead of thinking about it further, she went to the computer and turned it on. She knew she had to call Alex, but first she wanted to see if there was an e-mail from Renea waiting for her. The more information she had about the situation, the easier it would be to handle Alex.

It took a moment for Clarissa to access her mailbox, and she found not one but three messages bearing Renea's address. The first said: "Clarissa, I just saw your newspaper article, and I can't believe it. Where did you meet Slade Jacobson? And do you think it's wise to go off to Hawaii with him when you're in this frail and vulnerable state? You ought to wait a while to make these kinds of life-changing decisions. I hope you'll take a good look at what you're doing."

The second e-mail said: "Is that Elaina who Slade is carrying in the newspaper article? I printed out the picture and showed it to the entire family, but we can't agree on whether it's her because her hair looks so much darker in the picture. Maybe it's the lighting. Anyway, I can't believe you brought your daughter along on this little nervous breakdown of yours. I mean, I realize Slade Jacobson is gorgeous, but do you really think he's a good role model for Elaina?"

The third e-mail just said: "All of my friends want to know if you really know Tristan McKellips. And if you do, could you introduce him to us when you get back?"

Clarissa deleted the messages, then turned off the computer. The e-mails told her two things. First, Renea was an idiot. She'd known that all along, however, so it wasn't helpful. Second, Alex's entire family thought she'd run off with Slade for some sort of torrid affair. They undoubtedly now thought her immoral, an unfit mother, and were probably congratulating Alex on getting rid of her.

She sighed heavily, exited the Internet, and turned off the computer. She'd brought it all on herself, she knew. She'd been led by her pride when she e-mailed that picture to Renea. Clarissa had just wanted to prove to Renea that she didn't need Alex anymore, that she was capable of attracting someone like Slade Jacobson. But it wasn't the truth.

Was it?

Meredith had hinted that Slade was interested in her. She wouldn't have come up with the idea of the Cat Woman charade if she knew Slade felt nothing for Clarissa.

Or would she?

Maybe Meredith was just a romantic. Or hopelessly optimistic. Or senile.

The memory of every single middle school crush suddenly flooded into Clarissa's mind. How many times had a friend told her, sworn to her in fact, that a certain boy liked her, and then the next day the same boy would be hanging out with some other girl?

You just couldn't depend on a third-party opinion when it came to love. Which was just another reason Clarissa hated the whole dating thing.

Maybe it *would* be best to be disguised as someone else. It would give her the information she needed to decide how to go about telling him the truth.

Then again, maybe it would be easier just to resign immediately and go back to working two jobs.

She got up from the computer and went and sat back down on the couch. She looked over at the phone but didn't pick it up. Instead she tried to run through a scenario of possible scenes with Alex so she could plan how to react in advance.

He was probably upset she'd run off for a wild fling with Slade, thought she was now unstable, and thus no longer a capable mother. In this case, Clarissa would simply swallow her pride and tell Alex the truth. She was not Slade's girlfriend; she was his daughter's nanny.

And from now on she wouldn't let her pride lead her into making foolish decisions like sending things to Renea.

What an educational trip this was turning out to be. She had now committed to shun both dishonesty and pride. Before she boarded the plane for California, she'd most likely be dispensing with all her sins.

Clarissa picked up the phone. Her hand hovered over the buttons for a hesitating moment, then she quickly punched in Alex's work phone number.

A moment later she heard his voice say, "Hello?"

She waited for the stream of emotions that always came when she heard his voice. The hurt, the anger, the hollow sadness. None of them came this time. It was just Alex's voice.

"This is Clarissa," she said. "I heard you were trying to get hold of me."

"Yes," he said, and the word alone was an accusation. "What in the world is going on with you? First I get a call from a reporter and then I see this picture of you, Slade Jacobson, and Elaina together off in Hawaii, and I just—"

"That wasn't Elaina in the picture," Clarissa cut in, and suddenly it all seemed so ludicrous. He didn't even recognize his own daughter. "Elaina has straight blonde hair, not curly light brown hair, and she's a year younger than the girl in the picture."

"Well, if Elaina isn't with you, where is she?"

"I didn't say she wasn't with me. I just said that wasn't her in the picture. I thought you might want to know."

"My point is still the same," Alex said. "I gave you half of everything I own, *and* I'm paying child support to take care of Elaina, but if you've taken up with some bigwig rich guy, I don't think I should have to give you any money at all. You're probably better off now than I am. You ought to be paying me."

It wasn't the hurt that made her take a deep inward breath, it was the surprise. He wasn't upset about her immorality, or her failings as a mother, or even about Elaina at all. It was about money.

She thought about arguing the fact that he paid hardly anything as it was. She thought about accusing him of all the ways he wasn't a good father. She thought about bringing up how she'd worked two jobs over the last few months in an attempt to make ends meet. But somehow, as she held onto the phone, she realized it was a useless waste of emotional energy.

I *am* better off than you are, she wanted to say, but not in the way you think. I'm better off because somehow I'm going to get through this a better person.

In a calm voice she said, "The judge made a decision, and you're obligated to it. If you don't like it, you can discuss it with your lawyer, but I don't want to talk about it."

"Well, maybe I *will* talk to my lawyer," he said, and then sharply hung up the phone.

She knew he wouldn't. The fees he'd have to pay his lawyer to take the case to court again would far exceed anything he'd get in reduced child support.

Alex was just being purposely difficult again—which didn't bother her as much as the fact that he hadn't been at all concerned about Elaina. He didn't ask to speak to her. He didn't even ask how she was.

Clarissa put down the phone, then went and peeked in on Elaina sleeping.

"I love you, Elaina," Clarissa whispered to her, even though she knew Elaina couldn't hear her.

She needs a father who cares about her, Clarissa thought. *Someone who wants to see her color letters and talk to her on the phone. Just like I need a husband, someone who'll love and support me.*

And the only way she'd ever get either was if she opened herself up enough to care about someone, even if it meant getting hurt in the process. Without risk, there could be no love.

17

Slade and Bella didn't stay long at the Aloha Tower. Bella found it only a mildly interesting building and wanted to go walk around the harbor. So they did. At lunch they stopped at a seafood restaurant, and Slade tried to eat his shrimp cocktail without remembering Clarissa jumping around the hotel dining room, shaking her dress while little pieces of fish fell to the floor.

He momentarily considered not leaving for California in the morning. It would be so nice to stay here vacationing with Clarissa.

But he knew it wasn't the right thing to do. The sooner they got home, the better off they'd all be. Then Clarissa would be back safely with her perfectionist husband, and Slade would stay as far away from her as he possibly could.

He already had it figured out. When he had Clarissa tend Bella, he would leave before Clarissa came and not come home until after she was gone. Meredith would be there during the transition times and could take care of all payments and correspondence. That way Bella would still have the nanny she wanted, and he'd be far out of temptation's reach.

After lunch Slade and Bella walked around the marketplace, looking at shells and tourist items. He bought her a Hawaii T-shirt, a child-size grass skirt, and a shaved ice.

"Are we gonna get something for Elaina and Clarissa?" Bella asked as they walked along.

"I think that would be a good idea," he said. "Why don't you pick something out for Elaina, and I'll pick something out for Clarissa."

Bella quickly found a shell necklace she thought Elaina would like, but Slade couldn't find anything he thought would be appropriate to give Clarissa. He wanted something that would tell her how much she meant to him, and somehow a T-shirt just didn't convey the right message.

After looking for quite some time, Slade decided to forget tourist items, and they drove to a jeweler's. "You can help me choose," he said to Bella as they walked in. Because, after all, Clarissa couldn't turn down a gift Bella had picked out.

He wanted to get her a ring. Instead he settled for a pair of black pearl earrings. He would tell her they were for going above and beyond the call of a nanny by subjecting herself to a dress full of dead fish in order to retrieve his child from underneath the salad bar.

She couldn't refuse that, could she?

He picked up a pearl brooch for Meredith. She liked brooches, and besides if he gave a gift to Meredith, too, then it would make his gift to Clarissa seem less . . . inappropriate.

A little after five o'clock they drove home. Bella was tired but still overly excited to show Elaina her gift. She held tightly onto the bag the shell necklace was in during the entire drive home. Upon arriving at the hotel, she insisted they take it directly to Clarissa's room.

It wasn't Clarissa who opened the door, however, it was Meredith. She smiled at the two of them. "Did you have a nice day?"

"Yes," he said. "Where's Clarissa?"

"I gave her the afternoon off. I thought it would be better if I watched the girls, you know, in case Zorro showed up."

Slade smiled despite himself. "You mean better for Clarissa or better for you?"

She returned his smile without missing a beat. "I'm still deciding."

Bella ran into the room and over to where Elaina sat in front of a coloring book and 264 different shades of crayons. Without waiting another second, Bella took her gift from its bag and put it around her friend's neck.

"Isn't it pretty?" Bella asked.

"Ooooh," Elaina said with wonder.

Slade walked over to the girls. "It's a present for you," he told Elaina. "Bella picked it."

"And I helped picked out the earrings for Clarissa too," Bella said.

Slade frowned over at Bella. "Hey, that was supposed to be a surprise." Then to Elaina he said, "I want to show them to your mom before anyone tells her about them. So can you keep it a secret?"

Elaina nodded and held the shell necklace up so she could look at it better. "I'm a good secret keeper," she said. "I haven't told about the D force at all."

"The D force?" Slade asked. "What's that?"

"That's why we don't live at Daddy's house anymore."

Slade stared at her, letting the words sink in, and feeling their full impact.

"You don't live with your daddy anymore?"

"Nope," Elaina ran her fingers across the shells without even looking up at Slade. "But he still loves me."

"Your mother is divorced?" he asked again.

Now Elaina held a finger to her lips. "It's a secret."

He stood up and turned back to Meredith. "Where is Clarissa?"

"Out sightseeing somewhere," she said calmly.

"Could you be a little more specific?" He had already pulled the car keys from his pocket and was walking toward the door.

"You can't go looking for her now," Meredith said. "It's a big island, and you're in no mood to talk to her about it anyway."

"I'm in exactly the mood to talk to her about it," he said back.

Meredith glanced over at Elaina, then walked over closer to Slade. In a lowered voice she said, "It's always shocking to find out someone has lied to you, but I'm sure Clarissa had her reasons. If you talk to her about it now, you'll just end up yelling, and I don't think that's what you really want to do."

"It is exactly what I want to do," he whispered back. "I trusted her. I tried to protect her from Tristan. I thought I was going to hell. The least she owes me is a really good explanation."

"You need to think about this rationally first," Meredith said. "You'll have time to talk to Clarissa later. Right now you need to think about Kim and about all the people who are expecting you to show up with her." She looked down at her watch. "You've only got an hour until it's time to jump in the Batmobile and pick up your favorite feline friend."

"I'll call Kim and cancel," Slade said stiffly. "I doubt I'll be very good company tonight."

Meredith shook her head. "You can't do that. She's been looking forward to this for a long time. And besides, she probably has her cat suit halfway peeled on by now." Meredith patted Slade's arm. "You're an actor. Just smile a lot and tell her she looks lovely. You'll do fine."

Slade put his car keys back into his pocket but didn't leave the room. He turned back to Meredith and looked at her narrowly. "You don't seem terribly surprised by any of this." And then his eyes narrowed even further. "Did you know all along that Clarissa was single?"

Meredith put up one hand as though pledging. "I can honestly say that before today I thought she was a married woman."

He grunted but opened the door to leave anyway. "When Clarissa comes in, tell her I need to talk to her. Tonight."

"I'll tell her," Meredith said and closed the door behind him.

❖ ❖ ❖

Clarissa sat on a cheap plaid couch in the lobby of the Sunset Park Motel and changed her mind every thirty seconds as to whether she should stay or not.

It was ridiculous. The whole scheme was ridiculous, and the sooner she called it off the better. She needed to get up, walk out of the building, go back to her rental car, and find some service station where she could change back into normal clothes.

She glanced over at the lobby clock. 6:50. She still had ten minutes to escape. Or ten minutes to sit here and be stared at by each and every person who walked by.

Why couldn't Kim have wanted to be something normal for Halloween like everyone else? A surgeon or an Arabian princess, perhaps. But no, it had to be Cat Woman, and now Clarissa was stuck on a couch in a skintight leather and spandex outfit, looking like a hooker with an identity crisis.

The only saving grace of the whole thing was that she was sure none of the people who were now staring at her would ever recognize her again. Besides the holes around her eyes and lips, every inch of her skin was covered. And just to make the outfit complete, she had worn blood red lipstick and dark gray eyeshadow. When she'd looked in the mirror, she'd hardly recognized herself. Certainly no one else would.

Of course, that still didn't mean she was going to be able to pull off the whole charade. Clarissa had no idea how to act like a botanist, let alone an English one. Meredith had let Clarissa read all of Kim's undeleted e-mails, but there weren't many of them, and they certainly weren't very informative. All Clarissa knew about Kim was that she was specializing in something called systematics, that she thought the inevitable extinction of a quarter of Hawaii's natural plant species was a tragedy of epic proportion, and that she worshiped someone named Greg Koob. Clarissa had no idea who he was. Her only hope was that Slade would never actually bring up the subject of botany.

The English accent was another thing to worry about. As Clarissa sat tapping her cat claws—which protruded out of her black gloves—against the couch, she tried to think of every British English word she could. In England elevators were lifts, apartments were flats, gas was petrol, policemen were bobbies, and flashlights were torches. Something on a car was a boot, and something else was a bonnet, although she couldn't remember which was what. Probably none of these things would come up in the conversation anyway.

Why hadn't she watched more of those educational British shows on PBS?

Clarissa looked up at the clock again. It read 6:54. If she got up right now and ran all the way to the parking lot, which she vaguely remembered in England was called a "car park," she might make it without Slade seeing her at all. He'd never know what she'd done. It still wasn't too late.

Clarissa shifted on the couch but didn't get up. For all the horrible images she had of the night, another image, a better one, kept replaying in her mind. In this scenario everything went fine. She and Slade had a wonderful time talking and dancing together. Then as Slade drove her back to her hotel, she asked him about his nanny. He hesitated for a moment, then told her in awed, reverent tones how much he cared about Clarissa. A look of longing filtered through his eyes, and he murmured, "If only . . ."

Then the moment of Clarissa's bravery came. She said, "Slade, you once told me how we all wear masks. Since then I've thought a lot about the masks I wear. Some masks are just for politeness—just for social wear, but I've realized I have other masks—masks I use to protect myself.

"I have a self-reliant mask, so I won't have to need anyone else. I have a cynical mask, so I won't have to trust anyone else. And I have a victim mask that allows me to stay in my sorrow, so I won't ever have to move on with my life. But being with you makes me want to take the chance of unmasking myself." Then she would reach up and peel off her mask.

In this fantasy scenario, her hair was still lush and beautiful after taking off her mask, not stuck to the back of her neck in a sweaty clump, as it undoubtedly would be. In the fantasy Slade always wore an expression of pleasant surprise.

In real life it might be very different.

She looked up at the clock. 6:57. Maybe he'd be late. Maybe he was stuck in traffic somewhere, or lost, and wouldn't show up at all. Maybe she still had hope for an escape.

And then she saw him walking through the lobby doors.

Slade always had a powerful presence, but now as he strode into the lobby dressed in black, a cape flowing behind him, Clarissa didn't know whether to laugh or simply gasp and stare.

He walked toward her. "Kim?"

She stood. "You must be Slade, either that or the masked crusader has finally tracked me down." The accent didn't come out as well as she would have liked. She sounded a little too much like a nervous Eliza Doolittle, but now she was stuck with it.

He cocked his head, smiled at her, and for a moment said nothing.

"What?" she asked. "Are my ears still on straight?"

"Yes, it's just that . . ." his smile grew. "You're much . . . taller than I remember."

"Well, I should hope so. I was only eight when you last saw me."

He looked her up and down, shaking his head. "You don't look eight years old anymore."

No, she thought, *now I look like a streetwalker with a personality disorder.* She smiled and said, "I'm glad to hear it."

He held his hand out to her. "Shall we go?"

"Let's." She took his arm, and they walked out of the lobby.

Slade smiled all the way to his car. In fact, Clarissa couldn't remember when she'd seen him so uncommonly happy.

During the car ride he asked her about her flight, the weather in Sheffield, and how she liked her room in the motel. Then he said, "Now tell me all about what you'll be doing while you're here in Hawaii."

"I'll be studying the plant life," she said, tapping one claw against her knee.

"I've always found plants so fascinating," he said. "What exactly is it you do?"

"Well . . ." she shrugged as though not even she found it interesting to talk about. "Basically, what I do is gather plants. And then look at them under a microscope."

"Oh. And what do you look for under the microscope?"

"Different things," she said. "Cell structure. Disease. Photosynthesis. That sort of thing."

"Photosynthesis? You can see that happening under a microscope?"

Umm. Maybe not. She had no idea.

She cleared her throat uncomfortably. "Well, if you have the right type of microscope." She should have brought a beeper, she realized. If she'd brought a beeper she could have faked some sort of emergency and insisted he take her back to the motel. Now she was trapped in the car trying to remember the difference between chlorophyll and chloroform and hoping she didn't have to use either of those words in the near future.

"I've never understood how photosynthesis works," he said. "Could you explain it to me?"

She glanced over at the dashboard and faked a gasp. Slade looked first at her and then at the dashboard. "What is it?"

She let out an exaggerated sigh. "Oh, nothing, it's just that for a moment I thought we were out of petrol. And wouldn't it be horrible to be stuck out here without even so much as a torch? Or what if we had some other car trouble? I mean, can you see us crawling around the boot or the bobbie dressed like this?"

"The bobbie?" he asked.

"Bonnet," she said. "I meant bonnet."

He nodded. "Oh, right. Bonnet means hood in England, doesn't it?"

"Yes, that's what I meant." She cleared her throat again. "A bobbie is a policeman. And I can tell you, there's never a bobbie around when you need one, so it's a good thing we have enough petrol."

"You were telling me about photosynthesis," he said.

"Oh, you don't want me to talk about my work." She turned slightly toward him. "Why don't you tell me about your job? How have things been for you in Hawaii?"

Now he shook his head. "I pitched a script, and it was rejected."

"I'm so sorry." And then because he didn't say anything else she added, "What will you do with it now?"

"I don't know. I've gone through about every producer I can think of." He took his gaze from the road for a moment. "What do you think I ought to do with it?"

"Could you produce it yourself?"

"Perhaps," he said. "These things cost a lot of money, though. It would be the equivalent of putting all my eggs in one basket. If the film bombed I'd be—"

"Chickenless?"

"Exactly. And of course I'd have to find the right actors and actresses." He glanced over at her again. "Perhaps that wouldn't be so hard though. These days it seems everyone is trying their hand at acting."

She smiled back at him weakly, feeling more trapped by the minute.

"Besides," he went on. "I don't know that I have the stamina to do the whole movie. I'm not sure it's worth it to try."

"If you believe something will make the world better, then it's always worth it to try, even if you fail."

He shrugged. "You may be right. But it would take a lot of my time, and I don't have the best of luck balancing work and my daughter."

Just the segue she needed. "Don't you have someone to help you?" she asked brightly.

"I have a nanny."

"Is she a good nanny?" Clarissa asked. "I mean, do you like her?"

Slade smiled. "She's a very good nanny. Although . . ."

"Although what?"

"Although sometimes she does these things that make me want to wring her neck."

Clarissa gulped and ran her hand along the door handle absentmindedly. "That doesn't sound like you get along well."

"Sometimes we get along well. Very well."

"Oh." She tried to analyze what this meant, but couldn't quite grasp its meaning. She decided to press the point. "So you consider her a friend?"

"Yes, except that friends listen to you more. Clarissa refuses to listen to me. That's one of those areas I'd like to strangle her over."

The friendship part was good to hear. She didn't listen to the rest of his comment. She just ruminated about friendship for a moment and wondered if he meant "friends" as in the same way he felt about Meredith, or "friends" as in there could be more to it. She tried to devise a question that would help her find this out, but the resort came into view, and Slade pointed it out.

"There's the Mahalo Regency," he said. "Isn't it beautiful? You drive up to it and sort of get the feeling you've been here before."

Clarissa shifted in her seat uncomfortably. "Um, yes, you do." *He knows*, she suddenly thought. *Somehow he knows, and any moment now he's going to reach over and pull off this mask for me.*

"There's something I need to talk to you about before we go inside."

"Oh?" She braced herself for the accusation.

"You see, while I was attempting to avoid the advances of a certain woman, I gave several people the impression you and I were dating seriously. If it isn't too much to ask, could you play along for tonight?"

"Of course," she said. "I mean, if it would help you out."

He slowed the car down as they drove up to the front of the building. "It will be our own little masquerade within a masquerade," he said and winked over at her.

She smiled back at him and fiddled with her claws.

So he didn't know.

Of course he didn't know. How could he have known? She was just being paranoid, and if she didn't start acting with more confidence, she'd end up giving herself away before she meant to.

Slade put the car in park, and a valet came and opened the door for her. She stepped out, then waited for Slade to join her. When he did, she held out her arm for him to take, but instead he put his hand around her waist and drew her close.

"Remember," he said, "we're in a serious relationship."

He guided her up the stairs and then led her to the ballroom with his arm around her waist the entire time.

The room was decorated with pumpkins, fake spiderwebs, and cornstalks, but it was the people and not the room that caught her attention. With one sweep of her gaze, she saw Robin Hood, Rapunzel, The Grim Reaper, Pikachu, and a couple of Klingon warriors. She also noticed Zorro. He stood in a corner with one arm around a Xena warrior princess and the other around a blonde and buxom genie. She wore her bottle around her neck and very little else. He seemed quite engrossed with both women and not at all concerned about what Cinderella might be doing. Which is why, Clarissa supposed, he hadn't dressed as Prince Charming.

Slade saw her staring in that direction and smiled. "You've noticed Zorro at work."

"Is that what he's supposed to be? I thought he was Don Juan."

"No, Don Juan is what he is in real life. As Zorro he gets to ride a horse—" Slade suddenly stopped himself. "But I've forgotten. You mentioned once that Tristan was one of your favorite actors. I need to introduce you to him."

And she wanted to talk to him, but not like this. Not as Kim, and not with Slade beside her.

Slade took a step in that direction, but Clarissa didn't move. "That's all right. I think I know him well enough right now."

He smiled at her. "Yes, I suppose you do."

Slade then led her in a different direction, introducing her to the people he knew, all the while keeping his hand on her waist—except for the few times he ran his hand slowly up her back and put it on her shoulder. It was hard to breathe during those times.

He was all smiles and compliments as he made the introductions, calling her "dear" and telling people they'd met while he was researching some plants for a possible script idea. "It was love at first sight," he told everyone. "I knew I was hooked when she spoke, and suddenly I found mold and spores to be the most interesting things in the world." Here he always ran his hand up and down her back. "Yep, since then I've been likin' lichen."

Clarissa just smiled and tried to say as little as possible.

They danced a few dances. Clarissa enjoyed the break, enjoyed not having to worry about what to say while the music played, and enjoyed being so close to Slade.

When they went to the refreshment table, Tristan and Brandy sauntered up beside them. Brandy wore a black wig, a Wonder Woman costume, and held a golden lasso, which she swung against her thigh absentmindedly.

Tristan looked from Slade to Clarissa and said, "Well, look at what the cat dragged in."

Slade rested his hand in between Clarissa's shoulder blades. "Tristan, Brandy, this is my date, Kim Jones."

Clarissa stuck her paw out to shake Tristan's hand, but he took it and kissed it instead. "You look lovely enough to make me want to take up a life of crime."

"You better not say that too loudly," Clarissa told him. "After all, you're standing next to Batman and Wonder Woman."

Tristan's gaze went from her hand to her eyes, and his look held hers for a second longer than normal. For a moment Clarissa thought he suspected something, but the next moment he turned back to Slade. "Zorro can take on Batman any day. Anyone who needs a boy wonder to help him fight crime can't be a serious superhero."

Slade picked up a donut from the table and held it in his free hand. "You're just jealous because I have a cool car, and all you have is a horse."

Brandy put her hands on her hips in Wonder Woman style. "Hey, I'm even cooler. I've got an invisible jet."

"What's cool about that?" Slade said. "It just means you can never find where you parked the thing."

Tristan elbowed her. "Yeah, and the people on the ground get a really interesting view as you fly overhead."

"Watch it," Brandy told him. "Or you'll find yourself lassoed to the refreshment table."

Clarissa put one claw to her lips and tapped her teeth in thought. "I don't have any cool gadgets or gizmos. I don't even have a horse. How does Cat Woman ever get anything done?"

"She has magical dancing powers," Tristan said.

"I don't remember that being in the movie," Clarissa said.

Tristan reached out and took hold of her hand. "I'll prove it to you." Then he pulled her from Slade's side and out to the dance floor. Slade stood, donut still in hand, shaking his head, but he didn't try to stop him. Clarissa didn't try to stop him, either. Somehow, seeing Brandy right next to Tristan, joking as though they were friends, bothered her beyond belief. She would tell Tristan about the letter right now . . . just as soon as she figured out a good way to do it.

A slow song was playing, and as Tristan held her in position he asked her where she was from and how she knew Slade. She responded with the Kim answers she'd rattled off all night. In the back of her mind, however, she kept trying to formulate the right way to bring up Brandy.

So I noticed you're with that woman, and I was just wondering if you've ever told her any personal secrets that might embarrass you if they were printed in the tabloids.

255

This was not going to be easy. Perhaps she could fake some psychic powers or something . . .

The song was nearing its end before she got up her courage. She leaned in close to him and blurted out, "This is going to sound a bit peculiar, but I have a message to pass on to you from a friend."

"Oh? What is it?"

"Never trust a woman who was named after an alcoholic beverage."

He nodded with a smile. "And I thought all this time you were Cat Woman. You're actually the Riddler, right?"

"I'm serious."

He glanced back to the refreshment table where Slade and Brandy were both biting into pastries. "You're wondering about Wonder Woman?"

Clarissa almost forgot her English accent but caught herself before she spoke. "She sold you out, Tristan. She tried to tell Sylvia about your father's problems."

Tristan actually stopped dancing. He stood on the dance floor, staring at Clarissa with complete seriousness. It struck her, as she watched his face, that it was probably the first time she'd ever seen him not acting, not putting on a performance. "How do you know about my father?"

"I told you. I'm just delivering a message from a friend."

He still stood without dancing. "Who?"

Who, yes, and then the next questions would be why and how. Maybe she should have gone with the psychic powers after all.

"Is the message from Slade?" he asked.

"No, not Slade, don't mention it to him." She pulled at his hand to move him forward a bit. "People will start to wonder why you're just standing here."

Tristan moved his feet and hands in a poor imitation of dancing. "What exactly did Brandy do?"

The music ended, and Slade was watching them expectantly.

"I can't tell you right now. We'll talk about it later." But only if she couldn't find a way to avoid Tristan for the rest of the night.

She took his hand and pulled him back to Slade and Brandy, who had moved away from the refreshment table and farther along the wall. Slade was holding two soda cans in his hands, and as Clarissa walked up to him, he handed her one. "I think Zorro was right. You do have magical dancing powers."

Tristan didn't say anything. He just stared at Brandy and then stared off across the room.

Slade pointed toward two uniformed police officers who walked through the door not far from them. "It seems like law enforcement is the costume of choice tonight," he said. "You picked the wrong time to be a criminal, Kim."

The officers stopped a passing Bo Peep, talked with her for a moment, and then headed across the floor toward A.J.

"I don't think those are costumes," Clarissa said.

"Of course they're costumes," Slade answered, but they all watched silently as the men reached A.J.

Decked out in cowboy boots, spurs, vest, hat, and holster, A.J. turned to the officers. One of them said something to him, and A.J.'s jaw dropped. The officers gestured toward the door, and a moment later A.J. stormed across the room, shaking his head, with the officers following close behind him. As he walked past Clarissa to the door, she heard him say, "That is absolutely the most ridiculous thing I've ever heard!"

A.J. disappeared into the lobby, continuing his verbal assessment of the situation and using increasingly colorful adjectives. Slade took a sip of his soda. "I don't think those were costumes."

"What would A.J. be in trouble for?" Tristan asked.

So she wouldn't have to offer an opinion, Clarissa took a quick drink of her soda.

"It's probably just another security problem or something," Brandy said, but she took a couple steps sideways and craned her head to get a better view out the door where A.J. had gone.

Without moving the soda can from her lips, Clarissa surveyed the room. Sylvia was here somewhere. Clarissa knew it. She looked for a costume that could plausibly conceal the reporter. A witch maybe.

"Do you see anything out the door?" Slade asked Brandy.

"Just a few people waiting in the lobby. A.J. went down the hallway."

Clarissa scooted forward in order to see out the door. Along with a few hotel personnel and miscellaneous others, Sylvia and Grant Rockwell both stood in the lobby, looking expectantly down the hallway.

So, not only had Sylvia taken the bait, she'd taken the police out fishing with her.

Clarissa glanced around the room again, wondering if S.W.A.T. team members were close by, scaling the resort walls in commando fashion. Then she took another sip of her drink.

Tristan walked over to the doorway, to better see what was happening, and the rest of the group followed, hovering just inside the door. For several minutes there wasn't any activity in the lobby, unless you counted Sylvia pacing around a bit, saying something—though Clarissa couldn't hear what—to Grant.

And then A.J. and the police officers came back down the hallway. A.J. had the swagger back in his step and laughed as he walked. In a booming voice he said, "Well, officers, you'd be hard pressed to shoot anyone with those, but if you get any other people complaining about my guns, direct them to me, and I'll try."

"I'm sorry we bothered you, sir," one of the officers said as they reached the lobby. "Thanks for cooperating with us."

The pair had turned toward the front door, one already talking into his hand-held radio, when Sylvia approached them.

"You didn't find anything?" she asked incredulously. "Did you look in all of the crates? He's probably just hiding them."

The police officer said, "We looked at the prop weapons, ma'am. We have no reason at this point to issue a warrant."

Sylvia took a few steps forward until she stood between the

officers and the door. "So that's it? You're just going to leave and let him get away with weapon smuggling? You're going to let him hand over assault rifles to the mob just because they weren't sitting out in the open where you could see them?"

The police officer said something back to her, but since his voice didn't have nearly the volume of Sylvia's, Clarissa couldn't tell what it was. But after a moment the officers stepped around her and went to the door, while Sylvia stood looking after them with clenched fists.

A.J. put his thumbs through his belt loops, stepped sidewise so his feet were slightly apart, and for a moment did indeed look like an actual cowboy about to take down a heifer.

"So that's what you've sunk to in order to get your scoop," he called over to her. "Now you're making up wild stories accusing us of illegal activities and trying to get the police to believe them." A.J. nodded to her with a smirk. "I think you've stepped over the bounds of reporting and into the field of harassment, Ms. Stoddard, and I just wonder what my lawyer will have to say about all of this."

Without waiting for a response, A.J. turned on his boot heels and strode back into the party, shaking his head.

Grant was the next to nod and smile at Sylvia. "And to think I was afraid I wouldn't get a story on this trip." He held one hand up as though showing her something suspended in the air. "How does this sound: 'Celebrity Reporter Has Paranoia Attack and Calls In Police to Search Props'?" He laughed, then held up the other hand. "Or how about: 'Sylvia Stoddard Reassigned to Cover Cultural Issues in Borneo'?"

Sylvia took two steps toward Grant and shook a finger at him, her lips pursed into a scowl, but just as she was about to speak, she caught sight of Brandy standing in the doorway. Her finger and her scowl immediately turned to the actress. "You," she spat out. "You set me up!"

Brandy took a startled step backward, shaking her head. "I don't know what you're talking about, lady."

Sylvia's face flushed red, and her eyes narrowed into tiny slits. "Yes, you do, and don't think I'll let you get away with it." She turned then and stormed across the lobby.

As she heaved open the glass door, Grant called out to her, "What are you going to do about it, Sylvia? Call the police?"

Brandy stepped away from the doorway and back into the ballroom. She was shaking, and her face was pale against her dark red lipstick. "I don't know what she was talking about," she said again. "I don't know why she said those things."

Slade, who stood closest to her, took hold of her arm. "You look like you need to sit down." He led her to where tables and chairs were set up, and she went with him without protest.

Tristan started to follow them, but Clarissa reached out and took his arm. He looked back at her questioningly.

"Do you hear that sound?" she asked.

He stopped and listened, glancing around the room as he did. "What sound?"

"Shhh," she said, and then leaned closer to him. "It's the sound of a favor being paid off."

He looked down at her narrowly. "What do you know about all of this?"

"It has to do with blackmail, or in this case, greenmail. Maybe Brandy will explain it to you."

Slade returned then, taking hold of Clarissa's elbow and smiling down at her. "And you know what the funny thing about tonight is?"

She shook her head.

"This won't even make A.J.'s list of the top ten memorable things that have ever happened at his parties." He turned to Tristan. "What do you think would have to be the most memorable, when the Backstreet Boys challenged N'Sync to a yodeling contest, or when George Stephanopolous passed out during the limbo?"

Tristan shrugged but didn't say anything.

Slade's hand moved from Clarissa's hand to her elbow.

"You've yet to meet A.J. Why don't we stroll over, and I'll introduce you."

She would have liked to protest on the grounds that A.J. needed time to recover from his visit with the police, but as Clarissa's gaze fell on him, she could tell his recovery was complete. He stood in the middle of a group of people, waving one hand in the air in reenactment, and laughing uproariously.

Nataly stood beside him, quietly watching him with her arms folded. Clarissa was half surprised they were together at all. But perhaps they had worked things out. Or perhaps Nataly had found a way to convince A.J. that Bella hadn't told the truth. Maybe they just hadn't decided to make their breakup official yet.

Nataly also wore a cowboy hat and boots, but the rest of her outfit was less traditional. Her black jeans were so tight they were probably just one size away from being classified as a tourniquet, and her black halter top, equally tight, was covered with silver studs.

"So," Slade said as they approached the couple, "you've gone from a gunslinger to a gun smuggler?"

A.J. grinned at him. "Yeah, sure. I figured it would be less stressful than the TV business."

Nataly also smiled at Slade but less enthusiastically.

A.J. reached out his hand to Clarissa. "And you must be the botanist we've heard so much about."

Clarissa took his hand in hers and tried to shake it without gouging him with her claws. "Kim Jones. Lovely party you have here. Absolutely smashing."

Nataly's gaze slid over Clarissa. "You're a doctor of botany?"

"That's right."

She raised one eyebrow. "So what exactly do you do?"

"Oh, well, I specialize in systematics."

"Systematics? What does that mean?"

"That means I do what I do systematically." Clarissa laughed as though it weren't meant to be a joke and then looked around the room desperately for a reason to change the subject.

"What kind of plants do you like to study?" A.J. asked.

She smiled at him broadly while she mentally ran through a list of every single plant name she knew. Ferns, moss, vegetables, pine trees, flowers—botanists didn't study those, did they? Wasn't that florists? Botanists studied only exotic plants whose names she couldn't pronounce. Or did they? She knew only one plant for sure that was being studied by a botanist. "My favorite would have to be algae blooms," Clarissa said. "Over in England we like to say there's nothing like a bloomin' algae bloom."

Nataly smirked. "Really? That sounds absolutely fascinating."

A.J. surveyed the room. "Chuck from props is a Brit, too. You ought to introduce them, Slade. Chuck loves talking about England stuff." He craned his head about for a moment and then his gaze stopped suddenly. "Oh, there he is—over by the hors d'oeuvres table."

Slade looked down at Clarissa. "Shall we?"

"Not right now," Clarissa said. "Not when they're playing our song." She waved a clawed good-bye to A.J. and Nataly, then took Slade's hand and pulled him to the dance floor.

Slade walked with her slowly. "Our song is 'The Monster Mash'?"

"I'm sorry, but I didn't want to meet anyone else. I've hardly had a chance to talk to you all night."

Even though it wasn't a slow song, Slade took hold of one of Clarissa's hands and pulled her closer to him. "I'm sorry to be so forward," he whispered into her ear, "but people may be watching, and, well, it's all part of our masquerade."

It occurred to her as he held her, his body moving just inches away from hers, that she was supposed to be finding out what Slade felt about his nanny. But she couldn't think of a suitable way to bring up the topic. Standing close to Slade made everything else seem muddled. It was easier to sway to the rhythm of the music next to Slade. Here, like this, she could pretend that nothing else mattered, that there were no masks or masquerades.

"This Batman costume is really hot," he said.

"I thought so the moment I saw you in it."

He laughed again and said, "You know what I mean. That Cat Woman suit has got to be just as stuffy. I think after this song I'm going to take off my mask. Do you want me to help you off with yours?"

"No." She said the word too quickly and then added more slowly, "I mean, I don't want to mess up my makeup. I'll wait until sometime when I'm in front of a mirror."

"Suit yourself," he said, "literally, in this case."

She jarred slightly at the phrase. She'd said the same words to him the night she'd gone swimming, but of course the fact that he had repeated them now didn't mean anything. She was just being paranoid again.

The music ended, and he bent his head toward her ear. "Seeing as this is our song, I ought to give you a kiss now—for appearances' sake."

"Oh, well, yes. For appearances' sake," she repeated.

He reached with his hand, tilted her chin up, then kissed her lightly on the lips. Afterward, he gazed into her eyes and continued to hold her closely. "Of course, seeing that we're in love and you've just flown in from England to see me, I probably ought to give you a better kiss than that."

"Probably," she said.

He kissed her again, more ardently this time.

Breaking their embrace, he glanced around the room. "It's too hot to dance. Do you want to go for a walk outside and cool down?"

"Yes, I like walks."

She caught the hint of a smile on his lips. "Good. We'll take one."

He took her hand, and they walked out of the room and through the lobby to the front entrance of the hotel. Once outside they turned down the path that led to the resort's garden. Slade still held her hand, dropping it only while he peeled off his Batman mask.

Once the mask was off, he shook his head, then ran a hand through his still-wavy hair. "That thing is awful. I don't know how George Clooney and Val Kilmer stood it." He turned his attention back to Clarissa. "Are you sure you don't want to take yours off? You'll feel better."

"Maybe in a bit."

Even though there was no one to keep up appearances for, he took her hand back in his, and they continued down the path. It was the perfect time to say something. Clarissa fought for courage, trying to think of some casual way to bring up women, relationships, or nannies and wishing he'd say something so she wouldn't have to.

He didn't.

They walked in silence for a few more moments, and then she decided on the direct approach. "You probably know a lot of different types of women."

"I suppose so," he said.

"And you probably know exactly what type of woman interests you."

"I suppose so," he said again, this time with a slight smile on his lips.

"So what kind is it? I mean, the type of woman that interests you."

He glanced around, saw they were alone, then leaned up against a half wall that ran beside the path.

"You really want to know?" he asked, then pulled her slowly to him. He looked into her eyes for a moment, intently, then bent down and kissed her.

It was a strong kiss, an insistent one, completely without the pretense of being for anyone else's benefit. And Clarissa wondered, as she wound her arms around his neck, if it was wholly appropriate for someone to hold her this way when he hadn't seen her since she was eight years old. Perhaps he was just used to moving fast when it came to women. Or perhaps this meant he wasn't at all interested in his nanny. Kissing him made it hard to figure things out.

She kissed him for a few more moments as Clarissa, then pulled away as Kim.

"What's wrong?" he asked.

"We still don't know each other very well."

He let her go and again leaned back against the wall, surveying her. "I feel like I know you very well."

"Do you?"

"Yes, and the funny thing is, you've changed so much since we were kids."

"Oh? In what way?"

He folded his arms, cocked his head, and looked at her lazily. "Well, for one thing you used to be black."

His words hit her like a gunshot.

He'd known all along, and all along had been laughing at her.

Or perhaps he didn't quite know everything. He knew she was an impostor, but he couldn't know who she was, could he? Certainly he wouldn't have kissed her if he'd known she was Clarissa. Without another word she turned and started back up the path. She was prepared to jog all the way back to the Sunset Park Motel if need be. She got only two steps away before he called after her.

"Clarissa, don't you dare run away from me."

So it was worse than she thought. He knew everything—no, not everything. Just enough to really make her look despicable. She wanted to say, "I can explain." But how could she? Instead she turned and asked, "How did you know it was me?"

One of his eyebrows lifted. "Besides the fact that you're white?"

"There are a lot of white girls who could have fit into this costume," she said, as though it were a perfectly normal thing to protest.

"I've been looking into your eyes for almost a week now. You thought I wouldn't recognize them?"

"Oh." She would have been flattered by this comment if she didn't know that every other sentence in this conversation was going to be in the form of harsh criticism.

"You're probably wondering why I kissed you," she said.

He said something low under his breath, then walked over to where she stood. "I'm wondering why you lied to me about being married."

"You know that, too? How long have you known?"

He looked down at his watch. "For about three hours. Elaina told me how well she keeps secrets. She hasn't told anyone about the 'D force' at all."

Was it anger she heard in his voice? Disappointment? Clarissa closed her eyes momentarily in an attempt to shut everything off. "I didn't mean to lie to you. I just needed the job. And the only reason the job interviewer even sent me to your house was because he knew Alex. I couldn't tell him what a jerk Alex had turned out to be."

"And you couldn't tell me because . . . ?"

"I knew you'd be angry."

He tilted his head down at her. "And . . . ?"

"And because I wasn't sure it would matter to you in the way I wanted it to matter."

He nodded, although she wasn't sure if that meant he agreed it didn't matter to him, or only that he understood why she'd done it. Holding one hand out to indicate her costume, he said, "And you decided to have a night out as Cat Woman because . . . ?"

"I wanted to find out how you felt about me."

"You were going to accomplish this by pretending to be a completely different woman?"

"Well, it made sense when Meredith suggested it."

"And exactly what did you do with the real Kim? Is she tied up in a coat closet or something?"

She couldn't tell whether he was teasing or not. "Um, no. There was an algae bloom off the Gulf of Mexico she had to attend to."

Slade folded his arms and stared at her with an expression she couldn't discern.

"I was going to tell you eventually," she said. "I was just waiting for the right moment." Then, because she really longed to be free of it, she stepped away from him and unsnapped her mask from where it attached to the rest of the suit. She pulled it off and ran her fingers through her damp hair in an attempt to revive it. Softly she said, "I'm sorry, Slade."

He watched her, arms still folded, and didn't speak.

"Will you please say something?" she asked.

"All right," he said. "I can't believe it, but I think A.J. was right about my script. At this moment I have absolutely no desire to talk about the meaning of life."

"I don't know what you mean," she said. And then a bit more defensively added, "But would you like to comment on the fact that you knew who I was and just kissed me several times anyway?"

"Those were for each of the times over the last week that I wanted to kiss you and then went back to my room and told myself I was going to hell."

"Oh," she said, and then, "I'm sorry. I mean, sort of. I'm sorry about deceiving you. If it's any consolation, I can't tell you how many times I went to my room feeling miserable because I had lied to you."

He still stared at her, but now a small smile played on his lips. "Come here," he told her. "I'm still about seventeen kisses short."

And so she came to him, and set the balance straight.

About the Author

Sierra St. James has four children, all of whom have embarrassed her at one time or another with the comments they've made in public. Prime example:

Bishop to six-year-old son: What's your name?
Son: Luke Joshua Moroni.
Bishop: Well, that's quite a name. What does your mother call you when she wants to get your attention?
Son: Brat.
Author's note: I have never called my son a brat, only his older sister does that. Of course, try explaining that to the bishop during tithing settlement.

Sierra likes to write romances—because she's always been a romantic at heart, and, hey, where else do you get the chance to use the words *wry* and *brooding*?